# WOUNDS

Also by Nathan Ballingrud

*North American Lake Monsters*

# WOUNDS

## SIX STORIES FROM THE BORDER OF HELL

# NATHAN BALLINGRUD

SAGA PRESS

LONDON SYDNEY **NEW YORK** TORONTO NEW DELHI

SAGA PRESS
AN IMPRINT OF SIMON & SCHUSTER, INC.

1230 AVENUE OF THE AMERICAS, NEW YORK, NEW YORK 10020

Compilation copyright © 2019 by Nathan Ballingrud
Previously published in *Fearful Symmetries*: "The Atlas of Hell" (2014),
*Monstrous Affections*: "The Diabolist" (2014), *Nightmare Carnival*: "Skullpocket"
(2014), *Dark Cities*: "The Maw" (2017), *This Is Horror* : "The Visible Filth" (2015).
"The Butcher's Table" is original to the collection.
Jacket photograph copyright © 2013 by Robert Offner

SAGA PRESS and colophon are trademarks of Simon & Schuster, Inc.
For information about special discounts for bulk purchases, please contact Simon &
Schuster Special Sales at 1-866-506-1949 or business@simonandschuster.com.
The Simon & Schuster Speakers Bureau can bring authors to your live event.
For more information or to book an event, contact the Simon & Schuster Speakers
Bureau at 1-866-248-3049 or visit our website at www.simonspeakers.com.
Also available in a Saga Press hardcover edition
Interior design by Tom Daly
The text for this book was set in Adobe Caslon Pro.
Manufactured in the United States of America
First Saga Press paperback edition April 2019
10  9  8  7  6  5  4
CIP data for this book is available from the Library of Congress.
ISBN 978-1-5344-4992-3
ISBN 978-1-5344-4994-7 (eBook)
ISBN 978-1-5344-4993-0 (pbk)

For Mia

# CONTENTS

*Now you are standing at the very crossroads of your life;
and all your roads lead to strange places.*

—Mike Mignola, *Hellboy: The Third Wish*

# The Atlas of Hell

He didn't even know he was dead. I had just shot this guy in the head and he's still standing there giving me shit. Telling me what a big badass he works for, telling me I'm going to be sorry I was born. You know. Blood pouring out of his face. He can't even see anymore, it's in his goddamn eyes. So I look at the gun in my hand and I'm like, what the fuck, you know? Is this thing working or what? And I'm starting to think maybe this asshole is right, maybe I just stepped into something over my head. I mean, I feel a twinge of real fear. My hair is standing up like a cartoon. So I look at the dude and I say, 'Lay down! You're dead! I shot you!'"

There's a bourbon and ice sitting on the end table next to him. He takes a sip from it and puts it back down, placing it in its own wet ring. He's very precise about it.

I guess he just had to be told, because as soon as I say it? Boom. Drops like a fucking tree.

I don't know what he's expecting from me here. My leg is jumping up and down with nerves. I can't make it stop. I open my mouth to say something but a nervous laugh spills out instead.

He looks at me incredulously and cocks his head. Patrick is a big guy; but not doughy, like me. There's muscle packed beneath all that flesh. He looks like fists of meat sewn together and given a suit of clothes. "Why are you laughing?"

"I don't know. I thought it was supposed to be a funny story."

"No, you demented fuck. That's not a funny story. What's the matter with you?"

It's pushing midnight, and we're sitting on a coffee-stained couch in a darkened corner of the grubby little bookstore I own in New Orleans, about a block off Magazine Street. My name is Jack Oleander. I keep a small studio apartment overhead, but when Patrick started banging on my door half an hour ago I took him down here instead. I don't want him in my home. That he's here at all is a very bad sign.

My place is called Oleander Books. I sell used books, for the most part, and I serve a sparse clientele: mostly students and disaffected youth, their little hearts love-drunk on Kierkegaard or Salinger. That suits me just fine. Most of the books have been sitting on their shelves for years, and I feel like I've fostered a kind of relationship with them. A part of me is sorry whenever one of them leaves the nest.

The bookstore doesn't pay the bills, of course. The books and documents I sell in the back room take care of that. Few people know about the back room, but those who do pay quite well. Patrick's boss, Eugene, is one of those people. We parted under strained circumstances a year or so ago. I was never supposed to see him again. Patrick's presence here makes me afraid, and fear makes me reckless.

"Well, if it's not a funny story, then what kind of story is it? Because we've been drinking here for twenty minutes and you haven't mentioned business even once. If you want to trade war stories, it's going to have to wait for another time."

He gives me a sour look and picks up his glass, peering into it as he swirls the ice around. He's always hated me, and I know that his presence here pleases him no more than it does me.

"You don't make it easy to be your friend," he says.

"I didn't know we were friends."

The muscles in his jaw clench.

"You're wasting my time, Patrick. I know you're just the heavy, so maybe you don't understand this, but the work I do in the back room takes up a lot of energy. Sleep is valuable to me. You've sat on my couch and drunk my whiskey and burned away almost half an hour beating around the bush. I don't know how much more of this I can take."

He has his work face on now, the one a lot of guys see just before the lights go out. That's good; I want him in work mode. It makes him focus. The trick now is to keep him on the shy side of violence. You have to play these guys like marionettes. I got pretty good at it back in the day.

"You want to watch that," he says. "You want to watch that attitude."

I put my hands out, palms forward. "Hey," I say.

"I come to you in friendship. I come to you in respect."

That's bullshit, but whatever. It's time to settle him down. These macho types are such fragile little flowers. "Hey. I'm sorry. Really. I haven't been sleeping much. I'm tired, and it makes me stupid."

"That's a bad trait. So wake up and listen to me. I told you that story for two reasons. One, to stop you from saying dumb shit like you just did. Make you remember who you're dealing with. I can see it didn't work. I can see maybe I was being too subtle."

"Patrick, really. I—"

"If you interrupt me again I will break your right hand. The second reason I told you that story is to let you know that I've seen some crazy things in my life, so when I say that what I'm about to tell you scares me shitless, maybe you'll listen to what the fuck I'm saying."

He stops there, staring hard at me. After a couple seconds of this, I figure it's okay to talk.

"You have my full attention. Whatever this is you're about to tell me, it's from Eugene?"

"You know this is from Eugene. Why else would I drag myself over here?"

"Patrick, I wish you'd relax. I'm sorry I made you mad. You want another drink? Let me pour you another drink."

I can see the rage still coiling in his eyes, and I'm starting to think I pushed him too hard. I'm starting to wonder how fast I can run.

But then he leans back onto the couch and a smile settles over his face. It doesn't look natural there. "Jesus, you have a mouth. How does a guy like you get away with having a mouth like that?" He shakes the ice in his glass. "Yeah, go ahead. Pour me another one. Let's smoke a peace pipe."

I pour us both some more. He slugs it back in one deep swallow and holds his glass out for another. I give it to him. He seems to be relaxing.

"All right, okay. There's this guy. Creepy little grifter named Tobias George. He's one of those rats always crawling through the city, getting into shit, fucking up his own life, you don't even notice these guys. You know how it is."

"I do." I also know the name, but I don't tell him that.

"Only reason we know about him at all is because some-times he'll run a little scheme of his own, kick a percentage back to Eugene, it's all good. Well, one day this prick catches a case of ambition. He robs one of Eugene's poker games, makes off with a lot of money. Suicidal. Who knows what got into the guy. Some big dream climbed up his butt and opened him like an umbrella. We go hunting for him, but he disappears. We get word he went farther south, disappeared into the bayou. Like, not to Port Fourchon or some shit, but literally on a goddamn boat into the swamp. Eugene is pissed, and you know how he is, he jumps and shouts for a few days, but eventually he says fuck it. We're not gonna go wrestle alligators for him. After a while we just figured he died out there. You know."

"But he didn't."

"That he did not. We catch wind of him a few months later. He's in a whole new ballgame. He's selling artifacts pulled from Hell. And he's making a lot of money doing it."

"It's another scam," I say, knowing full well that it isn't.

"It's not."

"How do you know?"

"Don't worry about it. We know."

"A guy stole money and ran. That sounds more like your thing than mine, Patrick."

"Yeah, don't worry about that either. I got that part covered when the time comes. I won't go into the details, 'cause they don't matter, but what it comes down to is Eugene wants his own way into the game. Once this punk is put in the ground, he wants to keep this market alive. We happen to know Tobias has a book that tells him how to access this shit. An atlas. We want it, and we want to know how it works. And that's *your* thing, Jack."

I feel something cold spill through my guts. "That's not the deal we had."

"What can I tell you."

"No. I told . . ." My throat is dry. My leg is bouncing again. "Eugene told me we were through. He told me that. He's breaking his promise."

"That mouth again." Patrick finishes his drink and stands. "Come on. You can tell him that yourself, see how it goes over."

"Now? It's the middle of the night!"

"Don't worry, you won't be disturbing him. He don't sleep too well lately."

I've lived here my whole life. Grew up just a regular fat-white-kid schlub, decent parents, a ready-made path to the gray fields of middle-class servitude. But I went off the rails at some point. I was seduced by old books. I wanted to live out my life in a fog of parchment dust and old glue. I apprenticed myself to a bookbinder, a gnarled old Cajun named Rene Aucoin, who it turned out was a fading necromancer who had a nice side business refurbishing old grimoires. I learned some things from him, which led to my tenure as a librarian at the Camouflaged Library at the Ursuline Academy. It was when Eugene and his crew stuck their noses in the business, leading to a bloody confrontation with a death cult obsessed with the Damocles Scroll, that I left the academy and began my career as a book thief. I worked for Eugene for five years before we had our falling-out. When I left, we both knew it was for good.

Eugene has a bar in Midcity, far away from the T-shirt shops, the fetish dens and goth hangouts of the French Quarter, far away too from the more respectable veneer of the Central Business and Garden Districts. Midcity is a place where you can do what you want. Patrick drives me along Canal and parks out front. He leads me up the stairs and inside, where the blast of cold air is a relief from a heat that does not relent even at night. A jukebox is playing something stale, and four or five ghostlike figures nest at the bar. They do not turn around as we pass through. Patrick guides me downstairs, to Eugene's office.

Before I even reach the bottom of the stairs, Eugene starts talking to me.

"Hey, fat boy! Here comes the fat boy!"

No cover model himself, he comes around his desk with his arms outstretched, what's left of his gray hair combed in long, spindly fingers over the expanse of his scalp. Drink has made a soft wreckage of his face. His chest is sunken in, like something inside has collapsed and he's falling inward. He puts his hands on me in greeting, and I try not to flinch.

"Look at you. Look at you. You look good, Jack."

"So do you, Eugene."

The office is clean and uncluttered. There's a desk and a few padded chairs, a couch on the far wall underneath a huge Michalopoulos painting. Across from the desk is a minibar and a door that leads to the back alley. Mardi Gras masks are arranged behind his desk like a congress of spirits. Eugene is a New Orleans boy right down to his tapping toes, and he buys into every shabby lie the city ever told about itself.

"I hear you got a girl now. What's her name, Locky? Lick-me?"

"Lakshmi." This is already going badly. "Come on, Eugene. Let's not go there."

"Listen to him now. Calling the shots. All independent, all grown up now. Patrick give you any trouble? Sometimes he gets carried away."

Patrick doesn't blink. His role fulfilled, he's become a tree.

"No. No trouble at all. It was like old times."

"Hopefully, not too much like old times, huh?" He sits behind his desk, gestures for me to take a seat. Patrick pours a couple of drinks and hands one to each of us, then retreats behind me.

"I guess I'm just trying to figure out what I'm doing here, Eugene. Someone's not paying you. Isn't that what you have guys like him for?"

Eugene settles back, sips from his drink, and studies me. "Let's not play coy, Jack. Okay? Don't pretend you don't already know about Tobias. Don't insult my intelligence."

"I know about Tobias," I say.

"Tell me what you know."

I can't get comfortable in my chair. I feel like there are chains around my chest. I make one last effort. "Eugene. We had a deal."

"Are you having trouble hearing me? Should I raise my voice?"

"He started selling two months ago. He had a rock. It was about the size of a tennis ball, but it was as heavy as a television set. Everybody thought he was full of shit. They were laughing at him. It sold for a little bit of money, not much. But somebody out there liked what they saw. Word got around. He sold a two-inch piece of charred bone next. That went for a lot more."

"I bought that bone."

"Oh," I say. "Shit."

"Do you know why?"

"No, Eugene, of course I don't."

"Don't 'of course' me. I don't know what you know and what you don't. You're a slimy piece of filth, Jack. You're a human cockroach. I can't trust you. So don't get smart."

"I'm sorry. I didn't mean it like that."

"He had the nerve to contact me directly. He wanted me to know what he was offering before he put it on the market. Give me first chance. Jack, it's from my son. It's part of a thighbone from my son."

I can't seem to see straight. The blood has rushed to my head, and I feel dizzy. I clamp my hands on the armrests of the chair so I can feel something solid. "How . . . how do you know?"

"There's people for that. Don't ask dumb questions. I am very much not in the mood for dumb questions."

"Okay."

"Your thing is books, so that's why you're here. We tracked him to this old shack in the bayou. You're going to get the book."

I feel panic skitter through me. "You want me to go there?"

"Patrick's going with you."

"That's not what I do, Eugene!"

"Bullshit! You're a thief. You do this all the time. Patrick there can barely read a *People* magazine without breaking a sweat. You're going."

"Just have Patrick bring it back! You don't need me for this."

Eugene stares at me.

"Come on," I say. "You gave me your word."

I don't even see Patrick coming. His hand is on the back of my neck and he slams my face onto the desk hard enough to crack an ashtray underneath my cheekbone. My glass falls out of my hand and I hear the ice thump onto the carpet. He keeps me pinned to the desk. He wraps his free hand around my throat. I can't breathe.

Eugene leans in, his hands behind his back, like he's

examining something curious and mildly revolting. "Would you like to see him? Would you like to see my son?"

I pat Patrick's hand, a weirdly intimate gesture. I shake my head. I try to make words. My vision is starting to fry around the edges. Dark loops spool into the world.

Finally, Eugene says, "Let him go."

Patrick releases me. I slide off the table and land hard, dragging the broken ashtray with me, covering myself in ash and spent cigarette butts. I roll onto my side, choking.

Eugene puts his hand on my shoulder. "Hey, Jack, you okay? You all right down there? Get up. God damn, you're a drama queen. Get the fuck up already."

It takes a few minutes. When I'm sitting up again, Patrick hands me a napkin to clean the blood off my face. I don't look at him. There's nothing I can do. No point in feeling a goddamn thing about it.

"When do I leave?" I say.

"What the hell," Eugene says. "How about right now?"

We experience dawn as a rising heat and a slow bleed of light through the cypress and the Spanish moss, riding in an airboat through the swamp a good thirty miles south of New Orleans. Patrick and I are up front while an old man more leather than flesh guides us along some unseeable path. Our progress stirs movement from the local fauna—snakes, turtles, muskrats—and I'm constantly jumping at some heavy splash. I imagine a score of alligators gliding beneath us, tracking our progress with yellow, saurian eyes. The airboat wheels around a copse of trees into a watery clearing, and I half expect to see a brontosaurus wading in the shallows.

Instead I see a row of huge, bobbing purple flowers, each with a bleached human face in the center, mouths gaping and eyes palely blind. The sight of it shocks me into silence; our guide fixes his stare on the horizon, refusing to acknowledge anything unusual. Eyes perch along the tops of reeds; great kites of flesh stretch between tree limbs; one catches a light breeze from our passage and skates serenely through the air, coming at last to a gentle landing on the water, where it folds in on itself and sinks into the murk.

Our guide points, and I see a shack: a small, single-room architectural catastrophe, situated on the dubious shore and extending over the water on short stilts. A skiff is tied to a front porch that doubles as a small dock. It seems to be the only method of travel to or from the place. A filthy rebel flag hangs over the entrance in lieu of a door. At the moment, it's pulled to the side and a man I assume is Tobias George is standing there, naked but for a pair of shorts that hang precariously from his narrow waist. He's all bone and gristle. His face tells me nothing as we glide in toward the dock.

Patrick stands before we connect, despite a word of caution from our guide. He has one hand on his hip, like Washington crossing the Delaware. He has some tough-guy greeting halfway out of his mouth when the airboat's edge lightly taps the dock, nearly spilling him into the swamp, arms pinwheeling.

Tobias is unaffected by the display, but our guide is easy with a laugh and chooses not to hold back.

Patrick recovers himself and puts both hands on the dock, proceeding to crawl out of the boat like a child learning to walk. I'm grateful to God for the sight of it.

Tobias makes no move to help.

I take my time climbing out. "You wait right here," I tell the guide.

The guide nods, shutting down the engine and fishing a pack of smokes from his shirt.

"What're you guys doing here?" Tobias says. He hasn't even looked at me once. He can't peel his gaze from Patrick. He knows what Patrick's all about.

"Tobias, you crazy bastard. What the hell do you think you're doing?"

Tobias turns around and goes back inside, the rebel flag falling closed behind him. "Come on in, I guess."

We follow him inside, where it's even hotter. The air doesn't move in here, probably hasn't moved in twenty years, and it carries the sharp tang of marijuana. Dust motes drift across spears of light coming in through a window covered over in ratty, bug-smeared plastic. The room is barely furnished: There's a single mattress pushed against the wall to our left, a cheap collapsible table with a plastic folding chair, and a chest of drawers. Next to the bed is a camping cooker with a little saucepot and some cans of Sterno. On the table is a small pile of dull green buds, with some rolling papers and a Zippo.

There's a door flush against the back wall. I take a few steps in the direction and I can tell right away that there's some bad news behind it. The air spoils when I get close, coating the back of my throat with a greasy, evil film that feels like it seeps right into me. Violent fantasies sprout along my cortex like a little vine of tumors. I try to keep my face still as I imagine coring the eyeballs out of both these guys with a grapefruit spoon.

"Stay on that side of the room, Patrick," I say. I don't need him feeling this.

"What? Why?"

"Trust me. This is why you brought me."

Tobias casts a glance at me now, finally sensing some purpose behind my presence. He's good, though: I still can't figure his reaction.

"Y'all here to kill me?" he says.

Patrick already has his gun in hand. It's pointed at the floor. His eyes are fixed on Tobias and he seems to be weighing something in his mind. I can tell that whatever is behind that door is already working its influence on him. It has its grubby little fingers in his brain and it's pulling dark things out of it. "That depends on you," he says. "Eugene wants to talk to you."

"Yeah, that's not going to happen."

The violence in this room is alive and crawling. I realize, suddenly, why he stays stoned. "We want the book, Tobias," I say.

"What? Who are you?" He looks at Patrick. "What's he talking about?"

"You know what he's talking about. Go get the book."

"There is no book!"

He looks genuinely bewildered, and that worries me. I don't know if I can go back to Eugene without a book. I'm about to ask him what's in the back room when I hear a creak in the wood beyond the hanging flag and someone pulls it aside, flooding the shack with light. I spin around, and Patrick already has his gun raised, looking spooked.

The man standing in the doorway is framed by the sun: a black shape, a negative space. He's tall and slender, his hair like a spray of light around his head. I think for a moment that I can smell it burning. He steps into the shack and you can tell there's something wrong with him, though it's hard to figure just what. Some malformation of the aura, telegraphing a warning blast straight to the root of my brain. To look at him, as he steps into the shack and trades direct sunlight for the filtered illumination shared by the rest of us, he seems tired and gaunt but ultimately not unlike any other poverty-wracked country boy, and yet my skin ripples at his approach. I feel my lip curl and I have to concentrate to keep the revulsion from my face.

"Toby?" he says. His voice is young and uninflected. Normal. "I think my brother's on his way back. Who are these guys?"

"Hey, Johnny," Tobias says, looking at him over my shoulder. He's plainly nervous now, and although his focus stays on Johnny, his attention seems to radiate in all directions, like a man wondering where the next hit is coming from.

I could have told him that.

Fear turns to meanness in a guy like Patrick, and he reacts according to the dictates of his kind: he shoots.

It's one shot, quick and clean. Patrick is a professional. The sound of the gun concusses the air in the little shack and the bullet passes through Johnny's skull before I even have time to wince at the noise.

I blink. I can't hear anything beyond a high-pitched whine. I see Patrick standing still, looking down the length of his raised arm with a flat, dead expression. It's his true face. I see Tobias drop to one knee, his hands over his ears and his mouth working; he looks like he's shouting something. I see Johnny, too, still standing in the doorway, as unmoved by the bullet's passage through his skull as though it had been nothing more than a disappointing argument. Dark clots of brain meat are splashed across the flag behind him.

He looks from Patrick to Tobias and when he speaks I can barely hear him above the ringing in my head. "What should I do?" he says.

I step forward and gently push Patrick's arm down.

"Are you shitting me?" he says, staring at Johnny.

"Patrick," I say.

"Am I fucking cursed? Is that it? I shot you in the face!"

The bullet hole is a dime-size wound in Johnny's right cheekbone. It leaks a single rivulet of blood. "Asshole," Johnny says.

Tobias gets back to his feet, his arms stretched out to either side like he's trying to separate two imaginary boxers. "Will you just relax? Jesus Christ!" He guides Johnny to the little bed and sits him down, where he brushes the blond hair out of his face and inspects the bullet hole. Then he cranes his head around to examine the damage of the exit wound. "Goddamn it!" he says.

Johnny puts his own hand back there. "Oh man," he says.

I take a look. The whole back of his head is gone; now it's just a bowl of spilled gore. Little cinders are embedded in the mess, sending up coils of smoke.

"Patrick," I say. "Just be cool."

He's still in a fog. You can see him trying to arrange things in his brain. "I need to kill them, Jack. I need to. I never felt it like this before. What's happening here?"

Tobias pipes up. "I had a job for this guy all lined up at The Fry Pit! Now what!"

"Tobias, I need you to shut up," I say, keeping my eyes on Patrick. "Patrick, are you hearing me?" It's taking a huge effort to maintain my own composure. I have an image of wresting the gun from his hand and hitting him with it until his skull breaks. Only the absolute impossibility of it keeps me from trying.

My question causes the shutters to close in his eyes. Whatever tatter of human impulse stirred him to try to explain himself to me, to grope for reason amidst the bloody carnage boiling in his head, is subsumed again in a dull professional menace. "Don't talk to me like that. I'm not a goddamn kid."

I turn to the others. The bed is now awash in blood. Tobias is working earnestly to mitigate the damage back there, but I can't imagine what it is he thinks he can do. Brain matter is gathered in a clump on the bed; he seems to be scooping everything out. Johnny sits there forlornly, shoulders slumped. "I thought it would be better out here," he said. "Shit never ends."

"The atlas," I say.

"Fuck yourself," Tobias says.

I stride toward the closed door. If there's anything I need to know before I open it, I guess I'll just find out the hard way. A hot pulse of emotion blasts out at me as I touch the handle: fear, rage, a lust for carnage. It's overriding any sense of self-preservation I might have had. I wonder if a fire will pour through the door when it's opened, a furnace exhalation, and engulf us all. I find myself hoping for it.

Tobias shouts at me: "Don't!"

I pull it open.

A charred skull, oily smoke coiling from its fissures, is propped on a stool in an otherwise bare room no bigger than a closet. Black mold has grown over the stool and is creeping up the walls. A live current jolts my brain. Time dislocates, jumping seconds like an old record, and the world moves in jerky, stop-motion lurches. A language is seeping from the skull—a viscous, cracked sound like breaking bones and molten rock. My eyes sting and I briefly squeeze them shut. The skin on my face blisters.

*"Shut it! Shut the door!"*

Tobias is screaming, but whatever he's saying has no relation to me. It's as though I'm watching a play. Blood is leaking from his eyes. Patrick is grinning widely, his own eyes like bloody headlamps. He's violently twisting his right ear, working it like an apple stem. Johnny is sitting quietly, holding his gathered brains in his hands, rocking back and forth like an unhappy child. My upper arms are hurting, and it takes me a minute to realize that I'm gouging them with my own fingernails. I can't make myself stop.

Outside a sound rolls across the swamp like a foghorn, a deep, answering bellow to the language of Hell spilling from the closet.

Tobias lunges past me and slams the door shut, immediately muffling the skull's effect. I stagger toward the plastic chair but fall down hard before I make it, banging my shoulder against the table and knocking Tobias's drug paraphernalia all over the floor. Patrick makes a sound, half gasp and half sob, and leans back against the wall, cradling his savaged ear. The left side of his face is painted in blood. He's digging the heel of his hand into his right eye, like he's trying to rub something out of it.

"What the fuck was that!"

I think it's me who says that. Right now I can't be sure.

"That's your goddamn 'atlas,' you prick," Tobias says. He comes over to where I am and drops to the floor, scooping up the scattered buds and some papers. He begins to assemble a joint; his hands are shaking badly, so this takes some doing.

"A skull? The book is a skull?"

"No. It's a tongue inside the skull. Technically."

"What the Christ?"

"Just shut up a minute." He finishes making the joint, lights it, and takes a long, deep pull. He passes it to me.

For one surreal moment I feel like we're college buddies sitting in a dorm. It's like there's not a scorched, muttering skull in the next room, corroding the air around it. It's like there's not a man with a blown-out head moping quietly on the bed. I start to laugh, and I haven't even had a toke.

Tobias exhales explosively, the sweet smoke filling the air between us. "Take a hit, man. I'm serious. Trust me."

So I do. Almost immediately I feel an easing of the pressure in the room. The crackle of violent impulse, which I had ceased even to recognize, abates to a low thrum. My internal gauge ticks back down to highly frightened, which, in comparison to a moment before, feels like a monastic peace.

I gesture for Patrick to do the same.

"No. I don't pollute my body with that shit." He's touching his ear gingerly, trying to assess the damage.

"Patrick, last night you single-handedly killed half a bottle of ninety-proof bourbon. Let's have some perspective here."

He snatches the joint from me and drags hard on it, coughing it all back out so violently I think he might throw up.

Johnny laughs from his position on the bed. It's the first bright note he's sounded since his head came apart. "Amateur!"

Johnny's head seems to be changing shape. The shattered bone around the exit wound has smoothed over and extended upward an inch or so, like something growing. A tiny twig of bone has likewise emerged from the bullet wound beneath his eye.

"We need to get out of here," I say. "That thing is pretty much a live feed to Hell. We can't handle it. It's time to go."

"We're taking it with us," Patrick says.

"No. No, we're not."

"Not up for debate, Jack."

"I'm not riding with that thing. If you take it, you're going back alone."

Patrick nods and takes another pull from the joint, handling it much better this time. He passes it back to me. "Okay, but you gotta know that I'm leaving this place empty. You understand me, right?"

I don't, at first. It takes me a second. "You can't be serious. You're going to kill me?"

"Make up your mind."

For the first time since his arrival at my shop last night, I feel genuine despair. Everything to this point has had some precedence in my life. Even this brush with Hell isn't my first, though it's the most direct so far. But I've never seen my own death staring back at me quite so frankly. I always thought I'd confront this moment with a little poise, or at least a kind of stoic resignation. But I'm angry, and I'm afraid, and I feel tears gathering in my eyes.

"Goddamn it, Patrick. That doesn't make any sense."

"Look, Jack. I like you. You're weak and you're a coward, but you can't help those things. I would rather you come with me. We take this skull back to Eugene, like he wanted. We deliver Tobias to his just reward. You go back to your stupid bookstore and all is right with the world. But I can't leave this place with anybody in it."

Tobias doesn't seem to be paying attention. He's leaning back against the bed, a new joint rolled up and kept all to himself. I can't tell if he's resigned to his own death or if he's so far away he doesn't even know it's being discussed.

I can't think of anything to say. Maybe there isn't anything to be said anymore. Maybe language is over. Maybe everything is, at last, emptied out. I still feel the skull's muted influence crawling through my brain. It craves the bullet. I anticipate the explosion of the gun with a terrible relish. I wonder if, when my brains are launched into the air, I'll feel myself flying.

The bellow from the swamp sounds again. It's huge and

deep, like the ululating call of a mountain. It just keeps on going.

Johnny smiles. "Brother's home," he says.

Patrick looks toward the flag-covered doorway. "What?"

Tobias holds his hand aloft, finger extended, announcing his intention to orate. His eyelids are heavy. The joint he made for himself is spent. "There's a Hell monster. Did I forget to tell you?"

I start to laugh. I can't stop myself. It doesn't feel good.

Johnny smiles at me, mistaking my laughter for something else. "It showed up the same time I did. I think it followed me. Toby calls it my brother." He sounds wistful.

Patrick uses the gun barrel to open the flag a few inches. He peers outside for a moment, then lets it fall closed again. He looks at me. "We're stuck. The boat's gone."

"What? He left us?"

"Well . . . it's mostly gone."

I take a look for myself.

The airboat is a listing heap of bent scrap metal, the cage around its huge propeller a tangled bird's nest. Our guide's arm, still connected to a hunk of his torso, rests on the deck in a black puddle. The thing that did this is swimming in a lazy arc some distance away, trackable by the rolling surge of water it creates as it trawls along. Judging by the size of its wake, it's at least as big as a city bus. It breaches the surface once, exposing a mottled gray hide and an anemone-like thistle of eye stalks lifting skyward. The thing barrel-rolls until a deep black fissure emerges from below the waterline, and from this suppurated tear comes that stone-cracking call, the language of deep earth that curdles something inside me, springs tears to my eyes, brings me hard to my knees.

I scramble away from the door. Patrick is watching me with sad, desperate hope, his intent to murder momentarily forgotten, as though by some trick known only to me this thing might be banished back to its home, as though I might fix this scar that Tobias George, that mewling, incompetent little thief, has cut into the world.

I cannot fix this. There is no fixing this.

Behind us both, locked in its little room, the skull cooks the air.

It's the language that hurts. The awful speech. While that thing languishes in the waters out front, we're trapped inside, and I suspect that as long as the atlas speaks, the creature will not go far.

"Why would you do that to a man?" Patrick says. We're all sitting in a little huddled circle, passing the joint around. We might have been friends, in the eyes of someone who didn't know us. "Why would you send him a piece of his own dead son?"

"Are you serious? No one deserves it more than Eugene. He humiliated me. He made me feel small. All those years sending him a cut from money I earned, or doing errands for him, or tipping him off when I hear shit I think he should know. Never a 'thank you.' Never a 'good job.' Just grief. Just mockery. And his son was even worse. He would lay his hands on me. Slap the back of my head. Slap my face, even. What am I going to do, challenge Eugene's son? So I became everybody's bitch. The laughingstock."

Patrick shakes his head. "You didn't, though. Truth is we barely ever thought about you. I didn't even know your name until you knocked over that poker game. Eugene had to remind me."

This is hard for Tobias to hear. He stares at the floor, his jaw tight. He looks at me. "See what I mean? Nothing. You just have to take it from these guys, you know? Just take it and take it and take it. It was one of the happiest days of my life when that kid finally got wasted."

He goes on. We have nothing but time. He robbed the poker game in a fit of deranged anger and then fled south, hoping to disappear into the bayou. The reality of what he'd just done was starting to sink in. He's of the vermin class in criminal society, and vermin come in multitudes. One of the vermin friends told him about this shack where his old grand-daddy used to live. He got a boat and came out here, only to find a surprise waiting for him.

"The skull was in a black, iron box," he says. "Sitting on its side in the corner. There's a hole in the bottom of the box, like the whole thing was meant to fit around someone's head. It had a big gouge in the side of it, like someone had chopped it with something. I don't know what cuts through metal like that though. And inside, this skull . . . talking."

"It's one of the astronauts," Johnny says.

I rub my fingers in my eyes. "Astronauts? What?"

Johnny leans in, grateful for his moment. He tells us that occasionally there are men and women who wander through Hell in thin processions, wearing heavy gray robes and bearing lanterns to light their way. They are invariably chained together and led through the burning canyons by a loping demon: some malformed, tooth-spangled pinwheel of limbs and claws. They tour safely because they are shuttered against the sights and sounds of Hell by the iron boxes around their heads, which give them the appearance of strange astronauts on a pilgrimage through fire.

"I recognized the box," Johnny says. "This skull is from one of the astronauts of Hell. The box was broken, so I guess something bad happened to him."

"Where is it?"

Tobias shrugs. "I threw it out in the bayou. What do I need a broken box for? I started asking for things, and it sent them. The rock, the shard of bone."

"Hold on. How did you know to ask it for things? You're leaving something out."

Tobias and Johnny exchange a look. The extending bone around Johnny's head has grown further, into a kind of bowl, while the burning embers seem to have gathered more life, spitting little tongues of flame. It looks like a brazier, and it gives him an oddly regal aspect. The bone growing from his face has sprouted little offshoots, like a delicate branch.

Patrick picks up on their glance and retrieves his gun from the floor. He holds it casually in his lap.

"Everything that's brought here has a courier," Tobias says. "That's how Johnny got here. He brought the bone. And there was one already here when I found the skull. It told me."

"It?"

"Well . . . it was a person at first. Then it changed. They change over time. Evolve."

Patrick gets it before I do. "The thing in the water."

"Holy Christ. You mean Johnny's going to turn into something like *that*?" I look again at the fiery bowl his head is turning into.

"No no no!" Tobias holds out his hands, as if he could ward off the idea. "I'm pretty sure that's only because the other one never went away. I think it's the proximity of the skull that does it. There was one other courier, the girl who brought me the rock. I sent her away."

"Jesus. Where?"

"Just . . ." He waves, vaguely. "Away. Into the bayou."

"You're a real sweetheart, Tobias."

"Well, come on, I didn't know what to do! She was just—there! I didn't know anybody was going to be coming with it! I freaked out and told her to get out! But the important thing is I never saw any sign that she changed into anything. I haven't seen or heard anything from her since. You notice how the plants get weird as you get close to this place? It's gotta be the skull's influence."

"That's not exactly airtight logic, Tobias," I say. "What if it's not just the skull? What if it comes from them, too? I could tell something was fucked up about Johnny as soon as I saw him."

"Well, I'm taking the fucking chance! If there are going to be people coming out, they need to have a chance at a better life. That's why I got Johnny here a job. He'll be far away from that skull, so maybe he won't change into anything." He looks at his friend and at the lively fire that's crackling inside his head. "Well, he wouldn't have if you guys hadn't fucked it all up. I've got this all worked out. I'm going to find them jobs in little places, in little towns. I got money now, so I can afford to get them set up. Buy them some clothes, rent them out a place until they can start earning some money of their own. A second chance, you know? They deserve a second chance."

He's getting all worked up again, like he's going to break down into tears, and I'm struck with a revelation: Tobias is using this skull as a chance to redeem himself. He's going to funnel people out of Hell and back into the world of sunlight and cheeseburgers.

Tobias George may be the only good man in a fifty-mile radius. Too bad it's the most doomed idea I've ever heard in a life rich with them. But there are several possibilities for salvaging this situation. One thing is clear: Eugene cannot have the atlas. The level of catastrophe he might cause is incalculable. I need to get it back to my bookstore and to the back room. There are books there that will provide protections; at least I hope so.

All I need is something to carry it in.

I know just where to get it.

"Patrick. You still want to bring this thing to Eugene?"

"He's the boss. You change your mind about coming?"

"I think so, yeah. Tobias, we're going into the room."

He goes in gratefully. I think he feels in control in this room in a way that he doesn't out there with Patrick. It's almost funny.

The skull sits on the moss-blackened stool, greasy smoke seeping from its fissures and polluting the air. The broken language of Hell is a physical pressure. A blood vessel ruptures in my right eye and my vision goes cloudy and pink. Time fractures again. Tobias moves next to me, approaching the skull, but I can't tell what it's doing to him: he skips in time like I'm watching him through strobe lights, even though the light in here remains a constant, sizzling glare. I try not to vomit. Things are moving around in my brain like maggots in old meat.

The air seems to bend into the skull. I see it on the stool, blackening the world around it, and I try to imagine who it once belonged to: the chained Black Iron Monk, shielded by a metal box from the burning horrors of the world it moved through. Until something came along and opened it like a tin can, and Hell poured inside.

Who was it? What order would undertake such a pilgrimage? And to what end?

Tobias is saying something to me. I have to study him to figure out what.

The poor scrawny bastard is blistering all over his body. His lips peel back from his bloody teeth.

"Tell it what you want," he says.

So I do.

The boy is streaked with mud and gore. He is twelve, maybe thirteen. Steam rises from his body like wind-struck flags. I don't know where he appears from, or how; he's just there, two iron boxes dangling like huge lanterns from a chain in his hand. I wonder, briefly, what a child his age had done to be consigned to Hell. But then, it doesn't really matter.

I open one of the boxes and tell the boy to put the skull inside. He does. The skin bubbles on his hands where he touches it, but he makes no sign of pain.

I close the door on the skull, and it's like a light going out. Time slips back into its groove. The light recedes to a natural level. My skin stops burning, the desire to commit violence dissipates like smoke. I can feel where I've been scratching my own arms again. My eye is gummed shut with blood.

When we stumble back into the main room, Patrick is on his feet with the gun in his hand. Johnny is sitting on the bed, the bony rim of his open skull grown farther upward, elongating his head and giving him an alien grace. The fire in the bowl of his head burns briskly, crackling and shedding a warm light. Patrick looks at me, then at the boy with the iron boxes. "You got them," he says. "Where's the skull?"

I take the chain from the boy. The boxes are heavy together; the boy must be stronger than he looks. Something to remember. "In one of these. If it can keep that shit out, I'm betting it can keep it locked in, too. I think it's safe to move."

"And those'll get us past the thing outside?"

"If what Johnny said is true."

"It is," Johnny says. "But now there's only one extra box."

"That's right," I say, and swing them with every vestige of my failing strength at Patrick's head, where they land with a wet crunch. He staggers to his right a few steps, the left side of his face broken like crockery, and he puts a hand into the rancid scramble of his own brain. "Put that down, Jack," he says, "Don't be stupid."

"You're dead," I tell him gently. "You stupid bastard."

He accepts this gracefully and collapses to his knees, and then onto his face. Dark blood pours from his head as though from a spilled glass. I scoop up the gun, which feels clumsy in my hand. I never got the hang of guns.

Tobias stands in shock. "I can't believe you did that," he says.

"Shut up. Are there any clothes in that dresser? Put something on the kid. We're going back to the city." While he's doing that, I look at Johnny. "I'm not going to be able to see. Will you be able to guide me out?"

"Yes."

"Good," I say, and shoot Tobias in the back of the head.

For once, somebody dies without an argument.

I don't know much about the trip back. I open a slot on the base of the box and fit it over my head. I am consumed in darkness. I'm led out to the skiff by Johnny and the boy. The boy rides with me, and Johnny gets into the water, dragging us behind him. His personality is diminished, and I can't tell if it's because he mourns Tobias, or because that is changing too, developing into something cold and barren.

The journey takes several hours. I know we pass the corpse flowers, the staring eyes and the bloodless faces pressing from the foliage. I am sure that the creature unleashes its earth-breaking cry, and that any living thing that hears it hemorrhages its life away, into the still waters. I know that night falls. I know the unfurling flame of our new guide lights the undersides of the cypress, runs out before us across the water, fills the dark like the final lantern in a fallen world.

I make a quiet and steady passage there.

The bar is closed upstairs and the man at the door lets us in without a word. He makes no comment about my companions, or the iron boxes hanging from a chain. The world he lives in is already breaking from its old shape. The new one has space for wonders.

Eugene is sitting behind his desk in his darkened office. I can tell he's drunk. It smells like he's been here since we left, almost twenty-four hours ago now. The only light comes from the fire rising from Johnny's empty skull. It illuminates a pale structure on Eugene's desk: an immense antler, or a tree made of bone. There are human teeth protruding along some of its tines, and a long crack near the wider base of it reveals a raw, red meat, where a mouth opens and closes.

"Where's Patrick?" he says.

"Dead," I say. "Tobias, too."

"And the atlas?"

"I burned it."

He nods, as though he'd been expecting that very thing. After a moment he gestures at the bone tree. "This is my son," he says. "Say hi, Max."

The mouth shrieks. It stops to draw in a gasping breath, then repeats the sound. The cry is sustained for several seconds before stuttering into a sob, and then going silent again.

"He keeps growing. He's going to be a big boy before it's all over."

"Yeah. I can see that."

"Who're your friends, Jack?"

I have to think about that before I answer. "I really don't know," I say, finally.

"So what do you want? You want me to tell you you're off the hook? You want me to tell you you're free to go?"

"You told me that before. It turned out to be bullshit."

"Yeah, well. That's the world we live in, right?"

"I guess it is. You're on notice, Eugene. Leave me alone. Don't come to my door anymore. I'm sorry things didn't work out here. I'm sorry about your son. But you have to stay away. I'm only going to say it once."

He looks at Johnny and the boy, and then he smiles at me. He must have to summon it from far away. "I'll take that under advisement, Jack. Now get the fuck out of here."

We turn and walk back up the stairs. It's a long walk back to my bookstore, where I'm anxious to get to work on the atlas. But I have a light to guide me, and I know this place well.

# The Diabolist

For many years, we in the town of Angel's Rest knew your father. Our monster. He was a middle-aged man, prickly of temperament and reclusive of habit, but of such colorful history, and of such exotic disposition, that we forgave him these faults and regarded him with a fond indulgence. He was our upstart boy. Our black sheep. He lived in a faded old mansion by the lake and left us to gossip at his scandalous life story. It was a matter of record that he'd been drummed out of his place of employment at the university down in Hob's Landing some years ago, his increasingly eccentric theories and practices costing him his job, his reputation, and—it was whispered (and we believed because it was too wonderful not to)—the life of his own beloved wife.

Dr. Timothy Benn, metaphysical pathologist.

Theomancer.

Sometimes the sky around his house lit up after dark with whatever wicked industry kept him awake, bright reds and greens and yellows igniting the bellies of the clouds like a celestial carnival show, or like an iridescent bruise. Once he seemed to tip the axis of gravity, so that loose objects—pebbles in the road, dropped key rings, babies tossed into the air by their fathers—fell sideways toward his house, instead of toward the ground. This only lasted a few minutes, and we responded with bemused patience. It was just one of the quirks of sharing a small town with a known diabolist.

And so it was that we enjoyed the company of our resident monster and the particular glamour he afforded us, until the day he died, and you found him slumped in his favorite chair.

Dearest Allison.

We didn't know you like we knew him. Like him, you were sullen and withdrawn, but you lacked any of the outlandish characteristics that made him so charming to us. You did not puncture holes in time and space. You did not draw angels from the ether and bind them with whores' hair. You only lived, like any awkward girl, attending high school in a cloud of resentment and distrust, hiding your eyes behind your bangs and your body beneath baggy clothes and a shield of textbooks clutched to your chest. We saw you in class, sitting in the back row with your head down; we saw you weaving like an eel through hallways choked with strangers; we saw you when you came down from the mansion on pilgrimages to the grocery store, where even the items you bought were disappointing and mundane. Not even the minor spectacle of a kumquat.

After school, after shopping, we'd watch you climb into your father's car with the tinted windows, engine growling at the curb, and disappear up the hill into the mansion.

For all the attention you paid us, you might as well have been moving through a world erased of people.

We loved your father, but we did not love you.

~ ~ ~

The miracle began the night of his death. We imagine the scenario: He bid you good night as you went to bed, with a light kiss on the forehead. You asked him a small, domestic question: about high school, or about something you might have seen on TV. He answered you noncommittally; he wanted to be present for you, but after all there was work to be done. He walked downstairs and retired to his study, in the room overlooking the lake. He poured himself a healthy measure of single-malt Scotch and retrieved a crime novel from his bookshelf. We like to think that he enjoyed these small pleasures for a little while, as he reclined in his easy chair. Then he closed his eyes, leaned back, and quietly died, felled by the surrender of some mysterious inner function.

You came downstairs the next morning, Allison, and you found him there. Oh, how we would have loved to see your expression. To watch that tide of grief.

Instead, there is only this frustrating period of darkness in our narrative, lasting that whole day, in which you might have said anything, done anything, and there was no one there to see it. All that beautiful sorrow, lost forever.

You did not call any of us for help.

What did you do, Allison?

Did you cry? Did you scream?

Did you think of us at all?

We found you again the next morning. A Saturday, early. We saw your feet and ankles poised at the top of the cellar stairs. You paused there, at the edge of this dark gulf, uncertain of yourself. A quiet, unsteady hiss emerged from somewhere below, like an unending exhalation. You'd never been allowed in your father's laboratory before; simply standing there was a transgression. But after that pause, you descended with purpose, and we saw you: pale white legs, pink shorts, wrinkled black shirt; and finally your face, moonlike and frightened. You swept your hand over the light switch and threw the laboratory into flickering clarity.

Rows of shelving and workbenches filled the vast work space, each one crowded with repurposed wine boxes or milk crates, holding overstuffed three-ring binders or notebooks or jars of formaldehyde densely packed with biological misadventures. There was an aquarium empty of fish, but with two severed blue eyes lolling on the bright blue gravel, tracking you as you passed; a massive telescope dominating the cellar's far corner, its wide glass eye raised toward the closed root-cellar doors; a broken, bloody mason jar sitting at the center of a pentagram chalked onto the floor beneath one of the workbenches; and six large double-stacked dog crates with children's names and ages stenciled on the outsides, all empty save one, which was home to an abandoned stuffed lion. The walls were covered with parchment bearing a strange pictographic alphabet. Hanging among them were your own endeavors, paintings your father had retained from your elementary school days.

And then there were the small accumulations of a normal life: the desk chair with the wheels that stuck; the crumpled, empty bags of potato chips on the floor; the Minnesota Twins mug sitting beside the dormant laptop, still holding an inch of milky coffee, like dirty water at the bottom of a well.

And in the back of the room, nearly hidden by the clutter, was the vat. It was huge, slightly taller and wider than a refrigerator, mounted on an industrial-capacity cooling unit. It was filled with a luminescent green gel. A radio was affixed to the side of the vat with duct tape and twine; a spaghetti snarl of wires trailed from it to the vat's base, where it disappeared into the side.

This was where the hiss was coming from. It sputtered as you approached. When you stood at your father's desk—close enough to the vat to caress it, if you had wanted to—the static barked, and a voice, genderless and faint, swam up from the deeps of chaos and noise to speak to you.

"I know you," I said. This was my time in isolation and darkness—the time before I became "we" again.

Just briefly your face shone with the hard light of hope.

"I know you," I said again, willing my speech through the long black crush of empty space. "You're the daughter."

And you spoke to me, too, for the first time: "Who are you?"

I never had a name until your father gave me one. I was a wretch, one imp among a numberless multitude of imps working in the Love Mills on the Eighty-Fourth Declension of Hell. I did not know language until I was pulled here by your father's sorcery, and learned it after hearing him speak a single word; I did not know of my own individuality until I was peeled from a shared consciousness and from my own body, to be imprisoned as an isolated scrap of thought in that vat; and I did not know love, though my whole existence was bent to its creation, until I saw your father's expression crumple in despair when he realized that the thing he had plucked from Hell was not the one he had sought.

I knew something had happened to him, though I had no word for death. In the middle of the night I was engulfed by a falling tide of his dreams, thoughts, and memories, which came raining through the ceiling like gouts of ash, as if a volcano were expunging all the dry contents of the earth. It was a bewildering experience, vertiginous and exhilarating—

like nothing I had ever known. It did not abate all night and continued even as you came down to the cellar. I could tell immediately that you did not see it or feel it. Your father's dead brain was geysering, filling the air with all its accumulated freight, and you had no way to apprehend it.

I suppose that could be considered a waste.

"Your father called me 'Claire,' when I first arrived," I told you, each word spitting through the static, and I watched your face make a complicated movement: a mixture of sorrow and hope, which I have learned is part of love's vocabulary. You retreated to the desk and sat in your father's chair.

"That's my mother's name," you said.

"I know."

When you spoke again, your voice sounded strange, as though your throat were being squeezed: "Is that who you are?"

"No."

You were silent for a long time. The radio on my vat hissed, like rainfall, or like the sound of your father's spilling brain. You leafed through the pages of a journal he'd kept on the desk. You turned on the computer, but you didn't know the password to access it. Your search did not seem to be motivated by any real curiosity, though. You seemed stunned by something. Only partially there.

"Where is your father?" I asked you.

You sighed, as if I'd said something tedious. "He's dead."

"Oh," I said, understanding suddenly where the tide of dream ash was coming from. "Is that why you're upset?"

"I'm not upset." You looked at me, as if you thought I might challenge you. But I didn't know how to answer you, Allison. I envied your detachment. I was cast adrift from the rest of me, isolated for the first time. I had never known loneliness. It caused me great pain.

And pain, too, was something new.

How do your kind live like this? How do you not extinguish yourselves from the cold misery of it? How do you know each other at all?

"So, you're something Dad conjured up? Like a demon or something?"

"I'm not a demon. I'm an imp. I'm a laborer in the Love Mills."

"What are those?" You didn't even look at me as you asked these questions. Instead you walked slowly around the lab, tracing your finger across the pictographs or stopping to study one of your own early finger paintings.

"I don't know how to answer that in a way you can understand."

"Wow, you sound just like Dad."

It did not sound like a compliment.

"I want to go home," I said, hoping to turn this conversation along a more productive course.

You stopped at the dog cages with the children's names. "What did he do down here? I mean, I know he, like . . . summoned devils or whatever." You turned to look at me. "Is that what he did?"

"I don't know what he did before I arrived. I know that he was unhappy to see me."

"So you were an accident?"

"I think so."

You nodded and returned to his desk. You opened a manila envelope and a sheaf of photographs spilled out. They were of your mother. They were casual and unposed. Your father looked at them often. Sometimes they made him cry. Sometimes they pushed him into a rage. I couldn't understand how the same images could provoke such different reactions, and

I was curious to see how you would respond. You stared at them for a long time, too, but your expression did not change.

You put them down and said, "My dad's body is still upstairs. I haven't called anybody. I guess that's messed up."

"Is it?"

"It's what you're supposed to do. I'm supposed to cry, too."

"Why?"

You shrugged. "Because he's my dad."

"Then why don't you?"

"I'm a monster, I guess."

I didn't understand this, but it seemed unimportant, so I returned to my own concern. "I want to go home, Allison. I want my body back. I'm lonely here."

"Well, you can't," you said. "I don't know how to send you home. You're just going to have to suck it up."

"That's not acceptable."

You stood, calmly and with such poise, and approached the vat. This time you did put your hand on it, and though I should not have been able to, I felt the heat of your blood, the warmth of human proximity. I did not know what it meant, but it shocked me into silence.

"You were meant to be Mom. Did you know? He was trying to bring back Mom, and instead he got you."

I had nothing to say to that. I remembered his horrified reaction the night he pulled me here, and realized what he had done. It was my first glimpse of love's face.

"I'm going upstairs," you said, turning away from me.

I felt a wild and fearful longing. "Don't leave me here," I said, my voice lost in the crackle of the radio.

You just kept walking. You turned off the lights as you ascended and left me there, the green light from my vat and my strange liquid form throwing shadows into the dark air. I had never been alone like this. I began to understand that it would last forever.

Finally, you came down to us, in Angel's Rest. The day was overcast and windy; you descended the long road into town, your hair, for once, not obscuring your face but trailing behind you like a dark and unfurled flag. Maybe this unprecedented event should have been enough to let us know that something had gone wrong. But we were creatures caught in our own routine. We were unsuspicious and ignorant. It's hard to know a miracle for what it is until it blots out the sun with its beauty.

You went to the café in our local bookstore and bought a coffee, ignoring the clerk's open stare as you gave her your order. Her name was Maggie; she was a senior, three years ahead of you in school and bound for the very university that had driven your father out years ago. Her younger sister was in your computer science class, so she was privy to all the latest rumor and gossip surrounding you. She leaned forward a fraction and sniffed the air, to see if it was true that you didn't bathe, that you stank of body odor. She couldn't smell anything but assumed that this was because the jacket you were wearing obscured it. When she took your money, she was careful not to let her fingers touch yours, and she dropped the change onto the counter rather than put it into your hand.

Did you notice these minor insults?

Maggie was so close to leaving our town. If your father had only lived another six or seven months, she would have missed out on everything.

You waited out her shift, and then Joey came in. He saw you sitting there, and he felt a mixture of fear, anger, and excitement. He remembered going to the Devil's Willow with you earlier in the year, making out with you and wanting to go further but being told no. He remembered the humiliation he felt, the thwarted urge, and remembered too the fear of what people would say if they found out he'd tried to score with the town freak. He hadn't spoken with you or even looked at you since then. Your sudden presence scared him and excited him all over again.

You ignored Maggie's hostile stare as she walked away. When Joey was alone behind the counter, you approached him.

"Meet me there tonight," you said.

Something inside him twisted. He was afraid you were setting him up. Someone like you—an ugly girl, an unwanted girl—had no right. "What are you talking about, skank?" he said.

"You know what I'm talking about. Just be there tonight."

"I don't just come when you call. What makes you think you can even talk to me?"

"Whatever. Come or don't. This is your only chance."

You left him there. He spent the rest of his shift in a slow-burning rage, because although he was determined not to go, he knew that he would.

The Devil's Willow grew like a gnarled temple on the far side of the lake. Its brilliant green foliage spilled over and trailed into the water, like a suspended fountain, hiding the bent, blackened wood of the trunk. It got its name from the fact that we believed your father practiced infernal rites there. Some nights we'd see dozens of little candle flames arrayed beside it, or even suspended in the air around it, and there was that one whole week when the entire tree was engulfed in a cold green-white fire. Julie lost her virginity to Thom there last year, and although she never admitted this to anyone, she was afraid that she'd gotten pregnant and that her baby would be born with a goat's head. When she got her period she cried with relief and terror and her hands shook so badly at school that they sent her home early.

You went there after leaving Joey at the café. Were you planning the night ahead? Were you there for the silence, or were you trying to get closer to the dark energies of your father's practice? We saw the shape of you as you sat lakeside, your feet dipped into the water, leaning back on your hands like some pale white orchid.

You were always unknowable to us, Allison. We guessed at your motives, at your relationship with your father, and at your reactions to our taunts and provocations. Although we were content to imagine your interior life for all these years, now we want to know the truth. We don't want to guess at you anymore, Allison.

We want to know if you feel what we do.

We know a story of the lake.

There are no stories in the Love Mills. There is no one to tell them, and there is no one to listen; for an imp, there is nothing but the building and maintaining of the mills. It was not until I was pulled to this cold tomb of a world—torn from the plural into the singular—that an idea like "story" was ever introduced to me.

I did not hear it from your father, who did not forgive me for not being his wife. He worked at his various errands in silence. I only learned it after his death, when he sat up there in his study, reclining in his chair like a dead king, his head a volcano of dream ash, a ghostly plume of whatever made him a human being pouring out of him like a long sigh. It was beautiful, Allison, and it's a tragedy that you couldn't see it.

The story of the lake was a shower of cinders that fell through me after you left. I don't know if it's based on something he read or if it's something he made up. I don't even know whether or not he believed it. The story goes that there was once an angel that roamed these hills, in the early days of your kind, long before you had dominion over the world. The angel was a giant to men, a gyre of eyes and wings and talons, stranger and more fearsome than they could withstand. They ran from it in terror. The belief is that it was one of the last of the angels to join the Morningstar's rebellion. It arrived too late, and the gates of Hell were sealed. An outcast from both kingdoms, it wandered here alone until it could no longer bear the isolation. The angel found a deep lake—this one, Allison; this lake—and went to sleep at its bottom, where it would remain for the rest of time.

I don't know if the story is true. But I drew comfort from it. It made me less lonely. It's about the Morningstar, after all, and to hear Him spoken of, even in this secondary way, opened a cascade of beauty inside me. I felt a terrible yearning for my home and my work. It was by that yearning that I knew the Morningstar's grace was still upon me. The ache of need is a music in Hell.

Your father wondered if this town and everyone in it was just a dream itself, a figment the angel had created to keep itself company. Once I would have laughed at that. I would have told you that if it had wanted companionship, it would not have dreamt creatures such as you.

Now we're not so sure.

You came down to talk to me that night. You cooked yourself a dinner in the microwave and brought it downstairs, where you ate silently at your father's desk. You left the lights off, sitting in the green luminescence of the vat, listening to the quiet hiss of the radio. You did not acknowledge me at first, but your presence was a lovely surprise, and it went a great distance toward dispelling my loneliness. Though you didn't know it, it was an act of kindness.

"I like it down here," you said, once you'd finished. "It's like being at the bottom of the sea. No wonder Dad spent all his time here."

"I don't know what the sea is," I said.

"It's basically just like the lake outside, only a lot bigger."

"How much bigger?"

"It covers most of the world. Don't you know these things in Hell?"

The notion of a lake large enough to cover the world inspired that sense of yearning again. I didn't know how I could ache for a place I'd never been. My life had been defined by labor, by hard earth and turning bone and the pink blossoms of smoke rising from our industries, by striations of light across a sky obscured by a rosy curtain of ash. There was no sea. There was no lake. There was no wish for any other place.

It never occurred to me to wonder what it was we labored to create.

"I don't really know anything about Hell. I was in the Love Mills. That's all I know."

You shook your head and nearly smiled. "Trust me. If my dad brought you here? You're from Hell. That was basically his thing."

"If you say so."

You pushed your plate away and took one of your father's notebooks, leaning back in the chair and paging through it with apparent disinterest. "So did he talk to you about Mom?"

"He didn't say anything to me."

"Join the club." You shook your head, thinking about it. "She wanted to leave us, you know? She didn't care." You crossed your arms on the desk and rested your head there, turned away from me. "I guess he really loved her," you said, and for a long while you didn't say anything else. I heard you sniff once, and I knew you were crying. I recognized this as another manifestation of love. I was coming to know all of its wonderful facets. The kind you felt was like mine: a wanting that cannot be satisfied. The kind your father felt for your mother was different. It was the kind with hooks.

After a moment you lifted your head and looked at me. "Anyway, I came down here to see what I have to do to flush you out of there. It's right here in the notebook. I'm not sure what that'll do to you. Maybe send you back home, maybe kill you. So you might as well go ahead and enjoy your life for a little while longer, because I'm going to go upstairs and get wasted, then come down here and do it."

I did not know how to receive this information, so I said nothing. The only example I had of death was your own father, whose death seemed to have done little to change him, other than fixing him in place. After all, he still resided in his chair on the floor above us, unfurling his unspent thoughts into the air. The other possibility—being sent back home—was too wonderful to contemplate.

"And then I'm going to do one of Dad's rituals."

"What do you mean?"

"I've been looking through his notebooks. It doesn't look too hard. And since he just died, maybe I can get him back. Maybe he's not too far away yet."

"I don't understand. I thought you didn't care."

"I don't." The tears came back, but you made no move to hide them this time. "I don't care."

Even in its absence, love pulled at you with its terrible gravity. Your face was beautiful in anguish. I could see the work of my life there. The house was filled with it, Allison. Love in all its grandeur. What shapes it made of your lives. What shapes it makes, still.

Your father's thoughts had begun to cool, fluttering down to me now rarely, like leaves from an old tree, nearly spent. One drifted past, stately and blue. You were younger; you were on the couch watching TV with him. You'd had a good day; you were tired and warm. You leaned over and rested your head on your father's shoulder. He pushed you away. You apologized and leaned in the other direction. Shame consumed him.

He wanted to be touched with another kind of love, from another kind of person.

You flushed the vat as I considered that thought. The floor opened beneath me and I flowed through a narrow chute in a wild green torrent, sliding through darkness for several disorienting minutes until I splashed from the end of a culvert and flew through the clear air, landing finally in the warm lake and dissolving there.

It was like waking. It can only be like waking.

I saw the stars overhead. I felt the ripple of wind, the pull of the roots of the Devil's Willow as they sipped at me. I felt the bed of the earth below me, and I felt too the great, slow-beating heart of the thing buried beneath the cold mud.

I am the lake. You have made me anew.

Joey met you under the Devil's Willow. He was angry and scared, but just proud enough to believe that you had come to regret your earlier rejection of him, and now wanted him after all. He didn't come alone. He wanted to make you pay for the embarrassment you'd caused him, so he had two of his friends follow. They were meant to hide in the bushes several yards away and take pictures of you as you undressed, to pass around the school. Joey meant to have his revenge.

You were waiting for him beneath the willow. You had a picnic blanket spread out and half a dozen candles lit, their flames trembling in the cool night air. The sky was high and cold, icy with stars. You sat in the middle of the blanket, legs curled beneath you, a glass of whiskey already in your hand. Joey paused when he saw all of this. He considered doubling back to send his friends home.

But his fear of you was too great, so he didn't. He stopped at the edge of the blanket and stood frozen.

"Come on," you said.

"Are you drunk?"

"A little bit."

"Without me? That's not fair."

"So sit down and catch up with me."

He dropped to his knees and moved closer to you. You handed him the bottle, and he took it. You let him take a good swig, his head tilted back, before you slipped the knife cleanly between his ribs. You held it there for a moment, your hand wrapped tightly around the handle.

"Ow!" He looked down at what you had done. He hardly believed it was real. It felt so inconsequential; like a wasp sting. "You bitch! You stabbed me!"

You slid the knife free, and it was like pulling a stopper from a bottle of wine: Blood gushed from the wound, and Joey fell forward, catching himself with one hand while holding the other to his side. The pain careened through him now, unbelievable in its ferocity. "What?" he said, and his voice sounded small—like the child he still was.

I watched your face for a reaction. You looked pale, but otherwise betrayed no emotion.

"Help me," he said.

There was a rustling from the bushes several feet away, and you turned toward it, alarmed. His two friends—boys you must have seen at high school with Joey—crept uncertainly out of hiding. One held his phone at his side.

"Dude. Are you okay?"

You stood, the knife drooling in your hand.

"I think you better call an ambulance," Joey said, his voice pitched high with fear.

Because they were fools, the boys ignored him and ran forward. One dropped to Joey's side, and the other screamed at you, calling you filthy names, his body rigid with shock. You ignored them all; you were watching the tree.

A cold tongue of fire crept up from the roots and coiled around the trunk. Several more followed. In moments the Devil's Willow was a pale green-white conflagration, shedding no heat but filling the little valley with its weird radiance. I felt that thing that slept under the mud stir beneath my waters. Every slow thump of its heart brightened the willow's fire.

You spoke to it. "Bring him back. Please just bring him back. I'll do whatever you want. I'll kill everyone. I'll kill them all."

I realized then that you were talking to the Morningstar. Your unfilled want, Allison, the hollow in your heart and the love that goes unanswered, is a prayer to Him. Your whole life is a hymn to Hell.

I think that's when I fell in love, myself, for the first time.

"I don't know what to do," you said.

You couldn't bring back your father, though; whatever sorcery he practiced, you did not know it. You'd started something, but you did not know how to go further. In moments you would be brought down by these stupid boys, and what might happen after that I couldn't even guess.

But if the Morningstar could not respond to you, I could.

I couldn't speak to you without the radio. I would have to show you.

Joey made it easy. He lay gasping on the blanket, his friend's hand pressed into his side. The heel of his left shoe rested in the water. So I pulled him in. It only took a moment; it was easy. I had become the lake, diffused into it like a breath into the atmosphere. I poured myself into his eyes and down his throat; I filled him like a vessel. Then I used him to pull in his friend, and I filled him, too. In moments I had all three. I felt their life sparking in me. For the first time since being brought here, I knew a communal mind again. I was no longer alone. And so began the miracle you brought to our town.

We stood panting by the shore, feeling our new selves. We glanced at one another, ashamed by this new intimacy at first, at the torrents of knowledge that poured into us, all our shabby secrets and desires brought to sudden light. But the embarrassment dissipated quickly; there can be no secrets if we all share the same mind.

The same love.

We looked at you. We spoke to you in a chorus of voices: "Come here, Allison."

The look on your face—I didn't know it. Was it another kind of love? Was there more yet to learn?

"Who are you?" you asked.

"You know who we are," we said, in unison.

You turned and fled. It was a shocking rejection. We didn't understand. Isn't this what you wanted? To be welcomed? To be loved? Not to be alone anymore?

The tree lit the night and soon drew other people from town. They joined us, reluctantly at first—many had to be forced into the water, where I could pour into them—but they were grateful soon enough. By the time morning approached, we had everyone.

We decided to work. It was what we knew. The memory of the mills drove us. Many of us went into the lake to be consumed by the labor. Limbs were broken and reconfigured, bone grafted to bone, kites of skin stretched taut. It took two hundred people broken down and reassembled to make the skeleton of the mill's first wheel; there is more yet to be done.

As the sun crests the hills, the mill begins to turn in the lake. We lift our voice in a chorus of groans. We bend to you like reeds to the light. Why don't you respond, Allison? Why have you never responded to us, despite our every provocation?

We used to know our monster. Now we don't. We see you with ten thousand eyes, but we don't know you. You're standing at the window of your house, your hollow father still sitting behind you like a deposed king. His head gone cold and quiet. You're staring out at us. You press your hand to the glass. Can you feel the warmth of us, the way I felt your warmth once, through a different glass?

Your face makes a complicated movement, an expression we believe will tell us something about you. But before we can read it, the sunlight hits the windowpane and the glare of it reflects back to us, a tiny star in the morning light.

# Skullpocket

Jonathan Wormcake, the Eminent Ghoul of Hob's Landing, greets me at the door himself. Normally, one of his several servants would perform this minor duty, and I can only assume it's my role as a priest in the Church of the Maggot that affords me this special attention. I certainly don't believe it has anything to do with our first encounter, fifty years ago this very day. I'd be surprised if he remembers that at all.

He greets me with a cordial nod of the head and leads me down a long hallway to the vast study, lined with thousands of books and boasting broad windows overlooking the Chesapeake Bay, where the waters are painted gold by an autumn sun. I remember this walk, and this study, with a painful twinge in my heart. I was just a boy when I came here last. Now, like Mr. Wormcake himself, I am a very old man, facing an end to my life.

I'm shocked by the toll the years have taken on him. I know I shouldn't be; Mr. Wormcake's presence in this mansion extends back one hundred years, and his history with the town is well documented. But since the death of the Orchid Girl last year, he has withdrawn from public life, and in that time his aspect has changed considerably. Though his bearing remains regal, and his grooming is as immaculate as ever, age hangs from him like a too-large coat. The flesh around his head is entirely gone, and his hair—once his proudest feature—is no more. The bare bones of his skull gleam brightly in the late afternoon sunlight, and the eyes have fallen to dust, leaving dark sockets. He looks frail, and he looks tired.

To be fair, the fourteen children crowding the room, all between the ages of six and twelve, only underscore this impression. They've been selected for the honor of attending the opening ceremonies of the Seventieth Annual Skullpocket Fair by the Maggot, which summoned them here through their dreams. The children are too young, for the most part, to understand the significance of the honor, and so they mill about the great study in nervous anticipation, chattering to one another and touching things they shouldn't.

Mr. Wormcake's longtime manservant—formally known as Brain in a Jar 17, of the Frozen Parliament, but who is more affectionately recognized as the kindly "Uncle Digby"—glides into the room, his body a polished, gold-inlaid box on rolling treads, topped with a clear dome under which the floating severed head of an old man is suspended in a bubbling green solution, white hair drifting like ghostly kelp. He is received with a joyful chorus of shouts from the children, who immediately crowd around him. He embraces the closest of them with his metal arms.

"Oh my, look at all these wonderful children," he says. "What animated little beasts!"

To anyone new to Hob's Landing, Uncle Digby can be unnerving. His face and eyes are dead, and his head appears to be nothing more than a preserved portion of a cadaver, which never moves—it's as still as a walnut—but the brain inside is both alive and lively, and it speaks through a small voice box situated beneath the glass dome.

While the children are distracted, Mr. Wormcake removes a small wooden box from where it sits discreetly on a bookshelf. He opens it and withdraws the lower, fleshy portion of a human face—from below the nose to the first curve of the chin, kept moist in a thin pool of blood. A tongue is suspended from it by a system of leather twine and gears. Mr. Wormcake affixes the half face to his skull by means of an elastic band and pushes the tongue into his mouth. Blood trickles down the jawline of the skull and dapples the white collar of his starched shirt. The effect is disconcerting, even to me, who has grown up in Hob's Landing and is accustomed to stranger sights than this.

Jonathan Wormcake has not ventured into public view for twenty years, since the denuding of his skull, and it occurs to me that I am the first person not a part of this household to witness this procedure.

I am here because Mr. Wormcake is dying, and as the resident priest of the Church of the Maggot, it is my duty to preside over his end of life ritual.

We don't know how a ghoul dies. Not even he is sure; he left the warrens as a boy and was never indoctrinated into the mysteries. The dreams given to us by the Maggot, replete with images of sloughing flesh and great, black kites riding silently along the night's air currents, suggest that it's not an ending, but a transformation. But we have no experience to measure these dreams against. What waits for him on the far side of this death remains an open question.

He stretches his mouth and moves his tongue, like a man testing the fit of a new article of clothing. Apparently satisfied, he looks at me at last. "It's good of you to come, especially on this night," he says.

"I have to admit I was surprised you chose the opening night of Skullpocket Fair for this. It seems there might have been a more discreet time."

He looks at the children gathered around Uncle Digby, who is guiding them gently toward the great bay window. They are animated by excitement and fear, a tangle of emotions I remember from when I was in their place. "I have no intention of stealing their moment," he says. "This night is about them. Not me."

I'm not convinced this is entirely true. Though the children have been selected to participate in the opening ceremonies of Skullpocket Fair, and will be the focus of the opening act, the pomp and circumstance is no more about them than it is about the Maggot, or the role of the church in this town. Really, it's all about Jonathan Wormcake. Never mind the failed mayoral campaign of the mid-seventies, never mind the fallout from the Sleepover War or the damning secrets made public by the infamous betrayal of his best friend, Wenceslas Slipwicket—Wormcake is the true patriarch of Hob's Landing; the Skullpocket Fair is held each year to celebrate that fact, and to fortify it.

That this one marks the one hundredth anniversary of his dramatic arrival in town, as well as his imminent farewell to this particular life, makes his false modesty a little hard to take.

"Sit down," he says, and extends a hand toward the most comfortable chair in the room: a high-backed, deeply cushioned piece of furniture of the sort one might expect to find in the drawing room of an English lord. Wormcake maneuvers another, smaller chair away from the chess table in the corner and closer to me, so we can speak more easily. He eases himself slowly into it and sighs with a weary satisfaction as his body settles, at last, into stillness. If he had eyes, I believe he would close them now.

Meanwhile, Uncle Digby has corralled the children into double rows of folding chairs. He is distributing soda and little containers of popcorn, which do not calm the children, but do at least draw their focus.

"Did you speak to any of the children after they received the dream?" Wormcake asks me.

"No. Some of them were brought to the church by their parents, but I didn't speak to any of them personally. We have others who specialize in that kind of thing."

"I understand it can be a traumatic experience for some of them."

"Well, it's an honor to be selected by the Maggot, but it can also be pretty terrifying. The dream is very intense. Some people don't respond well."

"That makes me sad."

I glance over at the kids, seated now, popcorn spilling from their hands as they shovel it into their mouths. They bristle with a wild energy: a crackling, kinetic radiation that could spill into chaos and tears if not expertly handled. Uncle Digby, though, is nothing if not an expert. The kindliest member of the Frozen Parliament, he has long been the spokesman for the family, as well as a confidant to Mr. Wormcake himself. There are many who believe that without his steady influence, the relationship between the Wormcakes and the townspeople of Hob's Landing would have devolved into brutal violence long ago. Not everyone welcomed the new church, in the early years.

"The truth is, I don't want anyone to know why you're

here. I don't want my death to be a spectacle. If you came up here any other night, someone would notice, and it wouldn't be hard for them to figure out why. This way, the town's attention is on the fair. And anyway, I like the symmetry of it."

"Forgive me for asking, Mr. Wormcake, but my duty here demands it: Are you doing this because of the Orchid Girl's death?"

He casts a dark little glance at me. It's not possible to read emotion in a naked skull, of course, and the prosthetic mouth does not permit him any range of expression; but the force of the look leaves me no doubt of his irritation. "The Orchid Girl was her name for the people in town. Her real name was Gretchen. Call her that."

"My apologies. But the question remains, I'm afraid. To leave the world purely, you must do it unstained by grief."

"Don't presume to teach me about the faith I introduced to you."

I accept his chastisement quietly.

He is silent for a long moment, and I allow myself to be distracted by the sound of the children gabbling excitedly to one another, and of Uncle Digby relating some well-worn anecdote about the time the Kraken returned to the bay. Old news to me, but wonderful stuff to the kids. When Mr. Wormcake speaks again, it is to change course.

"You said the dream that summons the children is intense. You sounded as though you spoke from experience. This is not your first time to the house, is it?"

"No. I had the dream myself, when I was very young. I was summoned to Skullpocket Fair. Seventy years ago. The very first one."

"My, my. Now that *is* something. Interesting that it's you

who will perform my death ritual. So that puts you, what. In your eighties? You look young for your age."

I smile at him. "Thanks. I don't feel young."

"Who does, anymore? I suppose I should say welcome back."

The room seems host to a dizzying compression of history. There are three fairs represented tonight, at least for me: the Seventieth Annual Skullpocket Fair, which commences this evening; the inaugural Skullpocket Fair, which took place in 1944—seventy years ago, when I was a boy—and set my life on its course in the Church; and the Cold Water Fair of 1914, one hundred years ago, which Uncle Digby would begin describing very shortly. That Mr. Wormcake has chosen this night to die, and that I will be his instrument, seems too poetic to be entirely coincidental.

As if on cue, Uncle Digby's voice rings out, filling the small room. "Children, quiet down now, quiet down. It's time to begin." The kids settle at once, as though some spell has been spoken. They sit meekly in their seats, the gravity of the moment settling over them at last. The nervous energy is pulled in and contained, expressing itself now only in furtive glances and, in the case of one buzz-cut little boy, barely contained tears.

I remember, viscerally and immediately, the giddy terror that filled me when I was that boy, seventy years ago, summoned by a dream of a monster to a monster's house. I'm surprised when I feel the tears in my own eyes. And I'm further surprised by Mr. Wormcake's hand, hard and bony beneath its glove, coming over to squeeze my own.

"I'm glad it's you," he says. "Another instance of symmetry. Balance eases the heart."

I'm gratified, of course.

But as Uncle Digby begins to speak, it's hard to remember anything but the blood.

One hundred years ago, *says Uncle Digby to the children*, three little ghouls came out to play. They were Wormcake, Slip-wicket, and Stubblegut: best friends since birth. They were often allowed to play in the cemetery, as long as the sun was down and the gate was closed. There were many more children playing among the gravestones that night, but we're only going to concern ourselves with these three. The others were only regular children, and so they were not important.

Now, there were two things about this night that were already different from other nights they went aboveground to play. Does anybody know what they were?

No? Well I'll tell you. One was that they were let out a little bit earlier than normal. It was still twilight, and though sometimes ghouls were known to leave the warrens during that time, rarely were children permitted to come up so early. That night, however, the Maggot had sent word that there was to be a meeting in the charnel house—an emergency meeting, to arrange a ritual called an Extinction Rite, which the children did not understand, but which seemed to put the adults in a dreadfully dull mood. The children had to be got out of the way. There might have been some discussion about the wisdom of this decision, but ghouls are by nature a calm and reclusive folk, so no one worried that anything untoward would happen.

The other unusual thing about that night, obviously, was the Cold Water Fair.

The Cold Water Fair had been held every October for years and years. It was a way for Hob's Landing to celebrate its relationship with the Chesapeake Bay, and to commemorate the time the Kraken rose to devour the town but was turned away with some clever thinking and some good advice. This was the first time the fair was held on this side of Hob's Landing. In previous years it had been held on the northern side of the town, out of sight of the cemetery. But someone had bought some land and got grumpy about the fair being on it, so now they were holding it right at the bottom of the hill instead.

The ghoul children had never seen anything so wonderful! Imagine living your life in the warrens, underground, where everything was stone and darkness and cold earth. Whenever you came up to play, you could see the stars, you could see the light on the water, and you could even see the lights from town, which looked like flakes of gold. But this! Never anything like this. The fair was like a smear of bright paint: candy-colored pastels in the blue wash of air. A great illuminated wheel turned slowly in the middle of it, holding swinging gondola cars full of people.

*A Ferris wheel! shouts the buzz-cut boy who had been crying only a few minutes ago. His face is still ruddy, but his eyes shine with something else, now: something better.*

Yes, you're exactly right. A Ferris wheel! They had never even seen one before. Can you imagine that?

There were gaudy tents arranged all around it, like a little village. It was full of amazing new smells: cotton candy, roasting peanuts, hot cider. The high screams of children blew up to the little ghouls like a wind from a beautiful tomb. They stood transfixed at the fence, those grubby little things, with their hands wrapped around the bars and their faces pressed between.

They wondered, briefly, if this had anything to do with the Extinction Rite the adults kept talking about.

"Do you think they scream like that all the time?" Slip-wicket asked.

Wormcake said, "Of course they do. It's a fair. It's made just for screaming."

In fact, children, he had no idea if this was true. But he liked to pretend he was smarter than everybody else, even way back then.

*The children laugh. I glance at Mr. Wormcake, to gauge his reaction to what is probably a scripted joke, but his false mouth reveals nothing.*

Slipwicket released the longest, saddest sigh you have ever heard. It would have made you cry, it was so forlorn. He said, "Oh, how I would love to go to a place made only for screams." *Uncle Digby is laying it on thick here, his metal hands cupping the glass jar of his head, his voice warbling with barely contained sorrow. The kids eat it up.*

"Well, we can't," said Stubblegut. "We have to stay inside the fence."

Stubblegut was the most boring ghoul you ever saw. You could always depend on him to say something dull and dreadful. He was morose, always complaining, and he never wanted to try anything new. He was certain to grow up to be somebody's father—that most tedious of creatures. Sometimes the others would talk about ditching him as a friend, but they could never bring themselves to do it. They were good boys, and they knew you were supposed to stay loyal to your friends—even the boring ones.

"Come along," Stubblegut said. "Let's play skullpocket."

*At this, a transformation overtakes the children, as though a current has been fed into them. They jostle in their seats, and cries of "Skullpocket!" arise from them like pheasants from a bramble. They seem both exalted and terrified. Each is a little volcano, barely contained.*

Oh my! Do you know what skullpocket is, children?

*Yes, yes!*

*I do!*

*Yes!*

Excellent! In case any of you aren't sure, skullpocket is a favorite game of ghouls everywhere. In simple terms, you take a skull and kick it back and forth between your friends until it cracks to pieces. Whoever breaks it is the loser of the game and has to eat what they find inside its pocket. And what is that, children?

*The brain!*

*Eeeww!*

That's right! It's the brain, which everyone knows is the worst bit. It's full of all the gummy old sorrows and regrets gathered in life, and the older the brain is, the nastier it tastes. While the loser eats, other players will often dance in a circle around him and chant. And what do they chant?

*"Empty your pockets! Empty your pockets!" the children shout.*

Yes! You must play the game at a run, and respect is given to those who ricochet the skull off a gravestone to their intended target, increasing the risk of breaking it. Of course, you don't have to do that—you can play it safe and just bat it along nicely—but nobody likes a coward, do they, children? For a regular game, people use adults' skulls that have been interred for less than a year. More adventurous players might use the skull of an infant, which offers a wonderful challenge.

Well, someone was sent to retrieve a skull from the charnel house in the warrens, which was kept up by the corpse gardeners. There was always one to be spared for children who wanted to play.

The game was robust, with the ghouls careening the skull off trees and rocks and headstones; the skull proved hardy and it went on for quite some time.

Our young Mr. Wormcake became bored. He couldn't stop thinking about that fair, and the lights and the smells and—most of all—the screams. The screams filled his ears and distracted him from play. After a time, he left the game and returned to the fence, staring down at the fair. It had gotten darker by that time, so that it stood out in the night like a gorgeous burst of mushrooms.

Slipwicket and Stubblegut joined him.

"What are you doing?" said the latter. "The game isn't over. People will think you're afraid to play."

"I'm not afraid," said Wormcake. And in saying the words, a resolution took shape in his mind. "I'm not afraid of anything. I'm going down there."

His friends were shocked into silence. It was an awed silence, a holy silence, like the kind you find in church. It was the most outrageous thing they had ever heard anyone say.

"That's crazy," Stubblegut said.

"Why?"

"Because it's forbidden. Because the sunlight people live down there."

"So what?"

"They're gross!"

*At this, some of the children become upset. Little faces crinkle in outrage.*

Now, hold on, hold on. You have to understand how ghouls saw your people at the time. You were very strange to them. Hob's Landing was as exotic to them as a city on the moon would be to you. People went about riding horses, and they walked around in sunlight. On purpose, for Pete's sake! Who ever heard of such a thing?

*The children start to giggle at this, won over again.*

And when they came to the cemetery, they acted sad and

shameful. They buried their dead, the way a cat buries its own scat. They were soft and doughy, and they ate whatever came to hand, the way rats and cockroaches do.

*"We're not cockroaches!" cries one of the children.*

Of course not! But the ghouls didn't understand. They were afraid. So they made up wild ideas about you. And it kept their children from wandering, which was important, because they wanted the warrens to stay a secret. Ghouls had been living under the cities of the sunlight people for as long as there have *been* sunlight people, and for the most part they had kept their existence hidden. They were afraid of what would happen if they were discovered. Can you blame them for that?

But young Mr. Wormcake was not to be dissuaded by rumors or legends!

"I'm going down there. I want to see what it's all about."

Back then, the cemetery gate was not burdened with locks or chains; it simply had a latch, oiled and polished, which Wormcake lifted without trouble or fanfare. The gate swung open, and the wide, glittering world spread out before them like a feast at the banquet table. He turned to look at his friends. Behind them, the other children had assembled in a small crowd, the game of skullpocket forgotten. The looks on their faces ranged from fear to excitement to open disgust.

"Well?" he said to his friends. "Are you cowards?"

Slipwicket would not be called a coward! He made a grand show of his exit, lifting each foot with great exaggeration over the threshold and stomping it into the earth with a flourish. He completed his transgression with a happy skip and turned to look at Stubblegut, who lingered on the grave side of the fence and gathered his face into a worried knot. He placed his hands over his wide belly and gave it gentle pats, which was his habit when he was nervous.

At that moment of hesitation, when he might have gone back and warned the adults of what was happening, some unseen event in the fair below them caused a fresh bouquet of screams to lift up and settle over the ghouls like blown leaves. Slipwicket's whole body seemed to lean toward it, like he was being pulled by a great magnet. He looked at Stubblegut with such longing in his eyes, such a terrible ache, that his frightened friend's resolve was breached at last, and Stubblegut crossed the threshold himself with a grave and awful reluctance.

He was received with joy.

And before anyone could say "jackrabbit," Slipwicket bolted down the hill, a pale little gremlin in the dark green waves of grass. The others followed him in a cool breath of motion, the tall grass like a strange, rippling sea in the moonlight. Of course, they were silent in their elation: The magnitude of their crime was not lost upon them. Wormcake dared not release the cry of elation beating in his lungs.

But, children, they were in high rebellion. They were throwing off the rules of their parents and riding the wave of their own cresting excitement. Even Stubblegut felt it, like a blush of heat over his moss-grown soul.

Naturally, Uncle Digby's story stirs up memories of my own first fair.

The dream of the Maggot came to me in 1944, when I was twelve years old. The tradition of the Cold Water Fair had ended thirty years ago, on the blood-soaked night Uncle Digby is speaking of, and Hob's Landing had done without a festival of any sort since. But—though we didn't know it yet—this would be the year its replacement, the Skullpocket Fair, was born.

I was the sixth kid to receive the dream that year. I had heard about a couple of the others, so I had known, in some disconnected way, that it might happen. I didn't know what it meant, except that parents were terrified of it. They knew it had something to do with the Wormcake clan, and that was enough to make it suspect. Although this was in 1944, and the Wormcakes had been living in the mansion for thirty years at that point—peacefully, for the most part—there were still many in town who considered them to be the very incarnation of evil. Many of our parents were present that night of the Cold Water Fair, and they were slow to forgive. The fact that the Orchid Girl came into town and patronized the same shops we did, attended the same shows we did, didn't help matters at all, as far as they were concerned.

*She's putting on airs,* they said. *She thinks she's one of us. At least her husband has the decency to keep himself hidden away in that horrible old mansion.*

My friends and I were too young to be saddled with all of the old fears and prejudices of our parents, and anyway we thought the Orchid Girl was beautiful. We would watch her from across the street or through a window when she came to town, walking down Poplar Street as proud as you please, unattended by her servants or friends. She always wore a colorful, lovely dress that swirled around her legs, kept her hair pinned just so, and held her head high—almost defiantly, I can say now, looking back. We would try to see the seams on her face, where it would open up, but we never got close enough. We never dared.

We believed that anyone married to the Orchid Girl couldn't be all bad. And anyway, Mr. Wormcake always came to the school plays, brought his own children down to the ice skating rink in the wintertime, and threw an amazing Halloween party.

Admittedly, half the town never went, but most of us kids managed to make it over there.

We all knew about the Church of the Maggot. There were already neighborhoods converting, renouncing their own god for the one that burrowed through flesh. Some people our parents' age, also veterans of that night at the fair, had even become priests. They walked around town in shabby white vestments, talking on and on about the flesh as meat, the necessity of cleansing the bone, and other things that sounded strange and a little exciting to us. So when some of the children of Hob's Landing started to dream of the Maggot, us kids worried about it a lot less than our parents or grandparents did. At first, we were even jealous. Christina Laudener, just one year younger than I was, had the first one, and the next night it was little Eddie Brach. They talked about it in school, and word spread. It terrified them, but we wanted it ourselves nonetheless. They were initiates into some new mystery centered around the Wormcakes, and those of us who were left out burned with a terrible envy.

I was probably the worst of them, turning my jealousy into a bullying contempt whenever I saw them at the school, telling them that the ghouls were going to come into their homes while they were sleeping and kidnap them, so they could feed them to their precious Maggot. I made Eddie cry, and I was glad. I hated him for being a part of something I wasn't.

Until a couple of nights later, when I had the dream myself.

I'm told that everyone experiences the dream of the Maggot differently. For me it was a waking dream. I climbed out of bed at some dismal hour of the morning, when both my parents were still asleep, and stumbled my way to the bathroom. I sat on the toilet for a long time, waiting for something to happen, but I couldn't go, despite feeling that

I needed to very badly. I remember this being a source of profound distress in the dream, well out of proportion to real life. It terrified me and I felt that it was a sign I was going to die.

I left the toilet and walked down the hallway to my parents' room, to give them the news of my impending demise. In my dream I knew they would only laugh at me, and it made me hate them.

Then I felt a clutching pain in my abdomen. I dropped to my knees and began to vomit maggots. Copious amounts of them. They wouldn't stop coming, just splashed out onto the ground with each painful heave, in wriggling piles, ropy with blood and saliva. It went on and on and on. When I stood up, my body was as wrinkled and crushed as an emptied sack. I fell to the floor and had to crawl back to my room, boneless and weak.

The next morning I went down to breakfast as usual, and as my father bustled about the kitchen, looking for his keys and his hat, and my mother leaned against the countertop with a cigarette in her hand, I told them that I had received the dream everyone was talking about.

This stopped them both cold. My mother looked at me and said, "Are you sure? What happened? What does it mean?"

"They're having a fair. I have to go."

Of course this was absurd; there had been nothing about a fair in the dream at all. But the knowledge sat with all the incontrovertibility of a mountain. Such is the way of the Maggot.

"What fair?" Dad said. "There's no fair."

"The Wormcakes," I said. "They're having it at the mansion."

My parents exchanged a look.

"And they invited you in a dream?" he said.

"It wasn't really like an invitation. It's more like the Maggot told me I have to come."

"It's a summons," Mom told him. "That's what Carol was saying. It's like a command."

"Like hell," Dad said. "Who do those freaks think they are?"

"I think I have to go, Dad."

"You don't have to do a goddamned thing they tell you. None of us do."

I started to cry. The thought of disregarding the dream was unthinkable. I felt that familiar clenching in my gut and I feared the maggots were going to start pouring out of my mouth. I thought I could feel them inside me already, chewing away, as though I were already dead. I didn't know how to articulate what I know now: that the Maggot had emptied me out, and was offering to fill me again. To ignore it would be to live the rest of my life as a husk.

It was a hard cry, as sudden as a monsoon, my cheeks hot and red, the tears painting my face, my breath coming in a thin hiss. Mom rushed to me and engulfed me in her arms, saying the things moms are supposed to say.

"I have to go," I said. "I have to go, I have to. I have to go."

I watch the children sitting there in profile, their little faces turned to Uncle Digby and his performance like flowers to the sun, and I try to see myself there all those years ago. The sun is setting outside, and darkness is hoarding over the bay. The light in Uncle's glass dome illuminates the green solution from beneath, and his pale, dead face is graced with a rosy pink halo of light.

I must have seen the same thing when I sat there with the other kids. But I don't remember it. I only remember the fear. I guess I must have laughed at the jokes, just like the others did.

Skullpocket is, of course, a culling game. It's not about singling out and celebrating a winner. It's about thinning the herd.

Jonathan Wormcake does not appear to be listening to the story anymore. His attention is outside, on the darkening waters. Although her name has not come up yet, the Orchid Girl haunts this story as truly as any ghost. I wonder if it causes him pain. Grieving, to a ghoul, is a sign of weakness. It's a trait to be disdained. The grieving are not fit for the world. I look at the hard, clean curve of his skull and I try to fathom what's inside.

They were clever little ghouls, *Uncle Digby said*, and they kept to the outskirts and the shadows. They didn't want to be discovered. A ghoul child looks a lot like a human child when seen from the corner of the eye. It's true that they're paler, more gaunt, and if you look at one straight on you'll see that their eyes are like little black holes with nothing inside, but you have to pay attention to notice any of that. At the fair, no one was paying attention. There was too much else to see. So Wormcake and his friends were able to slip into the crowd without notice, and there they took in everything they could.

They were amazed by the striped, colorful tents, by the little booths with the competitive games, by the pens with pigs and mules, by the smells of cotton candy, frying oil, animal manure—everything was new and astonishing. Most of all, though, they marveled at the humans in their excitable state: walking around, running, hugging, laughing, and clasping their hands on one another's shoulders. Some were even crushing their lips together in a grotesque human version of a kiss!

*Here the children laugh. They are still young enough that all kissing is grotesque.*

There were many little ones, like themselves, and like you. They were swarming like hungry flies, running from tent to tent, waiting in lines, crackling with an energy so intense you could almost see it arcing from their hair.

It was quite unsettling to see humans acting this way. It was like watching someone indulging in madness. They were used to seeing humans in repose: quiet little morsels in their thin wooden boxes. Watching them like this was like watching a little worm before it transforms into a beautiful fly, but not as nice, because it was so much louder and uglier.

*A little girl raises her hand. She seems angry. When Uncle Digby acknowledges her, she says, "I don't think flies are beautiful. I think they're nasty."*

*"Well, I think you're the one who's nasty," Uncle Digby retorts. "And soon you'll be filling the little tummies of a thousand thousand flies, and they'll use you to lay eggs and make maggots, and shit out the bits of you they don't want. So maybe you should watch your horrid little mouth, child."*

*The little girl bursts into shocked tears, while the children around her stay silent or laugh unhappily.*

*Wormcake stirs beside me for the first time since the story began. "Uncle," he says.*

*"I'm sorry," says Uncle Digby. "Dear child, please forgive me. Tonight is a glorious night. Let's get back to the story, shall we?"*

*The children are quiet. Uncle Digby forges ahead.*

So they made their way amongst the humans, disturbed by their antics. They knew that it was only a matter of time before the humans all reached their true state, the condition in which they would face the long dark inside the earth; but this brief, erratic explosion of life stirred a fascinated shame in the ghouls.

"It's vile," said Stubblegut. "We shouldn't be seeing this. It's indecent."

"It's the most wonderful thing I've ever seen," said young Master Wormcake, and with the courage that had always separated him from the others, he strode out onto the midway, arms aswing and head struck back like the world's littlest worm lord.

You might be forgiven for thinking that *someone* would notice, provoking the humans to flee in terror, or cry out in alarm, or gather pitchforks and torches. But human beings are geniuses at self-delusion. Let's be honest, children, you are. You believe that your brief romance with the sun is your one, true life. Our little friend here, for example, becomes upset when contemplating the beauty of the fly. You cherish your comfortable delusions. That evening the humans at the fair just looked at the ghouls as wretched examples of their own kind. Sickly children, afflicted with some mysterious wasting illness that blues the flesh and tightens the skin around the bones. Pathetic creatures, to be mourned and fretted over, even if they also inspired a small thrill of revulsion. So the humans pretended not to see them. They ushered their own children to a safe distance and continued in their revels, in a state of constructed ignorance.

*Mr. Wormcake leans over to me and whispers in my ear, "Not entirely true. The human adults ignored us, yes. But the human children knew us for what we were. They pointed and quaked. Some burst into tears. It was all such fun."*

What was so difficult to tell my parents, all those years ago, was that I *wanted* to go to the fair. The summons was terrifying, yes, but it was also the touch of relevance I'd been wanting so badly. I was just like Christina Laudener now;

I was just like weepy Eddie Brach. Two other children had had the dream the same night I did, and by the time a week had finished, there were fourteen of us. The dreams stopped after that, and everyone understood that it was to be us, and only us.

We became a select group, a focus of envy and awe. There were some who felt the resentment I once did, of course, and we were the target of the same bullying I'd doled out myself. But we were a group by this time, and we found comfort and safety in that. We ate lunch together at school, hung out on weekends. The range of ages—six to twelve—was wide enough that normally none of us would have given one another the time of day. But the Maggot had changed everything.

The town was abuzz with talk. Of the fourteen summoned children, certainly, but also of the fair itself. Hob's Landing had been without anything like this since the night of Wormcake's arrival, thirty years before. That Wormcake himself should be the one to reintroduce a fair to the town seemed at once sacrilegious and entirely appropriate. Fliers began to appear, affixed to telephone poles, displayed in markets and libraries: *The First Annual Skullpocket Fair, To Be Held on the Grounds of Wormcake Mansion, on the Last Weekend of September 1944. Inaugurated by Select Children of Hob's Landing. Come and Partake in the Joy of Life with the Dapper Corpse!*

People were intrigued. That Mr. Wormcake was himself using the nickname he'd once fiercely objected to—he was not, he often reminded them, a corpse—was a powerful indicator that he meant to extend an olive branch to the people of Hob's Landing. And who were they to object? He and his family clearly weren't going anywhere. Wouldn't it be best, then, to foster a good relationship with the town's most famous citizens?

My parents were distraught. Once they realized I wanted to go, despite my panic of the first night, they forbade me. But that didn't worry me a bit. I knew the Maggot would provide a way. I was meant to be there, and the Maggot would organize the world in such a way as to make that happen.

And so it did. On the afternoon the first Skullpocket Fair was set to open, I headed for the front door, expecting a confrontation. But my parents were sitting together in the living room, my mother with her hands drawn in and her face downcast, my father looking furious and terrified at once. They watched me go to the door without making any move to interfere. Years later, I was to learn that the night before they had received their own dream from the Maggot. I don't know what that dream contained, but I do know that no parent has ever tried to interfere with the summons.

These days, of course, few would want to.

"Be careful," Mom said, just before I closed the door on them both.

The others and I had agreed to meet in front of the drugstore. Once we'd all assembled, we walked as a group through the center of town, past small gathered clusters of curious neighbors, and up the long road that would take us to the mansion by the bay.

The sun was on its way down.

They rode the Ferris wheel first, *said Uncle Digby*. From that height they looked down at the fair, and at Hob's Landing, and at their own cemetery upon the hill. Away from the town, near the coastline, was an old three-story mansion, long abandoned and believed to be haunted. Even the adult ghouls avoided the place, during their rare midnight excursions into town. But it was only one part of the tapestry.

The Cold Water Fair was a bloom of light on a dark earth. It was so much bigger than any of them had thought. As their car reached the height of its revolution, and they were bathed in the high cool air of the night, Wormcake was transfixed by the stars above them. They'd never seemed so close before. He sought out the constellations he'd been taught—the Rendering Pot, the Moldy King—and reached his hands over his head, trailing his fingers among them. As the gondola swung down again, it seemed he was dragging flames through the sky.

"Let's never go home again," Wormcake said. If the others heard him, they never said so.

And unknown to them, under the hill of graves, their parents were very busy setting up the Extinction Rite. Were the boys missed? I think they must have been. But no one could do anything about it.

What's next, children? What is it you really came to hear about?

*It's as though he's thrown a lit match into a barrel of firecrackers. They all explode at once.*

"The freak show!"

"The freak tent!"

"Freak show, freak show!"

*Uncle Digby raises his metal arms and a chuckle emits from the voice box beneath the jar. The bubbles churn with a little extra gusto around his lifeless floating head, and I think, for a moment, that it really is possible to read joy in that featureless aspect. Whatever tensions might have been festering just a few moments ago, they're all swept aside by the manic excitement generated by the promise of the freaks. This is what they've been waiting to hear.*

Yes, well, oh my, what a surprise. I thought you wanted to learn more about ghoul history. Maybe learn the names of all the elders? Or learn how they harvested food from the coffins? It's really a fascinating process, you know.

*"Nooooo!"*

Well, well, well. The freaks it is, then.

The ghouls stopped outside a green-and-white-striped tent, where an old man hunched beside a wooden clapboard sign. On that sign, in bright red paint, was that huge, glorious word: FREAKS. The old man looked at the boys with yellowing eyes—the first person to look at them directly all night—and said, "Well? Come to see the show, or to join it?"

He tapped the sign with a long finger, drawing their attention back to it. Beneath the word FREAKS was a list of words in smaller size, painted in an elegant hand. Words like THE MOST BEAUTIFUL MERMAID IN THE WORLD, THE GIANT WITH TWO FACES, and—you guessed it—THE ORCHID GIRL.

"Go on in, boys. Just be careful they let you out again."

They joined the line going inside. Curtains partitioned the interior into three rooms, and the crowd was funneled into a line. Lanterns hung from poles, and strings of lights crisscrossed the top of the tent.

The first freak was a man in a cage. He was seven feet tall, dressed in a pair of ratty trousers. He looked sleepy, and not terribly smart. He hadn't shaved in some time, his beard bristling like a thicket down his right cheek and jowl. The beard grew spottily on the left side, mostly because of the second face that grew there: flabby and half formed, like a face had just slid down the side of the head and bunched up on the neck. It had one blinking blue eye, and a nose right next to it, where the other eye should have been. And there was a big, open mouth nestled between the neck and shoulder, with a little tongue that darted out to moisten the chapped lips.

A sign hanging below his cage said, BRUNO: EATER OF CHILDREN.

The ghouls were fascinated by the second face, but the eating children part didn't seem all that remarkable to them. They'd eaten plenty themselves.

Next up was THE WORLD'S MOST BEAUTIFUL MERMAID. This one was a bit frustrating, because she was in a tank, and she was lying on the bottom of it. The scaly flesh of her tail was pressed up against the glass, so at first they thought they were looking at nothing more than a huge carp. Only after staring a moment did they notice the human torso that grew from it, curled around itself to hide from the gaze of the visitors. It was a woman's back, her spine ridged along her sun-dark skin. Long black hair floated around her head like a cloud of ink from an octopus.

Finally, they progressed into the next partition, and they came to THE ORCHID GIRL.

She stood on a platform in the back of the tent, in a huge bell jar. She was just about your age, children. She was wearing a bright blue dress, and she was sitting down with her arms wrapped around her legs, looking out balefully at the crowds of people coming in to see her. She looked quite unhappy. She did not look, at first blush, like a freak; the only thing unusual about her were what appeared to be pale red scars running in long, S-like curves down her face.

Well, here was another disappointing exhibit, the people thought, and they were becoming quite agitated. Someone yelled something at her, and there was talk of demanding their money back.

But everything changed when Wormcake and his friends

entered the room. The Orchid Girl sat a bit straighter, as if she had heard or felt something peculiar. She stood on her feet and looked out at the crowd. Almost immediately her gaze fell upon the ghoul children, as though she could sense them with some preternatural ability. And then, children, the most amazing thing happened. The thing that changed the ghouls' lives, her own life, and the lives of everyone in Hob's Landing forever afterward.

Her face opened along the red lines, and bloomed in brilliant petals of white and purple and green. Her body was only a disguise, you see. As everyone now knows, she was a gorgeous flower masquerading as a human being.

The people screamed or dropped to their knees in wonder. Some scattered like roaches in sunlight.

Wormcake and his friends ran too. They fled through the crowd and back out into the night. They were not afraid; they were caught in the grip of destiny. Wormcake, suddenly, was in love. He fled from the terror and the beauty of it.

It was the Orchid Girl who greeted us at the door when we arrived. She looked ethereal. She was in her human guise, and the pale lines dividing her face stood out vividly in the afternoon sun. I was reminded, shamefully, of one of the many criticisms my mother levied against her: "She really should cover that with makeup. She looks like a car accident survivor. It's disgraceful."

To us, though, she looked like a visitation from another, better world.

"Hello, children. Welcome to our house. Thank you for joining us."

That we didn't have a choice—the summons of the Maggot was not to be ignored—didn't enter our minds. We felt anointed by her welcome. We knew we'd been made special, and that everyone in Hob's Landing envied us.

She led us into the drawing room—the one that would host every meeting like this for years to come—where Uncle Digby was waiting to tell us the story. We knew him already through his several diplomatic excursions into town and were put at ease by his presence. The Orchid Girl joined her husband in two chairs off to the side, and they held hands while they listened.

I sat next to Christina Laudener. We were the oldest. The idea of romantic love was still alien to us, but not so alien that I didn't feel a twinge when I saw Mr. Wormcake and his wife holding hands. I felt as though I were in the grip of some implacable current, and that my life was being moved along a course that would see me elevated far beyond my current circumstance. As though I were the hero of a story, and this was my first chapter. I knew that Christina was a part of it. I glanced at her, tried to fathom whether or not she felt it too. She caught my look and gave me the biggest smile I'd ever received from a girl, before or since.

I have kept the memory of that smile with me, like a lantern, for the small hours of the night. I call upon it, with shame, even now.

The Maggot disapproves of sentiment.

Do you know what an Extinction Rite is, children? *Uncle Digby asks.*

*A few of the children shake their heads. Others are still, either afraid to answer the question or unsure of what their answer ought to be.*

On the night of the Cold Water Fair, one hundred years ago, the ghouls under the hill had reached the end of their age. Ghoul society, unlike yours, recognizes when its pinnacle is behind it. Once this point has been reached, there are two options: Assimilate into a larger ghoul city, or die. The ghouls under the hill did not find a larger city to join, and indeed many did not want to anyway. Their little city had endured for hundreds of years, and they were tired. The Maggot had delivered to the elders a dream of death, and so the Extinction Rite was prepared. The Extinction Rite, children, is the suicide of a city.

Like you, I am not a ghoul. I have never seen this rite performed. But also like you, I belong to the church introduced to Hob's Landing by Mr. Wormcake, so I can imagine it. I believe it must be a sight of almost impossible beauty. But I am glad he did not participate that night. Do you know what would have happened here in town, if he had?

*He looks at the little girl who talked back earlier.* What do you think, dear?

*She takes a long moment.* "I don't know. Nothing?"

Precisely. Nothing would have happened. They would have gone back inside when called, just like old Stubblegut wanted. They would have missed the fair. They would never have met the Orchid Girl, or dear old Bruno, or the lost caravan leader of the mermaid nation. I myself would still be frozen in the attic, with my sixteen compatriots, just another head in a jar. The Extinction Rite would have scoured away all the ghouls in the hill, and the people of Hob's Landing would have been none the wiser. Their little town would now be just another poverty-ridden fishing village, slowly dissolving into irrelevance.

Instead, what happened was this:

The ghoul children ran out of the tent that night, their little minds atilt with the inexplicable beauties they had just seen. It was as though the world had cracked open like some wonderful geode. They were exhilarated. They stood in the thronged midway, wondering what they ought to do next. Slipwicket and Stubblegut wanted to celebrate; the memory of their unfinished game of skullpocket was cresting in their thoughts, and the urge to recommence the game exerted itself upon them like the pull of gravity. Wormcake thought only of the Orchid Girl, imprisoned like a princess in one of the old tales, separated from him by a thin sheet of glass and by the impossible chasm of an alien culture.

And unbeknownst to them, in the warrens, the Extinction Rite reached its conclusion, and the will of the ghouls was made known to their god.

And so the Maggot spoke. Not just to these children, but to every ghoul in the city under the hill. A pulse of approval, a wordless will to proceed.

The Maggot said, DO IT.

What happened, then, was an accident. The Extinction Rite was not meant to affect the people of Hob's Landing at all. If Wormcake and the others had been at home, where they belonged, the Maggot's imperative would have caused them to destroy themselves. But they were not at home. And so what they heard was permission to indulge the desires of their hearts. And so they did.

Slipwicket fell upon the nearest child and tore the flesh from his skull like the rind from an orange, peeling it to the bone in seconds. Stubblegut, caught in the spirit of the moment, chose to help him. Bright streamers of blood arced through the air over their heads, splashed onto their faces. They wrestled the greasy skull from the body and Slipwicket gave it a mighty kick, sending it bouncing and rolling in a jolly tumble down the midway!

Wormcake made his way back into the tent, slashing out

with his sharp little fingers at the legs of anybody who failed to get out of his way quickly enough, splitting tendons and cracking kneecaps, leaving a bloody tangle of crippled people behind him.

Above them all, the cemetery on the hill split open like a rotten fruit. From the exposed tunnels beneath upturned clods of earth and tumbling gravestones came the spirits of the extinguished city of the ghouls: a host of buzzing angels, their faceted eyes glinting moonlight, their mandibles a-clatter, pale, iridescent wings filling the sky with the holy drone of the swarm.

People began to scream and run. Oh, what a sound! It was like a symphony. It was just what Wormcake and his friends had been hoping for, when they first looked down at the fair and heard the sounds carrying to them on the wind. They felt like grand heroes in a story, with the music swelling to match their achievements.

Slipwicket and Stubblegut batted the skull between them for a few moments, but it proved surprisingly fragile when careening off a fencepost. Of course, there was nothing to do but get another. So they did, and, preparing for future disappointments, they quickly decided that they should gather a whole stockpile of them.

Wormcake opened Bruno's cage and smashed the Orchid Girl's glass dome, but he was afraid to smash the mermaid's tank, for fear that she would die. Bruno—who had become great friends with her — lifted her out and hastened her down to the water, where she disappeared with a grateful wave. When he returned to the party, the ghouls were delighted to discover that he was called the Eater of Children for very good reason indeed. The Orchid Girl stood off to the side, the unfurling spirits of the cemetery rising like black smoke behind her, the unfurled petals of her head seeming to catch the moonlight and reflect it back like a strange lantern. Wormcake stood beside her and together they watched as the others capered and sported.

Beautiful carnage! Screams rising in scale before being choked off in the long dark of death, people swarming in panic like flies around a carcass, corpses littering the ground in outlandish positions one never finds in staid old coffins. Watching the people make the transition from antic foolishness to the dignified stillness of death reassured Wormcake of the nobility of their efforts, the rightness of their choices. He recognized the death of his home, but he was a disciple of the Maggot, after all, and he felt no grief for it.

What did the two of them talk about, standing there together, surrounded by death's flowering? Well, young Master Wormcake never told me. But I bet I can guess, just a little bit. They were just alike, those two. Different from everyone else around them, unafraid of the world's dangers. They recognized something of themselves in each other, I think. In any case, when they were finished talking, there was no doubt that they would take on whatever came next together.

It was the Orchid Girl who spotted the procession of torches coming from Hob's Landing.

"We should go to the mansion," she said. "They won't follow us there."

What happened next, children, is common knowledge, and not part of tonight's story. The Orchid Girl was right: The people of Hob's Landing were frightened of the mansion and did not follow them there. Wormcake and his friends found a new life inside. They found me, and the rest of the Frozen Parliament, covered by dust in the attic; they found the homunculus in the library; and of course, over time, they found all the secrets of the strange old alchemist who used to live there, which included the Orchid Girl's hidden history. Most importantly, though, they made themselves into a family. Eventually they even fashioned a peace with Hob's Landing and were able to build relationships with people in the town.

That was the last night the Cold Water Fair was ever held in Hob's Landing. With fourteen dead children and a family of monsters moved into the old mansion, the citizens of the town had lost their taste for it. For the better part of a generation, there was little celebration at all in the hamlet. Relations between the Wormcake family and the townsfolk were defined by mutual suspicion, misunderstanding, and fear. Progress was slow.

Thirty years later, relations had repaired enough that Mr. Wormcake founded the Skullpocket Fair. To commemorate the night he first came to Hob's Landing, found the love of his life, and began his long and beneficial relationship with this town, where he would eventually become the honored citizen you all know him as today.

How wonderful, yes, children?

And now, at last, we come to why the Maggot called you all here!

"So many lies."

This is what Mr. Wormcake tells me, after Uncle Digby ushers the children from the drawing room. The sun has set outside, and the purpling sky seems lit from behind.

"You know, he tells the story for children. He leaves out some details. That night in the freak tent, for instance. The people gathered around the mermaid were terrifying. There was a feral rage in that room. I didn't know what it was at the time. I was just a kid. But it was a dark sexual energy. An animal urge. They slapped their palms against her tank. They shouted at her. Said horrible things. She was curled away from them, so they couldn't see her naked, and that made them angry. I was afraid they would try to break the glass to get at her. I think it was only the fear of Bruno the cannibal, in the other room, somehow getting out too, that stopped them. I don't know.

"And that bit about me recognizing my 'destiny' when I saw the Orchid Girl—Gretchen. Nonsense. What child of that age feels romantic love? I was terrified. We all were. We'd just seen a flower disguised as a girl. What were we supposed to think?"

"I'm curious why you let Uncle Digby call her the Orchid Girl to the kids, when the name obviously annoys you."

"It's simplistic. It's her freak name. But you humans seem so invested in that. She was no more 'the Orchid Girl' than I'm 'the Dapper Corpse.' I'm not a corpse at all, for God's sake. But when we finally decided to assimilate, we believed that embracing the names would make it easier. And the kids like it, especially. So we use them."

"Is it hard to talk about her?" Probing for signs of blasphemy.

"No," he says, though he looks away as he says it. The profile of his skull is etched with lamplight. He goes on about her, though, and I start to get a sick feeling. "He would have you believe that she was a princess in a castle, waiting to be rescued by me. It's good for myth-making, but it's not true. She did need rescuing that night, yes, but so did Bruno. So did the mermaid. He doesn't talk about my 'destiny' with them, does he?"

I don't know what to say.

"Nothing but lies. We didn't want to go to the mansion. We wanted to go home. When we saw our home spilling into the sky, transfigured by the Extinction Rite . . . we were terrified."

I shake my head. "You were children. You can't blame yourself for how you felt."

"I was frightened for my parents."

I put a hand up to stop him. "Mr. Wormcake. Please. I can understand that this is a moment of, um . . . strong significance for you. It's not unusual to experience these unclean feelings. But you must not indulge them by giving them voice."

"I wanted my parents back, Priest."

"Mr. Wormcake."

"I mourned them. Right there, out in the open, I fell to my knees and cried."

"Mr. Wormcake, that's enough. You must stop."

He does. He turns away from me and stares through the window. The bay is out there somewhere, covered in the night. The lights in the drawing room obscure the view, and we can see our reflections hovering out there above the waters, like gentlemanly spirits.

"Take me to the chapel," I tell him quietly.

He stares at me for a long moment. Then he climbs to his feet. "All right," he says. "Come with me."

He pushes through a small door behind the chess table and enters a narrow, carpeted hallway. Lamps fixed to the walls offer pale light. There are paintings hung here too, but the light is dim and we are moving too quickly for me to make out specific details. The faces look desiccated, though. One seems to be a body seated on a divan, completely obscured by cobwebs. Another is a pastoral scene, a barrow mound surrounded by a fence made from the human bone.

At the end of the corridor, another small door opens into a private chapel. I'm immediately struck by the scent of spoiled meat. A bank of candles near the altar provides a shivering light. On the altar itself, a husk of unidentifiable flesh bleeds onto a silver platter. Scores of flies lift and fall, their droning presence crowding the ears. On the wall behind them, stained-glass windows flank a much larger window covered in heavy drapes. The stained glass depicts images of fly-winged angels, their faceted ruby eyes bright, their segmented arms spread as though offering benediction, or as though preparing to alight at a butcher's feast.

There is a pillow on the floor in front of the altar, and a pickax leans on the table beside it.

The Maggot summons fourteen children to the Skull-pocket Fair every year. One for each child who died that night in the Cold Water Fair, one hundred years ago, when Hob's Landing became a new town, guided by monsters and their strange new god. It's no good to question by what criteria the children are selected, by what sins or what virtues. There is no denying the summons. There is only the lesson of the worm, delivered over and over again: All life is a mass of wriggling grubs, awaiting the transformation to the form in which it will greet the long and quiet dark.

"The Church teaches the subjugation of memory," I say. "Grief is a weakness."

"I know," says Mr. Wormcake.

"Your marriage. Your love for your wife and your friends. They're stones in your pockets. They weigh you to the earth."

"I know."

"Empty them," I say.

And so he does. "I miss her," he says. He looks at me with those hollow sockets, speaks to me with that borrowed mouth, and for the first time that night I swear I can see some flicker of emotion, like a candle flame glimpsed at the bottom of the world. "I miss her so much. I'm not supposed to miss her. It's blasphemy. But I can't stop thinking about her. I don't want to hear the lies anymore. I don't want to hear the stories. I want to remember what really happened. We didn't recognize anything about each other at the fair that night. We were little kids and we were scared of what was going to happen to us. We stood on the edge of everything and we were too afraid to move. We didn't say a single word to each other the whole time. We didn't learn how to love each other until much later, after we were trapped in this house. And now she's gone and I don't know where she went and I'm scared all over again. I'm about to change, and I don't know how or into what because my home disappeared when I was little. No one taught me anything. I'm afraid of what's going to happen to me. I miss my wife."

I'm stunned by the magnitude of this confession. I'd been fooled by the glamour of his name and his history; I'd thought he would greet this moment with all the dignity of his station. I stand over him, this diminished patriarch, mewling like some abandoned infant, and I'm overwhelmed by disgust. I don't know where it comes from, and the force of it terrifies me.

"Well, you can't," I say, my anger a chained dog. "You don't get to. You don't get to miss her."

He stares at me. His mouth opens, but I cut him off. I grab the mound of ripe flesh from the altar and thrust it into his face. Cold fluids run between my fingers and down my wrist. Flies go berserk, bouncing off my face, crawling into my nose. "This is the world you made! These are the rules. You don't get to change your mind!"

Fifty years ago, when Uncle Digby finished his story and

finally opened the gate at the very first Skullpocket Fair, we all ran out onto the brand new midway, the lights swirling around us, the smells of sweets and fried foods filling our noses. We were driven by fear and hope. We knew death opened its mouth behind us, and we felt every living second pass through our bodies like tongues of fire, exalting us, carving us down to our very spirits. We heard the second gate swing open and we screamed as the monsters bounded onto the midway in furious pursuit: cannibal children, dogs bred to run on beams of moonlight, corpse flowers with human bodies, loping atrocities of the laboratory. The air stank of fear. Little Eddie Brach was in front of me and without thought I grabbed his shirt collar and yanked him down, leaping over his sprawled form in the very next instant. He bleated in cartoonlike surprise. I felt his blood splash against the back of my shirt in a hot torrent as the monsters took him, and I laughed with joy and relief. I saw Christina leap onto a rising gondola car and I followed. We slammed the door shut and watched the world bleed out beneath us. Our hearts were incandescent, and we clutched each other close. Somewhere below us a thing was chanting, "Empty your pockets, empty your pockets," followed by the hollow *pok!*s of skulls being cracked open. We laughed together. I felt the inferno of life. I knew that every promise would be fulfilled.

Six of us survived that night. Of those, four of us—exalted by the experience—took the Orders. We lived a life dedicated to the Maggot, living in quiet seclusion, preparing our bodies and our minds for the time of decay. We proselytized, grew our numbers. Every year some of the survivors of the fair would join us in our work. Together, we brought Hob's Landing to the worm.

But standing over this whimpering creature, I find myself

thinking only of Christina Laudener, her eyes a pale North Atlantic gray, her blond hair flowing like a stilled wave over her shoulders. We were children. We didn't know anything about love. Or at least, I didn't. I didn't understand what it was that had taken root in me until years later, when her life took her to a different place, and I sat in the underground church and contemplated the deliquescence of flesh until the hope for warmth, or for the touch of a kind hand, turned cold inside me.

I never learned what she did with her life. But she didn't take the Orders. She lived that incandescent moment with the rest of us, but she drew a different lesson from it.

"You tell me those were all lies?" I say. "I believed them. I believed everything."

"Gretchen wasn't a lie. Our life here wasn't a lie. It was glorious. It doesn't need to be dressed up with exaggerations."

I think of my own life, long for a human being, spent in cold subterranean chambers. My whole life. "The Maggot isn't a lie," I say.

"No. He certainly is not."

"I shouldn't have survived. I should have died. I pushed Eddie down. Eddie should have lived." I feel tears try to gather, but they won't fall. I want them to. I think, somehow, I would feel better about things if they did. But I've been a good boy: I've worked too hard at killing my own grief. Now that I finally need it, there just isn't enough. The Maggot has taken too much.

"Maybe so," Wormcake says. "But it doesn't matter anymore."

He gets up, approaches the windows. He pulls a cord behind the curtains and they slide open. A beautiful, kaleidoscopic light fills the room. The Seventieth Annual Skullpocket Fair is laid out on the mansion's grounds beyond the window, carousels spinning, roller coaster ticking up an incline, bumper cars spitting arcs of electricity. The Ferris wheel turns over it all, throwing sparking yellow and green and red light into the sky.

I join him at the window. "I want to go down there," I say, putting my fingers against the glass. "I want another chance."

"It's not for you anymore," Wormcake says. "It's not for me, either. It's for them."

He tugs at the false mouth on his skull, snapping the tethers, and tosses it to the floor. The tongue lolls like some yanked organ, and the flies cover it greedily. Maybe he believes that if he can no longer articulate his grief, he won't feel it anymore.

Maybe he's right.

He removes the fly-spangled meat from my hands and takes a deep bite. He offers it to me: a benediction. I recognize the kindness in it. I accept and take a bite of my own. This is the world we've made. Tears flood my eyes, and he touches my cheek with his bony hand.

Then he replaces the meat onto the altar and assumes his place on his knees beside it. He lays his head by the buzzing meat. I take the pickax and place the hard point of it against the skull, where all the poisons of the world have gathered, have slowed him, have weighed him to the earth. I hold the point there to fix it in my mind, and then I lift the ax over my head.

"Empty your pockets," I say.

Below us a gate opens, and the children pour out at a dead run. There goes the angry girl. There goes the weepy, buzz-cut kid. Arms and legs pumping, clothes flapping like banners in the wind. They're in the middle of the pack when the monsters are released. They have a chance.

They just barely have a chance.

# The Maw

**M**ix was about ready to ditch the weird old bastard. Too slow, too clumsy, too loud. Not even a block into Hollow City and already they'd captured the attention of one of the Wagoneers, and in her experience you could almost clap your hands in front of their faces and they wouldn't know it. Experience, though, that was the key word. She had it and he didn't, and it was probably going to get him killed. She'd be goddamned if she'd let it get her killed too.

She pulled him into an alcove and they waited quietly until the creature had passed, pushing its dreadful wheelbarrow.

"You need to rest?" she said.

"No, I don't need to rest," he snapped. "Keep going."

Mix was seventeen years old, and anybody on the far side of fifty seemed inexcusably ancient to her, but she reckoned this man to be pretty old even by that standard. He was spry enough to walk through streets cluttered with the debris of long abandonment without too much difficulty, but she could see the strain in his face, the sheen of sweat on his forehead. And a respectable pace for an old man was still just a fraction of the speed she preferred to move at while in Hollow City. She'd been stupid to take his money, but she'd always been a stupid girl. Just ask anybody.

They turned a corner and the last checkpoint—a small wooden shack with a lantern gleaming in a window—disappeared from view. It might as well have been a hundred miles away. The buildings hulked into the cloudy sky around them, windows shattered and bellied with darkness. The doors of little shops gaped like open mouths. Glass pebbled the sidewalk. Rags of newspapers, torn and scattered clothing, and tangles of bloody meat lay strewn across the pavement. Cars lined the sidewalks in their final repose. Life still prospered here, to be sure: rats, roaches, feral cats and dogs; she'd even seen a mother bear and her train of cubs once, moving through the ruined neighborhood like a fragment of a better dream. The place seethed with it. But there weren't any people anymore. At least, not in the way she used to think of people.

"Dear God," the man said, and she stopped. He shuffled into the middle of the street, shoulders slouched, his face slack as a dead man's. His eyes roved over the place, taking it all in. He looked frail, and lonely, and scared; which, she supposed, was exactly what he was. He reminded her of her parents in their last days, staring in befuddlement as the world changed around them, becoming this new and terrible thing. "Look what you've done," her father had said. As if she had somehow called this upon them herself.

She followed him, took his elbow, and pulled him back into the relative shadow of the sidewalk. "Hard to believe this is all just a few blocks away from where you live, huh?"

He swallowed, nodded.

"But listen to me, okay? You gotta listen to me, and do what I say. No walking out in the middle of the street. We stay quiet, we keep moving, we don't draw attention. Don't think I won't leave your ass if you get us in trouble. Do you understand me?"

He disengaged his elbow from her hand. At least he had the decency to look embarrassed. "Sorry," he said. "This is just my first time seeing it since I left. At the time it was just, it was . . . it was just chaos. Everything was so confused."

"Yeah, I get it." She didn't want to hear his story. Everybody had one. Tragedy gets boring after a while.

Hollow City was not a city at all, but a series of city blocks that used to be part of the Fleming and South Kensington neighborhoods, and had acquired its own peculiar identity over the last few months. Its informal name came from its emptiness: each building a shell, scoured of human life, whether through evacuation or the attentions of the Surgeons. The atmosphere had long turned an ashy gray, as though under perpetual cloud cover, even around the city beyond the afflicted neighborhood. Elsewhere in the city, lamps burned day and night; but not in here. Electricity had been cut off weeks ago. Nevertheless, light still swelled from isolated pockets, as though furnaces were being stoked to facilitate some awful labor transpiring beyond the sight of any who might venture in.

She had lived less than half a mile from here; she'd walked past it once, believing she'd feel nothing. But the echoes of that loveless place still lingered there. Whatever misery her parents had nurtured over the years, turning against each other and against their own child, still whispered to her from those broken windows.

When the change came here, it was like a benediction.

"There's things coming up that're gonna be hard to see," she said. "You ready for that?"

The old man looked disgusted. "I don't need to be lectured on what's hard to see by a child," he said. "You have no idea what I've seen."

"Yeah, well, whatever. Just don't freak out. And hustle it up."

Mix did not want to be here after the sun went down. She figured they had five good hours. Plenty of time for the old bastard to find who he was looking for, or—more likely—realize there was no one left to find.

They continued along the sidewalk, walking quickly but quietly. The rhythmic squeaking of unoiled wheels came from around a corner ahead, accompanied by the sound of several small voices holding a single high note in unison, like a miniature boys' choir. Mix put out her hand to stop him. He must not have been paying attention, because he walked right into her before stuttering to a halt. She felt the thinness of his chest, the sparrowlike brittleness of his bones. Guilt welled up from some long-buried spring in her gut: She had no business bringing him here on his maniacal errand. (*Stupid girl,* her father would have said. *Stupid work for a stupid girl.*) It was doomed, and he was doomed right along with it. She should have told him no. Another client would have come along eventually. Except that fewer and fewer people were paying to be escorted through Hollow City, and those who were tended to be adrenaline junkies, who were likely to get you killed, or—worse—religious nuts and artists, who felt entitled to bear witness to what was happening here due to some perceived calling. It was a species of narcissism that offended her on an obscure, inarticulate level. A few weeks ago she had guided a poet out to the center of the place and almost slipped away while he scribbled furiously, self-importantly, in his notebook. The temptation was stronger than she would have believed possible; she'd fantasized about how long she'd hear him calling out for her before the Surgeons stopped his tongue for good, or turned it to other purposes.

She didn't leave the poet, but she learned that there was an animal living inside her, something that celebrated when nature did its work upon the weak. She came to value that animal. She knew it would keep her alive.

This sudden guilt, then, was both unexpected and unwelcome. She waited for it to subside.

The prow of a wheelbarrow emerged from beyond the corner of the building, followed by its laden body, the wooden wheels turning in slow, wobbling rotations. The barrow was filled with gray, hacked torsos, some sprouting both arms, most with less, but all still wearing their heads, eyes rolled back to reveal the whites with little exploded capillaries standing in bright contrast to the gray pallor, each mouth rounded into an ellipse from which emitted that single, perfect note, as heartbreakingly beautiful as anything heard in one of God's cathedrals. Then the Wagoneer hove into view, its naked body blackened and wasted, comprised of just enough gristle and bone to render it ambulatory. The skin on its face was shrunken around its skull, and a withered crown of long black hair rustled like straw in the breeze. It turned its head, and for the second time that day they found themselves speared into place by a Wagoneer's stare. This one actually stopped its movement and leaned closer, as if committing their faces to memory, or transferring the sight of them via some infernal channel to a more distant intelligence.

Her gaze still fixed on the Wagoneer, Mix reached behind and grabbed the old man's wrist. "We have to run," she said.

## 2.

The dog was gone. Carlos realized it at once, and gravity took him, a feeling of aging so sudden and so complete that he half expected to die right there. He looked at the kitchen floor and wondered if he would hurt himself in the fall. Instead, he pulled a chair away from the table and collapsed into it. A great sadness welled up, turning in his chest, too big to be voiced. It threatened to break him in half.

Maria had been with him for fifteen years. She was a scruffy tan mutt, her muzzle gray and her eyes rheumy. They were walking life's last mile together. Carlos had never married; he'd become so acclimated to his loneliness that eventually the very idea of human companionship just made him antsy and tired. It was not as though he'd had to fight for his independence; his demeanor had grown cold and mean as he aged, not from any ill feeling toward other people, but simply from an unwillingness to endure their eccentricities. He had a theory that people warped as they aged, like old records left out in the sun, and unless you did it together and warped in conformity to each other, you eventually became incapable of aligning with anybody else.

Well, he'd grown old with Maria, that grand old dame, and she was all he needed or wanted.

When the ground first started to shake in Fleming, and the nights started filling with the screams of neighbors and strangers alike, he and Maria had huddled together in his apartment. He'd kept his baseball bat clutched in his thin, spotted hands while Maria bristled and growled at his side. She'd always been a gentle dog, frightened by visitors, scurrying under the bed at a loud knock, but now she had found a core of steel within herself and she stood between him and the door, her lips peeled from her yellowed teeth, prepared to hurl her frail old body against whatever might come through it. That, even more than the screaming outside, convinced him that whatever was out there was something to fear.

On the second night, the door was kicked in and bright lights sprayed into his apartment, the commanding voices of men piling into the room like something physical. Maria's whole body shook and snapped with fear and rage, her own hoarse barking pushing back at them, but when Carlos realized they were an evacuation team, he wrapped his arms around his dog and held her tight, whispering in her ear. "It's okay, baby, it's okay, little mama, calm down, calm down."

And she did, though she still trembled. The police, one of them sobbing unashamedly, loaded them both into a van parked at the bottom of the apartment building, not giving him any grief about taking the dog, thank God. He cast a quick glance down the street before a hand shoved him inside with a few of his terrified neighbors, huddled in their pajamas, and slammed the door behind him. What he saw was impossible. A man, eight feet tall or more, skinny as a handful of sticks, crossing a street only a block away with eerie, doe-like grace. He was a shape in the sodium lights, featureless and indistinct, like a child's drawing of a nightmare. He was stretching what looked like thin, bloody parchment from one streetlight to another; suspended from one end of the parchment was a human arm, flexing at the elbow again and again, like an animal in distress.

He looked at his neighbors, but he didn't know any of their names. They weren't talking, anyway.

Then the van surged to life, moving with ferocious speed to a location only a mile distant, behind a battery of checkpoints and blockades, and rings of armed officers.

Carlos and his dog were provided with a small apartment—

even smaller than the one they'd been living in—in tenement housing, with as many of the other residents of the besieged neighborhood as could be evacuated. The building was overcrowded, and over the ensuing months the existing residents received these newcomers with a gamut of reactions, ranging from sympathy to resentment to outright anger. The refugees responded to their new hosts in kind.

No one knew exactly what was happening in South Kensington and Fleming. Rumors spread that a tribe of kids, homeless or in gangs or God knows what, had started charging people to go in looking for people or items of value left behind, or sometimes even chaperoning people to their old homes. Though some minor effort had been made to quell these activities, the little industry managed to thrive. It disgusted Carlos; someone was always ready to make a dollar, no matter what the circumstance.

It was thanks to those kids, though, that news bled back of the old neighborhood transformed, stalked by weird figures pushing wheelbarrows or hauling huge carts of human wreckage, strange music drifting from empty streets, the tall figures—Surgeons, they came to be called—knitting people together in grotesque configurations. Buildings were empty, some completely hollowed out, as though cored from within, leaving nothing but their outer shells. The kids sneaking back inside started calling it Hollow City, and the name stuck. Which was just one more thing Carlos hated. The old neighborhoods had names. There were histories there, lives had been lived there. They didn't deserve some stupid comic book tag. They had belonged to humanity once.

A gray pallor hung over the place, slowly expanding until most of the surrounding city was covered. Carlos believed it was responsible for the way people acclimated too quickly to the transformation of the old neighborhoods. Apathy took root like a weed. Police kept up the blockades, but they were indifferently manned, and the kids' scouting efforts grew in proportion. The army never came in. No one in the tenements knew whether or not they were even called. There was nothing about this on the news. It was as though the city suffered its own private nightmare, which would continue unobserved until it could wake up and talk about it, or until it died in its sleep.

Carlos was resigned to let it play out in the background. He was nothing if not adaptive, and it did not take long for him to accept his reduced surroundings. It was noisy, chaotic, the walls were thin, but these things had been true of his old apartment, too. Sound was a comfort to him; he might not have friends, but his spirit was eased by the human commotion. He would have died there, as close to contentment as he might get, if only Maria had stayed with him.

He knew Maria was gone almost instantly, well before he hobbled out of bed and saw the apartment door ajar. He could feel her absence, like a pocket of airlessness. He suspected immediately that she'd gone back to her old home. What he didn't know was why. Was there something there that called her? Was she confused? Did the place mean more to her than he did? Her absence almost felt like a betrayal, like a spade digging into his heart.

But she was Maria. He would go and get her. He would bring her home.

Everything had gone lax at the border to the old neighborhood. The checkpoints seemed to be devoid of the police altogether; only these kids now, living in makeshift shacks, sleeping on mattresses harvested from local housing or perhaps from the afflicted area, living out of boxes and suitcases and school backpacks.

It took a while to find anybody willing to give him the time of day. He knew they considered him too risky: old, slow, fragile. But eventually he found one who would: a girl with a shaved head, dressed in a dark blue hoodie and jeans, who called herself Mix. Ridiculous name; why did they do that? Why couldn't they just be who they were? She considered the three crumpled twenties he offered her and accepted them with poor grace. She turned her back to him, reaching into a box she kept by her sleeping bag and jamming a backpack with bottles of water, a first aid kit, and what appeared to be a folded knife. She interrogated him as she packed.

"What are we looking for?"

"Maria," he said.

She stopped, turned and stared at him with something like contempt. "You know she's dead, right?"

"No. I don't know that at all."

"Do you know anything about what's going on in there?"

He flashed back to the tall man—one of the Surgeons, he supposed—stretching the twitching human parchment between streetlights. "Sure," he said. "It's Hell."

"Who knows what the fuck it is, but there's no one left alive in there. At least, no one that can be saved."

A swell of impatience threatened to overwhelm him. He would go in alone if he had to. What he would not do was stand here being condescended to by an infant. "Should I find someone else to take me?"

"No, I'll do it. But you have to follow my rules, okay? Stay quiet and stay moving. Keep to the sidewalks at all times, and close to the walls when you can. They mostly ignore stragglers, unless they're traveling in big groups or making some kinda scene. If one of them notices you, stay still. Usually they just move on."

"What if they don't?"

"Then I make it up on the fly. And you do exactly what I fucking say." She waited until he acknowledged this before continuing. "And whenever we realize this Maria or whoever is dead, we get the fuck out again. Like, immediately."

"She's not dead."

Mix zipped up her backpack and slung it over her shoulder. "Yeah, okay. Maybe you think you're the hero in a movie or something. You're not. You're just some old guy making a bad choice. So listen to me. Once *I'm* sure she's dead, I am leaving. If you come with me I'll make sure you get back out safe. If you stay behind, that's on you."

"Fine. Can we go?"

"Yeah, let's go. Where are we looking?"

"Home. She'll have gone home." He gave her the address.

She sighed. "Old man, that building's been cored. There's nothing inside."

"That's where she is."

Mix nodded, already turning away from him. Already, in some sense, finished. "Whatever you say."

## —— 3. ——

She yanked him around, as close to panic as she'd been in weeks, and they walked briskly back in the direction they'd come. She wanted to run, but either he couldn't or he wouldn't. It wasn't until he wrenched his wrist free of her grip, though, that she considered leaving him there. The animal inside her started to pace.

He stood resolutely in place, rubbing the spot on his wrist where she'd grabbed him. Behind him, in the dense gray air, the Wagoneer still watched, its lidless eyes shedding a dim yellow light. The thin choir of dismembered bodies held their sustained note. She'd been glanced at before, but none had ever stopped and stared until now. She thought about the knife in her backpack. An affectation. So stupid. Unless she gutted this old man right here and ran while the things fell upon him instead.

"Where are you going?" he said. He wasn't even trying to be quiet anymore. His voice bounced down the empty street, came back at them like a strange reflection of itself.

*Out,* she wanted to say. *We're getting out.* But instead, she said, "We'll go around. A detour. Hurry." She wasn't a dumb kid. She had a job. She would do it. She could handle this.

"Okay," he said, showing her a little deference for the first time. He joined her, even picking up his pace. "I thought you were going to leave me."

"Fuck you, I'm not leaving." She could hear the tears in her voice and she hated herself for it. Stupid girl. They were right all along.

They doubled back, turned a corner, pursuing a longer route to the address. Mix glanced behind her often, sure they were being followed, but the Wagoneer was nowhere to be seen.

The streets had continued to transform even in the few days since last she'd been here. The Wagoneers hauled their cartloads of human remains, coming from some central location and depositing them in moldering piles throughout Hollow City, where the Surgeons continued to stitch them together into grotesque, seemingly meaningless configurations: There were more torsos like the ones they had just seen strung like bunting from one side of the street to the other, each one tuned to a different pitch; great kites of skin flapped tautly in similar fashion, punched through with holes of varying sizes and patterns, as though a kind of Morse code had been pierced into them with an awl; skeletal structures made from the combined parts of a hundred rendered people loomed between the buildings in great, stilled wheels, fitting together like cogs in some demented engine. The bone wheels had been hastily assembled, still wet with blood and dripping with rags of meat. The eyes of the workers boiled with furnace light as they toiled, and the air grew steadily colder.

Mix stopped, hugging the corner of what had once been a twenty-four-hour drugstore. Blood splashed the interior of the picture window now, obscuring whatever was inside. The address he'd given was visible a little over a block away. The city block was a part of what formed the center of the affected area. She hadn't been this close to it before, herself.

If the old man was impatient with her stopping, he gave no sign. He was leaning against the wall too, breathing heavily. His eyes were unfocused, and she wondered how much of this he was taking in.

"You still alive back there?" she said.

"I think so. Hard to tell anymore." He made a vague gesture. "What is all this?"

"Shit, you're asking me? It's just another bad dream, I guess. You're the one with all the life experience, you ought to recognize one by now." When he didn't respond, she said, "So, you seen enough now?"

"What do you mean?"

She pointed ahead, to where his old apartment building hulked into the sky. The desiccated bodies of the Wagoneers came and went from inside with a clockwork regularity. "There's no one left in there, old man. That's fucking Grand Central Station."

"No. She's in there."

For a moment, Mix couldn't speak through the rage. The degree of obliviousness he was displaying, the absolute blind faith in an impossible outcome, had just crossed the border from desperate hope to outright derangement. He was crazy, probably had been for some time, and now he was going to get them both killed. Or worse than killed. The thing inside her paced and growled. She was ready to let it out at last.

She felt a curious dread about it. Not at his fate—he'd bought that for himself—but at the simple act of walking away, and at the border she would be crossing within herself by doing it. It was one she had always taken pride in being ready to cross, but now that the moment had come, she was afraid of it, and afraid of the world that waited for her on the other side. She pressed her forehead against the wall, closed her eyes, and listened to the strange sounds the new architectures of flesh created around her: the gorgeous notes, the flaglike snapping, the hollow echo of bones clattering in the wind. It reminded her of the various instruments in her school band being tuned before a concert. She heard him breathing beside her too, heavily and quickly, as he expended what she knew were his final energies on this suicidal quest.

"So who is she, anyway? Your wife? Your daughter?"

"No. She's my dog."

It was as though he'd said something in a foreign language. She needed a moment to translate it into something she could understand. When it happened, the last beleaguered rank of resistance inside her folded, and she started to laugh. It was quiet, almost despairing, and she couldn't stop it. She pressed her face into the stone wall and laughed through her clenched teeth.

The absurdity of it all.

"She's my dog," he said, a little defensively. "She's my only friend. I'm going to bring her home."

"Your home is gone," Mix said, the thin stream of giggles reaching its end, giving way instead to a huge sadness, the kind that did not seem to visit her but instead emerged from within, as much a part of her body as a liver or a spleen. She wanted to hate the old man but what she felt for him wasn't hate. It was something complicated and awful and unknown to her, but hate was too simple a word to describe it. If she had ever loved a child still innocent of its first heartbreak, still trusting in the goodness of the world, she might have known the feeling. But she wasn't a parent; and anyway, she couldn't remember love.

"A dog," she said.

The old man stood beside her, the aesthetic of Hell manifested around him, an abyssal acoustic being built by its wretched servants, and he looked like what he was: a slumped, fading old man, lonely in the world but for one simple animal. His speech was defiant, but his mind had already recognized the truth, and she could see it erode him even as she watched, like a sand dune in a strong wind.

Somewhere in this bloody tangle of bone and flesh, maybe even some still-muttering faces affixed to a wall with an unguent excreted from the lungs of the Surgeons, were her parents, their cold anger still seeping from their tongues, their self-loathing and their resentment still animating the flayed muscles in their peeled faces. She could hear them as clearly as ever.

Stupid girl.

Goddamn them anyway.

"All right," she said. "Let's go get your dog."

## — 4. —

The girl was careful, but there was no need to sneak. What could they do to him? Death wasn't shit. Carlos knew he should tell her to leave—it was obvious he wasn't going to be coming back, with or without Maria—but it was her choice to make. Life was long or short, and it meant something or it didn't. It wasn't his business to tell her how to measure hers.

The walls of his old apartment building bowed slightly, as though some great pressure grew from within. The doors had been torn off and the windows broken. He could see nothing inside but shadow. Walking the perimeter of the building were three dark-robed figures, their heads encased in black iron boxes. They exuded a monastic patience, moving slowly and with obvious precision. The lead figure held an open book in his left hand, scrawling something into it with his right. The one in the middle swung a censer, a black orb from which spilled a heavy yellow smoke. The scent of marigolds carried over to him. The figure in the back held aloft a severed head on a pole, which emitted a beam of light from its wrenched mouth.

Carlos waited for these figures to pass. He approached the doors as casually as if he belonged there. Mix made a sound of protest, but he ignored her. A Surgeon emerged from the doors just as he reached them, stooping low to fit, but though it cast him a curious glance, it did not interfere with him, or even break its stride. It stretched itself to its full height and walked away, thin hands trailing long needles of bone and gory thread. It moved slowly and languidly, like something walking underwater.

He moved to enter the building, but Mix restrained him from behind and edged in front of him instead. She held her left arm across his chest, protectively, as they crept forward;

in her right she held the knife she'd stashed in her backpack, unfolded into an ugly silver talon. He didn't know what had changed her mind about him, but he was grateful for it.

Though barely any light intruded into the building, he could see immediately that the girl had been right: The building's expansive interior had been scooped clean, leaving nothing but the outer walls, like the husk of an insect following a spider's feast. A great hole had opened in the earth beneath it, almost as wide as the building's foundation. The hole looked like a wound, raw and bloody, its walls sloping inward and meeting a hundred feet down in a moist, clutching glottis. Above it, the walls and ceiling had been sprayed with its meaty exhalations, red organic matter pasted over them so that they resembled the underside of a tongue.

Bodies of residents who'd been unable to evacuate were glued to the far wall with a thick yellow resin; even as they watched, one Carlos recognized as a young cashier at a local takeout was peeled from his perch and subjected to the attentions of a cleaver-wielding Surgeon, who quickly quartered him with a series of heavy and efficient chops. The cashier's limbs quivered, and his mouth gaped in wonderment at his own butchering. But instead of a cry or a scream, what emerged from him was a pure note, as clean and undiluted as anything heard on earth. Tears sprang to Carlos's eyes at the beauty of it, and ahead of him Mix put her hand over her lowered face, the curved knife glinting dully by her ear, a gesture of humility or of supplication.

"Maria," Carlos said, and there she was, snuffling through piled offal in a far corner, her snout filthy, her hair matted and sticky. The laborers of Hell walked around her without concern, and she seemed undisturbed by them as well. When she heard Carlos call her name, she answered with a happy bark and bounded over to him, spry for the moment, slamming the side of her body into his legs and lifting her head in grateful joy as he ran his gnarled fingers through her fur. Carlos dropped to his knees, heedless of the pain, of how difficult it would be to rise again. His dog sprawled into his lap. For a moment, they were happy.

And then Carlos thought, *You left me. You left me in the end. Why?* He hugged his dog close, burying his nose in her fur. He knew there was no answer beyond the obvious, constant imbalance in any transaction of the heart. *You don't love me the way I love you.*

He forgave her for it. There really wasn't anything else he could do.

## —— 5. ——

Mix watched them from a few feet away, the knife forgotten in her hand. She knew why the dog had come here. She could feel it; if the old man would leave the animal alone for a moment, he would too. The sound coming through that great, open throat in the ground, barely heard but thrumming in her blood, had called it here. She felt it like a density in the air, a gravity in the heart. She felt it in the way the earth called her to itself, with its promise of loam and worms, so that she sat down too, beside them but apart. The animal inside her recognized it, the same way the dog did. It settled into sleep at last. She wrapped her arms around herself, suddenly very cold.

*I'm not stupid,* she thought.

The sound from the hole grew in volume. It was an answer to loneliness, and a call to the forgotten. It was Hell's lullaby, and as the long note blew from the abyss it filtered out through the windows and the doors and it caught in the reed-like parchments of skin and set them to keening, it powered the wheels of bone so they clamored and rattled and chimed, and it blended with the chorus of sound from the suspended bodies until the whole of the city became as the bell of a great trumpet, spilling a mournful beauty into the world. Every yearning for love rang like a bell in the chest, every lonely fear found its justification.

The clangor of the song kept rising, until it filled the sky. Their ache stretched them until their bodies sang. In dark fathoms, something turned its vast head, and found it beautiful.

# The Visible Filth

The roaches were in high spirits. There were half a dozen of them, caught in the teeth of love. They capered across the liquor bottles, perched atop pour spouts like wooden ladies on the prows of sailing ships. They lifted their wings and delicately fluttered. They swung their antennae with a ripe sexual urgency, tracing love sonnets in the air.

Will, the bartender on duty, stood watching them, with his back to the rest of the bar. He couldn't move. He was bound by a sense of obligation to remain where he was, but the roaches stirred a primordial revulsion in him, and the urge to flee was palpable. His flesh shivered in one convulsive movement.

He worked the six p.m. to two a.m. shift at Rosie's Bar, a little hole-in-the-wall tucked back in the maze of streets of uptown New Orleans, surrounded by shotgun houses sagging on their frames, their porches bedazzled in old Mardi Gras beads and sprung couches. The bar's interior reflected its environment: a few tables and chairs, video poker machines lined up like totems against the back wall, a jukebox, ranks of stools against the bar.

He often had the misfortune of minding the place when the roaches started feeling passionate. It happened a few times a year, and each time it paralyzed him with horror.

At the moment Will's only customers were Alicia, a twenty-eight-year-old server at an oyster bar in the French Quarter, a longtime regular, and his best friend; and Jeffrey, her boyfriend of the moment, soon to be hustled into the ranks of the exes, if Will knew her at all. Jeffrey was one of those pretty boys with the hair and the lashes she liked, but he was not on her wavelength at all. Will gave him another month, tops.

"This place is disgusting," Alicia said.

"Don't slam the bar, babe," said Jeffrey. "It's just bugs."

"Fucking gross bugs who want to get busy on my bottle of Jameson."

Will just nodded. It was, indeed, disgusting.

"You should get an exterminator, brother," said Jeffrey. "Seriously."

The same conversation every time. Just different faces. "Yup. Talk to the boss."

"You know they say when you see one, there's thousands more in the walls."

"Oh yeah? Is that what they say?"

Alicia said, "Shut up, Jeffrey."

"Make me."

She pulled his face to hers and kissed him deeply. Apparently, love was in the air at Rosie's Bar that night. Jeffrey cupped the back of her head with one hand and let the other go sliding up her leg. He was a good boy. He knew what to do.

Will waited for the roach to relinquish its claim to the Jameson, then poured himself a shot. People from Louisiana liked to call the cockroach the official state bird; they were practically everywhere, and you couldn't worry too much if you saw one. No matter how clean you kept your place, they were going to get in. But when you got something like this, you were infested. There must be a huge nest somewhere in the wall, or underneath the building. Maybe more than one. He didn't think an exterminator would fix this problem. The whole wall needed to be torn out. Maybe the whole building would have to be burned down to the dark earth, and then you'd have to keep on burning, all the way down to their mother nests in Hell.

The roaches made little ticking noises as they scrambled about, and he had the brief, uncanny certainty that the noises would cohere into a kind of language if he listened carefully enough.

After a few more minutes, the bugs retired to their bedrooms, and the rows of bottles resumed their stately, lighted beauty. Jeffrey had his hand in Alicia's shirt.

"That shirt comes off, and it's free drinks all night," Will said.

Jeffrey pulled away, his face flushed. Alicia smoothed her shirt and her hair. "You wish, child."

"I really do."

Alicia circled her finger over the bar. "Shots. Line 'em up. Maybe you'll see something before the night is through."

He doubted it, but he poured them anyway.

Like most twenty-four-hour bars in New Orleans, the place did a decent business even on off nights. Most of the late-night clientele were made up of service industry drones like Alicia and Jeffrey, or cab drivers, or prostitutes, or just the lonely losers of the world, sliding their rent dollar by dollar into the video poker machines.

A few college kids filed in, finding a table some distance from the bar. After a moment one of them broke away and approached Will with an order for the table. Will cast his eye across the bunch— three girls and two guys, including the one placing the order. Almost certainly some of them were underage. College kids usually hit the Quarter for fun, but the Loyola campus was just a few blocks away, so inevitably a few of them drifted into Rosie's throughout the week, looking for a quiet night.

"Everybody twenty-one?" Will said.

The kid showed him his ID, sighing with the patience of a beleaguered saint. Legal less than a month.

"What about everybody else?"

"Yeah, man. Want me to get them?"

A weak bluff. Will thought about it; it was a Tuesday night, the shift was almost over, and the drawer was light. He decided he didn't care. "Don't worry about it."

Someone put some money into the jukebox and Tom Waits filled the silence. The college kids huddled around the table once they got their drinks, their backs forming a wall against the world. They seemed to be fixated on something between them. They were a lot quieter than he thought they'd be, though, which he considered a blessing. The night continued along its smooth course until Eric and his buddies walked in, staining the mood. They'd obviously already been on the bar circuit that night, coming in with beers in hand, descending on the pool table. Eric lifted his chin to Will in greeting; his three friends didn't trouble themselves.

"Hey, Eric. You guys need anything?"

"We're set for now, brother. Thanks."

Eric was a little plug of muscle and charisma. He was the sweetest guy in the world when sober. When he was drunk, though, every human interaction became a potential flash-point for violence. He lived in an apartment above the bar, so Will got to see that side of him a lot.

"How's Carrie?" Alicia asked, drawing him back.

Will shrugged, feeling a surge of unanchored guilt. "She's fine I guess. Head in the computer all the time, working on that paper she's doing for school. Same as always."

"You got yourself a smart one."

Jeffrey perked up, caught in a wash of inspiration. "Hey, we should all go out sometime. Does she like football? We could go to a Saints game."

The idea almost made him laugh. "No, man, she does not like football."

Alicia touched his hand. "That's totally a good idea though. Let's just hang out. I haven't seen her in weeks. We could double date!"

"Oh my God."

"Don't be a dick, Will. Make it happen."

"I'll suggest it to her. I'm telling you, though, she's living her schoolwork right now. I'm not even sure she remembers my name."

"Make it happen."

A bottle shattered somewhere by the pool table, followed by a muffled grunt. The bar went silent except for the sound of scuffling shoes and short bursts of breath, overlaid with a jaunty dirge from the Violent Femmes. Eric and one of the guys he'd come in with were grappled together, Eric's arm around the other guy's neck. He hit him in the face with three quick shots. The guy gripped the jagged neck of his beer bottle and swung it around to rake it across Eric's arm. Blood splashed to the grungy linoleum.

"Goddamn it!" Will said. "Somebody get that fucking bottle!"

Nobody wanted to get near them. One of the other guys Eric had come in with, some heavily muscled punk with his hat on backward and some kind of Celtic tattoo snaking down his right arm, leaned against the pool table and laughed. "God *damn*, son," he said.

Fights happened all the time, and sometimes you just had to let them play themselves out, but the jagged bottle changed everything. Will dialed 911.

Eric wouldn't let go of the guy's neck. He hit him again a few more times, and when the bottle came around once more he took it on the cheek. Blood sprayed onto the floor, the pool table, across his own face. Eric made a high-pitched noise that seemed to signal a transition into another state of being, that seemed to carve this moment from the rational world and hold it separate. The escalation of violence shifted the room's atmosphere. It almost seemed that another presence had crept in: some curious, blood-streaked thing.

Jeffrey flew in from the sidelines, like some berserker canary in a sky full of hawks. He threw himself against them both, wrapping his weak little hands around the wrist of the guy with the broken bottle. The momentum of his charge carried them all into the table where the college kids were sitting, and everybody went down in a clamor of toppling chairs and spilling glasses and shrieks of fear.

Alicia shouted something, running toward the tumble of bodies. Will rounded the bar—too late, he knew, he should have been the one to engage them—and followed her into the scrum. A camera flash leapt from the tangle of bodies, like lightning in the belly of a thunderhead.

By the time he arrived, it was already over. Eric had maneuvered on top of the other guy and was giving him a brutal series of jabs to the side of the head before somebody finally pulled him off. His antagonist, deprived of his weapon, moved groggily, his eyes already swelling shut, his face a bloodied wreck. His right hand looked broken. The kids who'd been at the table formed a penumbra around the scene, looking on with an almost professional calm.

One of the girls said, "Did you call the police?"

"Of course I fucking did."

She looked at the others and said, "Let's go." They dispersed immediately, pouring through the door and sublimating into the night.

Once freed from the entanglement, Eric had grown immediately calm, like a chemical rendered inert. The flesh on his cheek was torn in a gruesome display; the scar would pull his whole face out of alignment. He seemed not to feel it. His eyes were dilated and unfocused, but the rage seemed spent, and he went back to the pool table to retrieve what was left of his beer.

"Eric," Will said. "You need to get to a hospital. Seriously."

"Cops are coming?" he said. The words were a slush in his mouth.

"Yes."

"Fucking pussy." Will didn't know if that was meant for him or for the guy on the floor. "All right, come on," Eric said, and headed out the door. His remaining friends followed, not sparing a glance for their vanquished comrade.

Will, Alicia, and Jeffrey were left with the beaten man, who was only now pulling himself with glacial slowness into the closest upright chair. Will fetched a bar rag and gave it to him for his face, but he just held it limply, his hand suspended at his side. A thin stream of blood drooled from a cut on his face and pooled in a wrinkle on his shirt.

"You all right, man?"

"Just fuck off, dude."

"Yeah, you can say that to the cops, too, asshole." It was easy to be tough when the danger had passed. He felt a little ashamed by it, but not enough to shut himself up. "Grabbing a bottle in a fight is chickenshit."

The guy stood abruptly, knocking his chair over. Will flinched back a step. But the guy didn't waste any attention on him. He tottered briefly, achieved his bearings, and headed out the front door, into the warm night air. They watched him walk slowly down the sidewalk, into the lightless neighborhood, until he was obscured by parked cars and trees.

"What the hell was that?" Alicia said. Will turned to offer up some wry commentary about Eric and his friends but saw right away that the question was for Jeffrey, not him. "What did you think you were doing?"

"I don't know," Jeffrey said. "It was instinct, I guess."

"You're not some tough guy. You could have been really hurt."

"I know. But he had a broken bottle. He could have killed him."

Will had no stomach for listening to Jeffrey play the humble hero. He had a sudden urge to break a chair over his head. "You did good," he said.

Only now did he notice how much blood there was, all over his bar, like strange little sigils. On the green felt of the pool table, on the floor beside it, splashed on the chairs and pooled in a little puddle where the guy had been sitting just moments before. Stipples and coins of it making a trail over the floor where Eric had walked. A smear of it on the glass door, left there when he'd pushed his way out. Rosie's Bar felt curiously hollow, like a socket from which something had been torn loose, or like a voided womb.

Still no sign of the police. On a fucking Tuesday night. What else could they be doing?

The three of them spent the next twenty minutes restoring the tables and chairs to their places, wiping up as much of the blood as they could find. Will found a smartphone kicked into a corner, probably dropped by one of the college kids when their table was knocked into. He slid it into his pocket while he finished cleaning.

When they were done, he returned to his place behind the bar and poured himself a shot of Jameson. He knocked it down and poured three more, arrayed them on the bar, one for each.

They raised their glasses and touched the rims. His hand was shaking.

"To New Orleans!" Alicia said.

"This fucking town."

They drank.

Will liked coming home in the small hours. Carrie always left the light over the oven on for him before going to bed, creating a little island of domestic warmth: the clean white range, the fat green teapot, the checkered hand towel hanging from the oven door. Everything else was an ocean of quiet darkness. He set his keys softly on the countertop, retrieved a bottle of Abita Amber from the fridge, and settled down at the kitchen table. He'd given himself a buzz at the bar, and the world seemed pleasantly muddled to him now, not unlike the feeling of being half-asleep on a late morning.

He tried to push the fight out of his mind. The police finally did stroll in, well after Alicia and Jeffrey had gone home and Doug, the graveyard bartender, had taken over. Will had waited for them with growing impatience, nursing a beer in the corner. When they arrived—not Derek, who was a regular here, but a couple guys he didn't know—they took his statement, gave the place a cursory look, and ambled out again, looking fairly unimpressed by it all. Which was good. Nobody wanted uniformed cops hanging out in the bar. Just having the squad car parked out front—pale white in the dark, the reflective NOPD lettering on the doors flaring into a bright blue warning in the headlights of every passing car—was murder on business. When Will headed home, the bar had been empty, and Doug was leaned back against the counter, reading yesterday's newspaper.

Will had never seen Eric in a worse fight; he'd taken real damage from that broken bottle. Surely, this would slow him down a bit. At the very least, it might keep him from drinking while he waited for the stitches to heal. The thought brought Will some peace. He'd make a point of dropping in on him the next day, to make sure he'd wised up and gone to the emergency room.

Feeling restless, he wandered through the living room, navigating the darkness by muscle memory, and opened the door into the bedroom. Carrie was asleep, the sheets kicked down around her ankles in the heat. She ended up knocking half the covers to the floor every night, but couldn't sleep with the air conditioner on because it made her too cold. It was a battle Will had long ago surrendered, having resigned himself to making do with the ceiling fan. She was wearing a T-shirt and a pair of white granny panties which, once, he had found both odd and charming. Her short blond hair was rucked up against the pillow, and her face had the defenseless, wide-open innocence of deep sleep. It was easiest to love her when she was like this. He touched her cheek, hooked a strand of hair back over her ear.

He stood there for a moment, trying to decide if he was tired enough to join her. But the clangor of the evening still rang in his blood. He went back to the kitchen and grabbed another beer from the fridge.

A faint musical chime sounded somewhere, far away—a descending spill of notes in a minor key, like a refrain from a gloomy lullaby. He stopped in mid-stoop, the cold air from the refrigerator washing over him. There was nothing more, so he brought his beer back to the kitchen table and settled into his chair.

The sound came again, and this time he felt a vibration in his pants pocket. It was the cell phone from the bar, the one left behind by someone in that crowd of kids. He slipped it free and examined it: a bright yellow smartphone, fairly new judging by its condition, with a series of sparkling heart stickers affixed to its outer rim. The desktop was a picture of some Far Eastern mountain, snowcapped, radiant with reflected sunlight. He slid his finger across the screen to access the display, and there was a notification of two text messages received.

A momentary hesitation fluttered through his mind before he looked at them. Privacy be damned; she should have been more careful if she didn't want him to look.

The messages were from somebody named Garrett:

I think something is in here with me.

And then, sent two minutes later: I'm scared.

Will put the phone down and dropped his hands, staring at it. The fog in his head dissipated somewhat, and he was surprised to feel his heart beating. The screen remained lit for a few seconds and then blinked back to its inert state. He sat silently, unsure of what to do next. A sporadic ticking sounded somewhere in the darkness, beyond his little island of light. A scuttling roach. The phone chimed again, vibrating raucously against the tabletop. He leaned over and looked at the message.

**It knows I'm here. It's trying to talk. Please come.**

"What the fuck," Will whispered. He picked up the phone and scrolled through Garrett's messages. Maybe this was a game. Maybe they went back to the bar, knew he had the phone, and were fucking with him. Before these texts, there were only six messages exchanged between them. Arranging a study session for class, a mention of coffee; simple banalities. Nothing like this.

They were messing with him. He texted a reply: **You can pick up the phone tomorrow night at the bar. I go in at six.**

Enough time passed that he figured it was all over. He took another pull from his beer and decided it was just about time to join Carrie in bed after all. The roach scuttled somewhere over toward the cabinets, but his normal sense of revulsion was dimmed by his weariness and his irritation at the events of the night. His brain kept cycling around to Jeffrey. Again and again. Launching himself into the fray and maybe tipping the balance in Eric's favor. The look in Alicia's eyes afterward: She'd said she was pissed, and she probably was a little, but there was a heat in that look that did not come from anger. It made Will feel small.

The phone clamored again, making him jump. "Goddamn you," he said to it, and leaned over to see what it had to say.

**Tina?**

He sighed and texted back, against his own better judgement. **No, not Tina, asswipe. I have her phone.** He pressed send, immediately felt a swelling of guilt. Why the hostility? Maybe the guy really didn't know.

**Who are you? Get Tina.**

She left it at the bar. I'm the bartender. Tell her to pick it up tomorrow night. And stop fucking around.

He shut the ringer off and set it on the dish towel from the stove, to dull its vibrations. It sat there, a cheery yellow rectangle in the dark cave of his kitchen. He finished off the beer, trying to keep his mind unanchored, free-floating; but Jeffrey and Alicia kept bobbing to the surface, thwarting his efforts. He imagined them entangled in bed, a pale twist of limbs and sweat. Something dark turned over inside him, and he felt the sting of shame prickle his skin.

The scuttling sound intensified, and the roach veered into the open. It froze there, as if realizing its error. Its antennae searched the air, trying to gauge the severity of its predicament. Will considered the effort involved in getting up to kill it; it would be long gone before he even got close. He stomped his foot, trying to scare it. The roach did not flinch, brash as a rooster, unmoved by the sudden trembling of the world beneath it.

The phone vibrated quietly on its dish towel. Will didn't even bother to look at it. He got up from the table, placing the empty beer bottles into the recycling bin with a muted clink, and headed to bed. The roach disappeared under the refrigerator. Everything appeared clean, orderly, and quiet.

When he awoke, Carrie was already up, and the smell of coffee and frying bacon floated into the bedroom like a summons from God. He lay in the sweet fog of half sleep, relishing the bliss of it. He listened to Carrie's footsteps as she moved around in the kitchen, listened to her hum something quietly to herself, and felt a well of gratitude for this good life. He imagined Eric waking up in his own grim hovel, his face crusty with blood and bright with pain. Closing his eyes, he stretched in the cool sheets and derived a wicked pleasure from the contrast.

The clink of plates on the countertop finally dragged him out of bed.

She was still wearing only her T-shirt, her long legs gold and lean in the early light. He came up to her from behind, full-mast, and wrapped her in his arms, pressing himself against her and burying his nose in her hair.

"Good morning, pretty girl," he said.

She paused, smiled, and leaned her head to the side, baring her neck to him, which he dutifully kissed. A splinter of memory lanced through his mind: his shameful jealousy over Alicia. He blew it away like ash.

"Good morning," she said. She reached behind herself and wrapped her fingers around his cock through his boxers. "I thought you were going to miss breakfast."

"Madness."

"The eggs are going to burn."

He released her with a show of reluctance. She gave him a final squeeze and abandoned him to rescue the eggs from the range. He shambled to the coffeepot and poured himself a mug.

"Whose phone is that?"

He tensed. Her tone was light, but he heard the challenge in it. "Some chick's," he said. "She left it at the bar."

"So you brought it home?"

"I forgot I had it. There was a fight. She dropped it, and I was distracted."

Carrie scraped eggs onto two plates, lifted bacon still sopping with grease from a frying pan to join them. She sat at the table with him and together they ate in what he imagined was a comfortable silence.

"Was Alicia there with her new boyfriend?" she asked, after a while.

"Yeah. They want to have a double date with us."

"That sounds awful."

"I know. Maybe we could rope in a few more people and have a triple date, or even a mass date."

"Now it sounds like you're talking about murder."

"Right?"

Carrie reached across the table and pulled the phone toward her. Will felt an unaccountable twinge of anxiety. "What are you doing?" he said.

"Trying to find out whose phone it is, dummy. Why, should I not look? Am I going to see something I don't want to see?"

"No. Why would you say that?"

"I don't know."

"I'm not lying about the phone, Carrie."

"I know. I believe you."

But an unidentifiable discomfort had been introduced between them, which neither would directly acknowledge and which unfolded invisibly over the table like a sick bloom. Will got up and took his dish to the trash, where he scooped the remains of his breakfast. If Carrie noticed or cared, she gave no sign. Instead she took this as her cue to access the phone and begin her investigations.

Will was pouring himself a second cup of coffee when he heard Carrie yelp.

She put the phone on the table and pushed it away from her. "Fuck," she said. And then she grabbed it again. "Who the fuck were you talking to last night?"

"What do you mean? What's going on?"

"You were texting someone on this thing last night." She

delivered it like an accusation. He was about to snap a reply when she turned the face of it to him and he saw the last two texts, delivered after he had abandoned the conversation.

The first:

**PLEASE**

The second, delivered about ten minutes later, was simply a picture. Will squinted at it, couldn't make it out. He took the phone from her and held it closer to his face. A cold wave pulsed from his heart. It was a picture of half a dozen bloody teeth. They were arranged in a cluster on what appeared to be a wooden table; the roots were broken on most of them, as if they'd been wrenched out.

"Jesus Christ," he whispered.

"What the fuck is that?"

He considered it for a moment. He swiped his thumb across the screen and brought it back to the main menu. Weather, App Store, Google, Camera, Messages, Maps. All of it banal. Nothing on here, it seemed, to personalize it. He wondered what he would see if he checked the rest of her messages.

"Don't mess with it, Will. Take it to the cops. Somebody got hurt last night."

"Maybe. Or maybe they're just fucking with me." He knew it was ridiculous even as he said it.

She rose without a word and brought her plate to the sink. She kept her back to him as she ran the water over it.

"You know what? It's Wednesday; Derek will be in after his shift. I'll show it to him."

Derek was a cop in the Sixth District. He and his partner often spent time there on their off nights. He'd saved Will's bacon on more than one occasion—scaring off drug dealers, helping people out the door who didn't want to leave, and just generally making it known that Rosie's was protected. He was a good guy, and Will was happy to have him as a regular. He felt much better about the idea of showing the phone to him than bringing it into the precinct office, where he was pretty sure he'd be laughed out of the building.

Carrie seemed mollified by this. She shut the water off and faced him, leaning against the sink. "What if she comes back to claim it first?"

"I'll just tell her we haven't found it. I'll let the cops deal with it."

"Even though you just texted somebody that you have it? On this very phone?"

Will shrugged. "What's she going to do, call the police?"

She thought about that. "Yeah. Okay. I guess that works."

He put the phone back onto the table and pushed it away from him. "So did you get your paper written last night?"

She sighed, as if already exhausted. "Mostly. I have to go over it again before class. Probably rewrite the ending, since I was a zombie by the time I got to it. Then turn it in and hope Steve likes it."

Steve: her English Lit professor. It rankled him that she called him by his first name, but she claimed all the students did. He liked an "informal learning environment." Well, how progressive of him. The fucker. Carrie had been agonizing over a paper on T. S. Eliot's "The Hollow Men" for almost two months, and he was sick of hearing about it. She'd never fretted this much over a paper for any other professor. "I'm sure he'll love it," he said, making no effort to hide the sourness he felt. He knew it was petty, but it felt good anyway.

She cast him a look, which he could not interpret. "He better. It's a quarter of my grade."

"Right."

"What about you? What are you going to do?"

"I don't know. I feel like I should check up on Eric."

"Why?"

"He was the one in the fight last night. He got cut up pretty bad."

"Well, there's a shock. Let him hide under his rock. I'm sure he's fine. People like that always are."

"People like what?"

"The ones who start shit. It's always everyone else who suffers."

"I just want to make sure he's okay. Concern for others is a common human trait. You'll learn that about us in time."

She walked up to where he sat, standing over him and pressing herself close. "Asshole," she said, and kissed him. He felt himself rise to her, and she grinned as she pushed his hands away. "I have to work."

"Evil," he said, pulling her down for another kiss first, then watching as she went to her office in the next room, which was a calamity of stacked papers, earmarked books, discs, DVDs, and zip drives.

He shambled into the bathroom and started the shower, trying to decide what to do to fill his day after checking on Eric, and before he had to be back at work. Maybe just beers and video games. There was a lot of empty space until then, and empty spaces suited him just fine.

As he walked through the dense morning heat, heading toward the bar and Eric's apartment, Steve nested in the middle of Will's mind, bending every other thought toward him like some terrible star. He couldn't escape its pull.

Will had spent his life skimming over the surface of things, impatient with the requirements of engagement. He told himself that this was because he was open to experience in a way most people weren't, that you sapped the potential for spontaneity from life if you regimented your hours with obligation. This rationalization came upon him in college, shortly after he dropped out, converting all that money invested by his parents into so much tinder for the fire.

Most of the time he believed it.

And why not? Women liked him. He was tall, and he stayed fit without too much effort. He was generally cheerful and had an easy charisma. As long as he had a woman in his life and reasonable access to booze and the occasional line of coke, he figured he'd be okay. He'd been working as a bartender since dropping out of school six or seven years ago, and he believed he might just be able to live out the next fifty years of his life in this state of calibrated contentment.

He loved Carrie, he supposed, but love was a tide that came and went. Who knew how long she would stay with him? She was ambitious, and he could tell it annoyed her that he wasn't. He figured her patience would wear out sometime in the next six months. Another reason that being a bartender was an ideal job. The girls grew like fruits on a tree. You practically just had to reach out and pluck one.

Life so far seemed like a kind of dance to him, and he was pleased to discover that he was pretty good at it. If there was something hollow underneath it all, a well of fear that sometimes seemed to pull everything else into it and leave him clutching the stone rim to keep from falling into himself, well, that was just part of being human, he supposed. That's what the booze was for.

This line of thought brought him back around to Alicia, and her irritating infatuation with her little hipster douchebag beau-du-jour, Jeffrey. Alicia played the field even more shamelessly than he ever had, and while that intimidated him at first, he eventually came around to admiring her for it. She'd sit at the bar by herself and they'd bullshit about work, her latest boyfriend, his newest girlfriend. When Carrie came along and stuck around longer than most, Alicia had the good sense to spare her from attack, without even having to be asked. Will found that impressive. They hadn't ever slept together, and he enjoyed the steady sexual tension that resulted.

Still, he'd always figured it was just a matter of time, and he was content to wait until the moment was right—when Carrie was gone, or when they were just drunk enough that it didn't matter. But then Jeffrey happened along, and all of a sudden things were different.

He would have liked to say that he'd refrained from taking cheap shots at Jeffrey, returning the respect she'd shown his new relationship, but he hadn't. Sometimes he just couldn't resist. Alicia tolerated it for a while, deflecting his insults. Then she just started to ignore them, until it wasn't much fun anymore. He satisfied himself with the belief that Jeffrey couldn't last much longer, that Alicia's appetite and her impatience with ridiculous men would spell his doom. But he'd been waiting for a while now. He suspected Jeffrey's unlikely heroics last night had given him an extended lease.

He pulled out his phone and dialed Alicia.

"Get a beer with me," he said.

"Fuck, dude, what time is it?"

"Are you still asleep? It's like ten o'clock."

"I didn't get to sleep until sunrise."

So their night hadn't ended when they left Rosie's. That hurt, though he knew it was unreasonable. "So are you going to come get a beer with me?"

"No, asshole, I am not. I'm going back to sleep."

"When did you turn into a pussy?"

"That is so wrong. And so are you. Maybe I'll see you tonight. Have one for me, okay?"

She hung up.

He pocketed the phone again and kept walking. He had no right to feel rejected, but he did. He was skirting dangerously close to infidelity, was practically inviting it, but he didn't feel the pang of guilt he knew he should. There was just a need, and he had to answer it.

The thought of going in and having a beer without Alicia with him was too depressing to countenance, so he maintained his heading, resigned to checking in on Eric instead.

A metal staircase affixed to the side of Rosie's led up to a small balcony and Eric's front door. You could access the place without being noticed from inside the bar, for which he was grateful. Rosie herself worked the morning shift, and if she saw him, she'd want to call him in and fill his head with her outrageous opinions. He crept up the stairs and knocked on Eric's door.

Will found himself hoping that he wouldn't answer. He was having a hard time remembering the impulse that drove him here. They'd never been close—hell, they barely qualified as friends—and standing here in the heat of a bright Wednesday morning, Will felt mother-hennish and ridiculous.

But the thunk of a deadbolt retracting into the doorframe scuttled any hope he had of leaving unnoticed. The door swung open into a cool darkness, and Eric was standing there in his underwear, his hair matted with sweat despite the air conditioner Will could hear clattering away somewhere in the depths of the apartment. The right side of Eric's face was a Technicolor nightmare of scabbed and torn flesh. Dried blood speckled his face and shoulders.

"Holy shit, Eric."

Eric spoke without moving his jaw. He was clearly in vast pain. "What is it."

"I came to check on you. You need to go to the hospital, man."

"No."

"Fuck that. Yes. I'm gonna go get my car."

Eric took his elbow and brought him inside, shutting the door against the heat. "It's not as bad as it looks."

"Dude, you can barely talk!"

He made a vague gesture toward his face. "Swollen. That's all. Come inside."

Will followed him into the kitchen, which was cluttered in barfly chic: takeout boxes on the counter, trash overdue for removal, a few plates in the sink. In the living room he could see some clothing piled in a corner. Eric shook some pills out of a bottle on the counter and swallowed them dry. "Buddy of mine can stitch this up."

"A buddy of yours? What is this, Afghanistan?"

"Can't afford a hospital."

He moved slowly into the living room, one hand in front of him as though he were looking for balance. When he made it to the couch, he collapsed onto it and unfurled like a caterpillar. The blinds were drawn on the room's only window, and the apartment had the cool, dank atmosphere of a cave. "Thank your friend for me," he said.

"What friend?"

"Guy who saved my ass last night. The one banging your girl."

Will felt both irritated and irrationally thrilled. "Alicia isn't my girl."

"Okay, man." His voice was starting to drift.

"Who was that guy you were fighting with?"

Eric didn't answer. His breathing calmed, water finding its level.

"Okay. Anyway. I was just checking in. I'll let you sleep."

Eric, eyes still closed, put out a hand. For an awkward moment, Will thought he meant for him to hold it. "Don't leave me," he said, his voice bleary with painkillers and the proximity of sleep. "Nightmares."

Will felt a sudden shame at having witnessed this nakedly weak gesture, this plea in the dark; it was a gross and bewildering intimacy, and he wanted to pretend he hadn't heard it. Reluctantly, though, he found a place to sit down by moving a laundry basket from a chair to the floor. "Okay," he said. "I'll hang out for a little bit."

He waited for Eric to drift off to sleep, watching his face twitch, his eyes spin beneath his eyelids. He was growing cold in the frigid blast of the AC, but Eric was still covered in a thin sheen of sweat. Below them, in Rosie's Bar, someone fed some money into the jukebox and a dull bass throbbed its way up through the floor, ringing the bones in his body. It would drive him mad, that constant, subdermal growl. He watched Eric fade away, and wondered what black dreams slid through his brain.

Feeling aimless and obscurely unsatisfied, Will walked home, where he planned to crash on the couch and play video games until Carrie came back from class. He didn't like spending time by himself; silence unnerved him, left him feeling unanchored and threatened. The froth of the video games was partially successful in keeping that silence at bay, but after a while it started to chew through his little pixelated boundaries, and he would be forced to find some other distraction.

So it was with relief that he sensed someone else at home, as though a passage through the air had sent ripples brushing his skin as he entered.

"Carrie?" She should still be in class, but she might have returned early. No one answered. He passed through the kitchen, through the living room, and stopped in their bedroom. The place was empty. Feeling mildly foolish, he planted himself in front of the TV and booted up his video game console.

He was an American solider half an hour into a jungle heavily seasoned with hostiles and a good five minutes away from a hotly defended save point when his phone vibrated. He paused the game and fished it from his pocket.

Blank. No messages.

His blood cooled when he realized which phone it had been. He set his own down and removed the other one from his pocket, the bright yellow one with the hearts. Its face was lit, the little green text box signifying a message received. He tapped it with his finger. It was from someone named Jason.

**Hey bartender.**

He looked at it for several seconds before deciding not to answer. He leaned back and unpaused the game. A sniper took a shot at him from the dense foliage. He keyed himself into a crouch.

It buzzed again, and he glanced over.

**You looked.**

*Fuck you,* he thought.

Buzz: **It's yours now.**

He dropped the controller and typed a response. **Don't want your goddam phone. Pick it up at the bar tonight.**

A moment passed. **Did you look at all the pretty pictures yet?**

He typed. **Maybe I should take it to the police.**

**Take a look. Might like what you see.**

He waited, but nothing else came from the phone. The video game was frozen on the death screen. A blurry image of his avatar's bullet-riddled corpse lay behind the reset prompt.

He switched it off and gave his full attention to the yellow phone. It felt like a conduit of dark energy, and he felt uncomfortable holding on to it. He placed it on an end table beside the couch and called up the menu. The camera icon pulled his eye toward it, as though it exerted its own peculiar gravity. He touched the icon and scrolled over to the picture gallery.

There were four saved images and a video file. He stared at them a moment. He tried to come to terms with what he was seeing, tried to arrange the world in such a way that would accommodate his own mundane life, the daily maintenance of his ordinary existence, along with what he saw arrayed before him in neat little squares, like snapshots of Hell.

He tapped his finger on the first one so it ballooned to fill the screen.

It looked like a close-up shot of a sleeping man's face. He was middle-aged, balding, with a large, flat nose; his face was soft and rounded, like the features of a stone carving worn smooth by time. There was nothing sinister about this picture; it might be an intimate portrait taken by a lover, or a dear friend.

The second was the same man from the same angle but taken from a few feet farther away. In this picture the man was clearly dead, felled by a violent strike to the head. The rounded dome of the man's skull, cropped out of the first image, was here depicted in its shattered complexity: bone and brain and blood extruded from the crown like a psychedelic volcano caught in mid-expulsion. The man was lying on the sidewalk. The blood around his head reflected a disc of overhead light, a streetlamp or a flashlight. The picture had been taken at night. He noticed what appeared to be a wedding band on the man's left hand, which lay palm up, white and plump.

The third picture revealed a new setting. This one had been taken indoors, under a harsh light, probably a fluorescent. Seventies-style wood paneling covered the wall in the background. A utilitarian white drafting table occupied the foreground, and resting atop it was the same man's head, severed from its body. It sat planted straight on the table; someone must have taken the time to balance it, to arrange it just so. The wound in his head was not visible from this angle. No blood marred the scene, save the inevitable blackened ring around the neck. It seemed that some care had been taken to clean the blood from his head, primping him like a schoolboy for his yearbook photo. A slender red book lay on the table behind it, partially obscured, its spine facing the camera.

Will tried to slide on to the next one, but his fingers had gone numb and the phone clattered to the floor. He experienced a wild and irrational fear that someone had heard him and would see what he was looking at, and he felt an overwhelming shame—as though he'd been caught looking at the most outrageous pornography, or as though these ghastly photographs depicted his own work.

Putting the phone back on the table, he closed his eyes and forced himself to calm down. His breath was shaky, his nerves jumping. It occurred to him abruptly, like some divine communication, that he did not have to look any further. He knew something awful had happened, that a murder of grotesque proportions had been committed and documented, and that any further examination was unnecessary. He should go to the police right now and wash his hands of it.

But stopping was unthinkable. He scrolled to the fourth photograph.

In this one, someone had gone to work on the head with an almost medical precision, and an artisan's hand. Using the killing wound as a starting point, someone had sliced the man's scalp into a star pattern and pulled the skin down from the head in bloody banana peels. The soft, generous features of his face, which had suggested to Will only moments ago the close proximity of someone beloved, were obscured now by the bloody undersides of themselves. The skull had been scraped clean, or nearly so. The eye sockets had been scooped hollow. The table beneath the head was festooned with the gory splashes of the artisan's labor.

Only the video clip remained. Pressing the button was not like scrolling through the pictures; he could not pretend he was carried by momentum. This was a separate choice. It was his second chance to turn away.

He pressed play.

The video player took a moment to load, and then filled the screen with the shaky image of the head on the table. A blare of static shrieked from the phone as someone said something unintelligible. Will tapped the button to lower the volume, conscious of the sound intruding into the atmosphere of his apartment, like a species of ghost. He checked over his shoulder, the sense of proximity to another person prickling his nerves once more, and then held the phone close to his face to be sure he wouldn't miss anything. Shame, fear, and a weird thrill filled his body.

*"Tina! Hold it steady. Jesus."* A young man's voice.

The view stabilized, holding firm on the severed head,

which was canting to one side. The fourth picture had already been taken: careful ribbons of flesh suspended like wilted petals over the dead man's face. The top of the skull had been shaved down, leaving a red, raw hole just above the temple. A girl stepped into frame, her back to the camera. She had straight blond hair, an athletic body. She straightened the head again, held it a moment to make sure it stayed in place.

*"Oh my God I can feel it,"* she said, and jerked her hands away.

*"Get the fuck out of the picture!"* Another girl's voice.

She retreated, and a calm settled over the image. An almost imperceptible movement of the camera as the hand holding it trembled. A stifled, nervous giggle. The head shifted slightly, as if it had heard something and had to turn a fraction to listen more closely. Then it moved again, and something seemed to move in the darkness of its open skull.

*"Oh shit."* High-pitched, genderless.

Four thick, pale fingers extended from inside the hole and hooked over the forehead. Someone screamed off camera and the image skewed wildly. The video ended.

"Will?"

"Fuck!" He flipped the phone over, turning to see Carrie standing beside him. He felt slow and disjointed, as though he'd dropped a tab of acid. "When did you get home?"

"Just now." She wasn't looking at him, though. "What are you looking at?"

"Nothing."

"I thought you were going to turn that in to the police."

"Yeah. Tonight. I said I'd do it tonight. Jesus, what time is it?"

"I came home early. Skipped math. What are you looking at, Will?"

"I said nothing. Just . . ." He stood up and put his arms around her in a belated welcome. There was nothing genuine about the gesture, and she pushed him away, plainly irritated.

"Give it to me."

He just shook his head, avoiding her eyes. He could not let her see what he'd just seen. "No. Carrie, just trust me. You don't want to."

He felt her staring at him. "Is that Alicia's phone?"

"What? No! What does that even mean?"

"You know what the fuck it means."

"I can't believe this. I can't believe you're still hung up on this. My friends can only be guys? Really? What about Steve?"

This didn't get the rise out of her he was hoping for. She looked at him calmly and said, "What *about* Steve?"

"He's into you. He wants to fuck you."

"So what? I'm not fucking him."

"But you want to."

"No. I don't. You want to check my phone? See if I have any pictures of him on it? You want to see if I've sent him pictures of my tits? Go check it. It's in my purse in the kitchen. Go."

He shook his head, but the temptation was real. Was she bluffing? Did she know that he wouldn't do it? What if he surprised her and really looked? What would he find? "No," he said. "I trust you. I wish you trusted me too."

"I want to trust you. But you're fucking looking at *something* on that fucking phone and you're acting guilty as shit!"

Of course, she was right. Nothing about his behavior signaled anything good. He knew that. He retrieved the phone from the table and placed it into her hand. "You don't want to look," he said. "You really don't. It's awful."

"What is it?"

He thought about the fingers. "I don't know."

She sat down, and she opened the files.

He watched it all a second time with her. When she was done, she returned it to him, her hand shaking. He stared at her face the way he would a television screen, waiting for something to happen on it, waiting for it to give him something to react to.

"Is that Garrett? The one who was texting last night?"

That thought hadn't even occurred to him. "The guy on the table? I don't think so. These were taken earlier. They were already on the phone. I think he's part of this crowd though. He obviously knows Tina."

"Call him."

"What? No."

"Then give it to me. I'll do it."

He clutched the phone more tightly. "Why, Carrie? It's a bad idea."

"I want to know if he's still alive. Were those his teeth we saw this morning? I don't want to think about someone dying like that while you ignored him."

"*Ignored him?*"

"He was asking for help! He was begging you!"

"Oh, fuck that," he said, a surge of guilt turning quickly to anger. "This is stupid." He activated the screen and went back to Garrett's last written text.

**PLEASE**

He summoned Garrett's number and called it.

Carrie stared at him as he waited for an answer, the phone trilling lightly into his ear. After a moment it stopped ringing. He brought the phone away from his ear a fraction of an inch, thinking at first that it had been disconnected, but something about the quality of the silence told him otherwise.

"Hello?"

Something was alive in that silence.

"Garrett? Hello?"

It spoke. It sounded broken and wet, like something sliding itself together in a slurry of blood and bones. A tongue testing the border of language. Liquid syllables collided and slipped past each other. It sounded too close, like it was already living in his head.

He threw the phone across the room in a reflex of disgust, Carrie's barked cry of shock lost in the echo of the voice leaking from his ear like a thread of blood. The phone came apart in two pieces, and Carrie was already racing toward it, leaving him to rub at his ear with the heel of his hand, tears he didn't even know he was crying trailing down his cheek.

Carrie crouched on the floor, fitting the battery back into the phone, snapping its shell back into place. "Was that him? Was that Garrett?" She sounded panicked.

And why would that be, he wondered, the fear and the disgust of a moment ago settling into a thick soup of anger. She wasn't the one with that voice lingering in her head.

"No," he said. "It wasn't anybody."

Wednesdays were always among the slowest nights of the week, so there was plenty of time for fear to grind away at the levees he'd built against the panic. He felt it threaten to breach every time the door swung open, and he hated himself for it. He didn't know if he'd be able to recognize any of them again, even if they did show up. All college kids looked to him as if they came from the same homogenous gene pool, as if they were all grown in some remote basement laboratory. Arrogant, loud, their little faces as yet unmarked by the heart's weather—they were like bright, wriggling grubs. Members of the Larval Class.

He drank a little more than normal that night, riding his usual buzz a little further into the red. The clientele was sparse enough and familiar enough, though, that he could afford to work with dulled senses. They fetched beers from him and settled onto their stools or into their customary orbits around the pool table, the rails of normal activity so comfortable and rigid that it seemed nothing peculiar could possibly exist in the world.

Derek didn't show up that night after all. Will felt a curious relief. He didn't want to give it up. A distant alarm rang somewhere deep in his brain when he realized this, but he doused it with a shot of whiskey. He and Carrie hadn't discussed what they'd seen on the phone. They watched it a few more times after she put the phone back together. Somewhere in there, she cried. Then she stopped. When it was time for him to go, they didn't exchange any words, or kiss. Something dead was in the air with them, its limp black wings pressing them flat. He was happy not to have to think about it.

At some point Alicia came in without Jeffrey. He felt an immediate lightening of his spirit, and her arrival seemed like a kind of justice to him, like some secret communication from the universe, a kind gesture to balance the scales. She took her usual stool and he mixed her usual drink. The comfortable click of the pool balls punctuated the low chatter in the bar, Sam Cooke crooned easily from the jukebox, and the true order of the world nestled back into place.

"Quiet in here tonight," Alicia said. "You hear anything about Eric?"

He'd managed to forget about Eric. "Yeah, actually. Went to see him this morning. He's cut pretty bad, but he won't go to the hospital. He thinks he's Rambo."

"You tell Derek about it?"

"He hasn't been in. I'm sure it'll come up." He didn't want to talk about Eric. "So where's Jeffrey tonight?"

Alicia looked irritated and her gaze traveled along the rows of bottles behind him. "He's being an asshole. I'm punishing him."

"Really? What did he do?"

"Like I said. Being an asshole. Anybody come in to claim that phone?"

He poured them both a shot of Jameson. "Not yet."

"Just this one," Alicia said. "I have to go easy tonight."

"Why?"

"I just don't feel like being wasted. I want to try to cut back."

He wondered if that meant he'd be seeing less of her. The thought was terrifying in a way that even the strange video was not. A great sorrow, disproportionate and bewildering, moved through him. "You don't have to get wasted," he said, trying to sound normal. "Just do what I do. Maintain the buzz. It's like surfing."

"You don't have to tell me how to drink, Will."

They drank the shots; and then, as is the way of these things, they drank a few more. The night achieved its rhythm. The dull anxiety he felt each time the door opened to admit someone new did not abate completely, but as midnight swung around and receded, it faded to a quiet hum. Everything related to the phone and the college kids retracted into a dim kernel of absurdity. Alicia stayed the whole shift, easygoing and flirtatious, just like the old days. She laughed at his dumb jokes, made a few of her own. He felt like a human being again.

When Doug came in to relieve him at two, he snagged a half-full bottle of bourbon from the shelf and swung it like a pendulum in front of Alicia. "I don't want to go home yet," he said.

"Me neither."

"Let's go up to the levee and kill this thing."

Her eyes unfocused for a moment, and he could actually see the doubt pass over her face. It stung.

"Come on, woman."

"Okay. Let's go."

Once they were in his car and on the road, he said, "Listen to this, it's beautiful," and keyed in a Pines song called "All the While," a sweet, quiet rumination that filled the precarious space between them with warmth, a place for them to exist in soft and bleary community. The lights outside washed across the windshield, casting a glow onto her skin and then releasing it into darkness again. She rested her forehead against the window and said, "You know what I like about you, Will? When you say something is beautiful, it really is. That word means something to you." He absorbed the compliment. It filled him up.

He parked in the grass and together they ascended the levee's steep gradient, where a walking path snaked across the top. They crossed it and walked a little beyond, settling into the grass along the downward slope. The Mississippi was huge and silent at their outstretched feet, moving the earth's dark energy through the night. The air was humid and close; clouds cruised across the stars. Their shoulders were pressed together as they lay back and watched them. Will took a pull from the bottle and passed it to her; she did the same.

"This is nice," he said.

"Yeah. No people. I like no people."

"Me too."

She angled her head so that it rested on his shoulder, her

eyes closed sleepily. He turned to her, his nose in her hair. "You smell good," he said.

She smiled. "Mmm."

"You ever wonder how things could have been?"

She took a moment to answer, but only a small one. "Yes," she said.

He kissed her forehead. Her breath stilled. He did it again, and this time she turned her face up to him, her eyes still closed, and offered her lips. He kissed her there with disbelief that such a thing might be happening to him, with a sense of a great engine beginning at last to turn, with a cresting joy. They kissed tentatively, their lips only grazing, and then more deeply, until they turned their bodies to each other and he put a hand on her cheek. He grazed his fingers across her ear, down the side of her face, and then down to her breast. He felt her bra underneath her shirt, wanted to pull it aside, touch skin to skin. He felt her fingers dig into his hair and his back.

And then she pulled away, pressing her hand against his chest. "Stop, Will."

"But . . ."

"Stop. Please. I'm sorry. I'm really sorry."

He sat up, dismayed. "Why? What's wrong?"

"You know what's wrong." She sat up too, adjusting her shirt, brushing grass from her hair. There was more space between them now.

"Is it Jeffrey?"

"Of course it's Jeffrey. And it's Carrie, too. Come on, Will."

"Why? Why *him*, for Christ's sake? I don't understand it."

She shook her head. Her face was flushed, and her lower lip trembled. "I don't know. I'm sorry. I'm horrible."

He put his hand on her back. "No, Alicia."

Arching away from his touch, she said, "Don't."

He sat there, feeling ridiculous, feeling like something essential had been blasted away from inside him. "I'm sorry."

"Let's just go back."

They walked back to the car, and when he started the engine, she reached down and switched off the music. They drove back to the bar in a painful silence. He pulled in behind the place she'd parked, his headlights illuminating the license plate, the rear window. He saw the empty seats in there and imagined them both sitting inside, in a kinder universe, adjacent to this one, where that would be a normal thing, where they both belonged in the same place. He said, "She doesn't love me, you know."

She looked at him with genuine sorrow. "I'm sorry for that. If that's true, then I really am."

"Does he love you?"

She nodded. "I think he really does," she said.

"I do too, you know."

"I know you do." She put her hand on his cheek, and the gentleness of it nearly made him cry. "I'll see you tomorrow night, okay?"

"Yeah. Okay." He could feel the tears in his eyes, knew that she could see them. He didn't care.

She kissed him quickly, chastely. "You're a good man, Will. Maybe the best one. Good night."

"Good night," he said.

He was anything but a good man. He knew it. He watched her pull away from the curb and disappear around the corner. Then he rested his head on the steering wheel and sat there for a while.

~ ~ ~

By the time he arrived back home, the sun was bruising the sky in the east. He pulled in behind Carrie's car on the side of the road, shut the engine off, and leaned back in his seat with his eyes closed. Something big was trapped inside him, some great sadness, and he felt if he could cry, or even articulate it in speech, it would relieve the pressure and provide him some measure of relief. But he couldn't reach it. He couldn't find a way to address it. He wondered if it would become the thing that defined him. He imagined himself in the third person, as someone observed and understood by an invisible witness. Would there be room for sympathy? Or would he be damned by it?

The car was a liminal zone, a transitional place, and as long as he stayed there he would not have to face either Carrie or Alicia again. It seemed an attractive prospect. He could easily go to sleep here, let the heat of daylight wake him up in an hour or two. He could think of something to tell Carrie.

He was pretty sure he could think of something.

His phone chimed in his pocket, and he fumbled it hurriedly out, thinking for one incandescent moment that it might be Alicia.

It was Carrie. The disappointment was almost physical. He looked at their apartment across the street. The porch light was on, but everything inside was dark.

He accepted the call and said, "Hey. Sorry I'm so late. I'm right outside. I'm on my way in."

The call disconnected.

His skin prickled. He told himself she was just angry with him, that she had a right to be—more than she knew—and she'd simply hung up on him. That he would go inside and take what he had coming. But he knew it was something else. When the phone chimed a text received, he didn't want to look. He stared at the icon for a long time, feeling that strange, unreleasable presence swell inside of him. Finally he slid his thumb across the screen and looked at the text.

It was another picture. Taken from inside his house, the lights off. The perspective was from the kitchen, directed at the door to Carrie's study but angled in such a way that the picture did not afford a look into it. Only the cool blue glow of an active computer screen, radiating from inside her study like a heat signature, gave any hint of a human presence.

Will crossed the street, feeling powerfully dislocated from the world. The door was still locked. He unlocked it and stepped into the warm darkness of the interior, attuned to each convulsion of his heart. He knew he should find a weapon, but the actual doing of it seemed too complicated. Easier to just walk into the black cave of his home and accept what waited there.

"Carrie?"

He entered the kitchen. He stood precisely in the spot the photo had been taken. There, bleeding from her study, was the blue glow of the computer screen.

"Carrie? Are you awake?"

He got no answer.

He stepped up to the door and peered in.

She was sitting in her chair, elbows on the desk, leaning in close to the screen. Her right hand was on the mouse, still as a held breath. Something was moving on the screen.

"Carrie. Are you okay?"

"Huh?" She looked at him, blinking at the adjustment. "Oh. Hey. Sorry, I didn't know you were home. What time is it?"

"It's past five, honey." He looked at the screen. She was watching a video of a black tunnel. The walls glistened with moisture. The camera moved through it slowly and smoothly, as if it were gliding along a track.

"Oh man. Really? I lost track of time." She rubbed her eyes.

"What's that? Are you researching something?"

She switched off the screen. "No. That's something else." She arose from her chair and draped her arms around his shoulders. "Are you just getting home?"

"Yeah. I stayed after the shift. Played a few games of pool. Just hung out."

"Good. I like you to have fun." She kissed him sleepily. "Let's go to bed."

"Did you send me a picture a few minutes ago? Did you try to call me?"

She frowned, put her forehead on his shoulder. "No. Maybe? I don't think so. I can't really remember. I feel foggy."

"Are you drunk?"

"I'm just really tired, Will. Come on. Let's go to bed." She headed in that direction, attempting to drag him along behind her.

"I'll be right there, okay?"

She continued on by herself, walking like someone drugged, sagging from her own bones.

He checked the apartment thoroughly. In closets, under the bed, in the pantry. The place was empty. After double-checking the lock on the front door, he followed her to bed. He stared at the ceiling until the rising sun painted it with light, Carrie still snoring beside him. Only then did he manage to close his eyes and lose himself from the world.

They both slept into the early afternoon. They awoke groggy and irritable. A heavy weight swung in Will's head, moving at a slight lag to the rest of him. He trudged into the bathroom, where he took a scorching shower. He felt unaccountably filthy, as though he'd been steeped in sewage. The soap and hot water did nothing to change it. He considered, briefly, that he was feeling guilt about his encounter with Alicia, but in fact the only thing he felt about that was a horror at her rejection.

In the living room Carrie was sitting on the couch, staring at the window, her hands folded together on her lap. The blinds were still drawn, and the day was a pale white blur beyond them. She noticed him come in and gave him a wan smile. He had a hard time returning it, but he did.

"What do you think it is?" she said.

"What do you mean?"

She opened her hands, and the yellow phone was there. "The pictures. The video." Her face looked wrong. Maybe she was sick.

"I don't know."

"I thought you were going to give this to Derek."

"He didn't come in last night."

"Why not?"

"He has a life I guess, Carrie. He doesn't punch a clock there."

She didn't respond. Instead she activated the phone and opened the picture album.

"What are you doing?"

"I'm looking at them," she said simply.

He joined her on the couch and leaned in to her, looking as well. "I don't think this is a good idea," he said. She scrolled to the pictures of the severed head, pausing on the first one.

"I Googled that guy's name last night. Garrett? Checked if there were any references on nola.com to someone with that name who went missing or was hurt. I didn't find anything."

"We don't know that anything happened to him," Will said.

She ignored this. "Then I Googled other words."

He felt queasy. "Like what?"

"I don't remember. A bunch of stuff. Voices on the phone, trading images of violence, death cults, that sort of thing."

He shook his head, unable to process what he was hearing. "Death cults?"

"Well, I don't know, Will! What the fuck are these people doing? Texting each other these things?"

"Carrie, I feel weird about this. I don't think looking for this—whatever it is—is a good idea."

"I'm not looking for it, it's already here! Don't you feel it? I don't feel alone here, even when I know I am."

He stood and started pacing, his body sparking with an energy as much excitement as fear. "Well? Did you find anything?"

"I can't remember," she said quietly. He thought of the dark, wet tunnel on the screen last night.

"Don't go looking again," he said.

Carrie sighed, putting her forehead in her hand. The phone lay limply in her other one. "Don't tell me what to do, Will."

He put out his hand. "Give it to me."

"Excuse me?"

"Please. Please, Carrie. Give it to me. I'm going to give it to the police. I'm just going to drive to the station."

"No you won't." She set it on the end table and left him to fetch it himself. "You'll keep it. You're like them."

"What are you talking about? Like who?"

"People look so normal on the outside," she said. "Inside it's all just worms."

He snatched up the phone before she could change her mind. "I don't understand you," he said.

She arose from the couch and disappeared into the bed-room, emerging a while later dressed for the day.

"Have a good night at work," she said.

"Just like that?"

"Give up the phone tonight. Then we'll talk." With that she was gone.

He fell onto the couch, wanting to be angry. She had no right to give him an ultimatum. He was the one who'd found the damn thing, he was the one who'd seen the pictures and tried to protect her from them, he was the one who'd had to listen to that awful voice after she insisted he make the call. The more he thought about it all, the more righteous he felt.

But he still couldn't get angry.

He wasn't sure what he was supposed to feel. The spikes of fear he'd experienced earlier always seemed to retreat to a low-grade anxiety during the day. He knew she was right about one thing, though. He did not want to turn the phone in. It felt like a door opening into a dark room. It scared him, but something lived there that he wanted to see.

He took the opportunity to check Carrie's computer in her office, personal space be damned. He booted it up and toggled her history. Some .edu sites, links to papers on T. S. Eliot, a few celebrity gossip sites, a lengthy spell of window shopping at Amazon. Somewhere in that time the weight of what she'd seen shifted her focus; what started as a perusal of furniture and clothing ending with a browse through the true crime section, followed by books on the occult. There were links to a few sites after that, but not many—ancient, hor-ribly designed sites about Satanism and witchcraft, hosted on long-defunct platforms with rudimentary interfaces. It was a geological dig through the strata of the Internet's past. From there she seemed to have spent considerable time looking into something called *The Second Translation of Wounds*. The last recorded site visit was time-stamped 11:17. Several hours before he arrived home.

Clicking on links to *The Second Translation of Wounds* took him to crackpot religious sites, links to occult booksellers with titles like the *Codex Gigas*, *Dragon Rouge*, and *The Munich Manuscript*. *The Second Translation* was part of a three-volume set that addressed the manifestation of angels through human injury.

From there he followed her search history to a file sharing site devoted to the exchange of photographs of extreme violence. He'd seen the sites where they displayed photos from crime scenes or accidents; this was something different. Photos of smashed fingers, broken bones, impalements, drooling injuries. These looked like personal photos.

After that, there was no record of her activity. As if she'd shut the computer off. Or cracked through the lowest stratum to something else.

He remembered the black, glistening tunnel. Something moving through it.

He shut the computer down. The whole thing made him feel sick. He went into the kitchen and made himself a screwdriver. He kept thinking about it. He couldn't stop.

The night was surprisingly busy, and at first he was able to lose himself in the tide of work. Most of what he termed Rosie's Regulars made an appearance: Old Willard, the raisin-faced ex-POW from the Korean War, smiling through his sublimated rage and throwing nasty remarks at tough guys fifty years his junior; Naked Mary, the heavyset exhibitionist, who was good for two or three appearances a month and always concluded her stay with a pool game played in the nude; Scotty, the oyster-shucker from down in the Quarter, who sang Frank Sinatra tunes at the top of his lungs; along with the ordinary flotsam of an ordinary night, a number of whom Will counted among his friends—at least as far as a word like that stretched when they only came to see you for the booze.

Even the roaches were at a low ebb, as the bar had been visited by an exterminator earlier in the day. He found nearly a dozen of them on their backs, their legs moving lethargically, as though they'd been caught sweetly dreaming.

But for the absence of Alicia, it was shaping up to be a banner night at Rosie's.

Derek and his partner showed up too, drifting to their usual haunt at the pool table. Will felt the weight of the yellow phone in his pocket.

Around ten thirty, a pall settled over him. Alicia's continued absence started to feel like an indictment. The bar was full, the jukebox was rattling on its feet, the vibe was good, but the joy he'd been taking in the work seeped away, and his mind disengaged. She was blowing him off. He remembered their kiss with a beautiful, unkind clarity. He needed her to be here so that he could apologize to her, so that he could be reassured by her, and so that he could impress upon her with the force of absolute conviction that the love he bore her was the purest thing he had ever felt.

Perhaps it was because of this distraction that he did not immediately recognize the clean-cut kid leaning across the bar, his arms folded beneath him and an ugly half grin climbing up one side of his perfect face. Will looked at the kid, waiting for him to place his order, some pugilistic impulse keeping him from being the first to speak. If the kid was too cool to speak, he could fucking go without.

And then he recognized him. His face must have betrayed him, because then the kid gave him the full-wattage smile, the one that charmed the girls right out of their clothes, like snakes from their baskets. "Took you a minute," he said.

Will looked behind him for the other kids, the ones too young to come up and order for themselves. The bar was crowded, but he didn't see them. The table in the corner, where they'd roosted last time, was empty.

"What can I do for you?" Will said, trying to play down his momentary shock. Act like he was any normal customer.

"Well, I'm not going to stay long—I forgot my ID." He patted his pockets with a sad smile.

"Are you Garrett?"

The kid seemed to enjoy that. "Garrett? No. I'm Jason. We had a nice little exchange yesterday. Remember?"

"Is Garrett dead?"

"By no means. He's around. Who knows, maybe you'll see him. You don't have that phone on you, do you? You still want to give it back?"

"The phone belongs to someone named Tina. You don't look like a Tina to me."

Jason smiled. "That's okay. It's yours now anyway. I just came by to tell you we left you a little present."

The world blurred for a moment. He thought of Carrie, alone at home, staring into her computer screen. "Leave her alone," he said. He sounded weak, like a scared little kid.

Jason smiled and shook his head. "Your girlfriend? Nice tits, butch haircut? No, dude, I'm not talking about her. Hey, you got a thing for dykes or something?"

Will couldn't believe he was saying this to him. In his bar, of all places. Surrounded by his friends. The absolute arrogance of the move rendered him breathless. He had a vague sense of people waiting for his attention down the bar. They could keep waiting. "You need to get the fuck out of here right now," he said, "before something bad happens to you."

Jason held up his hands in mock surrender. "No problem, man, no problem."

"Who are you people, anyway?"

He seemed to consider this a moment, and then leaned in over the bar, gesturing Will closer. Against his better judgment, Will leaned in too.

"The truth?" he said. "We're nothing but a nice suit of clothes, waiting for somebody to put us on."

"What the fuck?"

"Open your present," he said, and turned to push his way through the crowd. In a moment he was gone.

Will sent Carrie a quick text, and she replied that she was fine. So he continued to work, agitated and jumpy.

When Alicia finally strolled in with Jeffrey, well past eleven, Will felt a thrill of relief. They took their positions at the end of the bar and turned in to each other, deep in conversation. He poured their drinks and set them down; no exchange of words was necessary. They were functions of an algorithm.

He wouldn't try to wedge himself into their conversation. Usually he was welcomed into it, but tonight they barely gave him notice. That was all right. What he had to say to Alicia would take time and her full attention. He could wait.

Derek tapped the bar for his attention. Will grabbed a cold bottle of Miller Lite from the cooler and went to meet him.

"I heard what happened to Eric," he said, taking the beer and turning it up to his mouth, never breaking eye contact. "Why didn't you call us, man?"

"I did. You guys didn't show up for like an hour."

"I don't mean Sixth Precinct, I mean *us*." He pointed to

himself and his partner. "You have my number, right?"

Will looked at dozens of business cards and personal notes tacked to the wall behind the bar phone, interlaced and overlaid like continental plates. "I know it's up here somewhere."

Derek slid him a card with his name and number on it. "Put this in your wallet. Next time, forget the precinct. You call me."

"Okay." Will felt both empowered and chastened.

"So is he all right? Who did it?"

He thought about Eric dwelling in darkness above them, solitary as a monk, cherishing his wound like some acolyte in a cult of pain. He considered what his reaction might be if a couple of police officers—even ones he drank with and played pool with sometimes—came into his apartment at Will's direction. It wasn't something he wanted to think about for long.

"He's okay. I checked on him yesterday. He's cut, but I think it's his pride that's hurt, more than anything." *I'm lying now*, he thought. *I'm actively lying to the police.*

"What about the guy that did it?"

"I've never seen him in here before. I figure that's between them."

Derek raised his eyebrows. "Dude swings a broken bottle in your bar and you figure that's just between them?"

"You know what I mean."

"No, I really don't. You see him, use that card. I want to talk to him. See how tough this bitch really is."

"Okay, Derek."

"I'm serious."

"I know. I will." Derek started to turn away, and Will stopped him. "Hey, Derek? You ever see like, websites where people post crazy shit?"

"Isn't that the whole Internet?"

"I'm talking about violent stuff. Maybe crimes."

"I mean, that's not really my department, but sure, I guess. That's probably more of a federal thing if it's online. Why, you see something?"

"I don't know."

Derek gave him his full attention. "You want to talk about it?"

Will looked around at all the customers. "I can't right now."

"Come by the precinct tomorrow. Just tell them you want to talk to me, they'll take you back. Okay?"

"Yeah."

"You all right, man?"

"Yeah, definitely. I'll be in tomorrow."

Derek returned to the pool table, placed some quarters on the edge, and watched his partner finish his game. Will gathered a few dirty mugs from the bar and brought them to the sink. He caught a glimpse of Alicia and Jeffrey from the corner of his eye and stopped what he was doing.

Jeffrey was staring at him with an expression Will found difficult to interpret. Alicia slouched beside him in an attitude of defeat, her head lowered, her hand cupped over her eyes.

*Well, here we go*, he thought, and he walked over to them.

"Need another beer, Jeffrey?"

Jeffrey looked at his bottle, which was still half full, and tipped it over with one finger. The contents splashed over the bar top, and the bottle rolled and fell over Will's side, where it landed with a glassy crunch. "Yeah," he said. "That one's empty."

Alicia lifted her head. "Please don't."

Will leaned over until he caught Jeffrey's gaze, and held it. "Are you okay, Jeffrey?" His tone of voice made it more of a challenge than a question.

Jeffrey was not okay. In fact he was grandly drunk, his eyes bloodshot and the skin hanging loosely from his face, like wet laundry. He gave Will a big grin, about as genuine as an alligator's, and clasped his hand. "Hey, Will, I'm good, I'm really good. How the fuck are *you*, Will?" His words stumbled against one another.

Will extracted his hand. "You're wasted, man. You should go on home." He looked at Alicia. "You guys started before you got here, didn't you?"

She didn't answer, just watched him with sadness in her gaze. It unsettled him; he didn't know how to read it. She was probably wasted too.

"Bring me another beer, Will," said Jeffrey.

"I think you're about done for the night, man."

"Bring me another beer, Will."

"Don't take this approach with me, Jeffrey." He looked at Alicia. "Maybe you should get him out of here."

She nodded vaguely. She looked devastated. Obviously, she'd told him. That's what Will had wanted, of course, but somehow he'd imagined that it would be different. That she would not be so upset herself. But Alicia was kind, and she would be distraught over the pain she was causing Jeffrey. It would run its course. He tried to catch her eye to signal his own understanding, but she was too involved in getting Jeffrey to his feet to notice.

Jeffrey did not resist too much. He let himself be guided off the stool, but some residual instinct of self-respect wouldn't allow a clean retreat: As she walked him away from where they were sitting, he flicked her half-empty bottle off the bar too. It shattered on the floor.

People were starting to look.

Alicia pulled him harder. "Jeffrey!"

"Bring me another beer, Will," he said.

"You're not a tough guy, Jeffrey," said Will. "Stop acting like one."

They were almost at the door by this time, drawing looks in their wake. It was too easy. Will was struck by a perverse impulse.

"Alicia," he said. "I'll call you later."

Jeffrey turned, wrenching his arm free of Alicia's grasp, and walked back toward the bar. Rage clouded his face. Will was fascinated; what was he going to do, vault over the bar? The presence of violence was in the room again, filling it like a gas. He felt ghostlike. A witness to his own life. Something fundamental was about to tip, and he waited for it with a hunger that was curiously distinct from any sense of self-preservation. What he wanted was an irrevocable action, the crossing of a bloody border.

Derek intervened. He stepped in front of Jeffrey, stopping him in his tracks. "We got a problem here?"

The frustration on Jeffrey's face was almost heartbreaking. You could see his heroic plans evaporating right before his eyes. "I thought we were friends," he said to Will, speaking over Derek's shoulder.

"We are friends," Will said. "Come on, man."

"What's the matter with you, you fucking prick?"

Derek poked him hard in the shoulder. "Don't talk to him. Talk to me."

Derek wanted it too; you could see it radiate from him like a stuttering light.

"I don't want to talk to you," Jeffrey said. He didn't sound confrontational; he just sounded sad. All the bravado he'd felt after breaking up the fight the other night, the masculine dream he'd allowed himself to indulge in, was gone. He just stood there, ashamed and ineffectual, tears gathering in his eyes. Alicia took his arm again, shooting a dark look at Will, and led him away. This time, he didn't resist. They pushed through the door, into the world outside.

"Was he crying?" somebody said, and there was a snicker. Then, as if a switch had been flipped, people returned to their own little endeavors. The noise rose, the pool balls clicked, and people approached the bar with money in hand. The night's slow engine began to turn once again.

Derek and his partner finished their pool game and left, waving amiably on their way out the door.

Will felt cheated, somehow. That old hollowness reasserted itself, and he felt a vertiginous pull, as though he stood on its crumbling edge. The image Carrie had been looking at the night before came back to him: the wet, black tunnel, and the silent, gliding passage through it to an unfathomable end.

Something waited down there.

He pulled his phone out of his pocket, ready to dial her.

There was already a message waiting for him. A text from Carrie. Two of them. He quickly slid it open.

**I think something is in here with me.**

The next was a picture: their own apartment. Their own bedroom. The lights off. A man sitting on the edge of their bed, facing the camera. His arms rested loosely between his legs, and he was buried in shadow. His face seemed somehow misshapen. Will felt his gut clench, felt adrenaline spike in his body. He was breathing hard. His hands shook. He tapped the picture to bring it to the fore and enlarged it. Squinted at it.

The picture seemed to move. Something behind the figure fluttered, like a wing.

*We left you a little present.*

A wave of nausea passed over him, and he felt something hot crowd the back of his throat. He stepped out from behind the bar without really thinking about what he was doing. He pushed his way through the crowd. His chest was too tight, he could barely breathe. Somebody called out to him.

"Watch the bar!" he said back. He didn't care who.

In seconds he was in his car and speeding through the narrow streets, slamming through potholes and across cracked pavement bucked up over the roots of oaks, gunning through intersections. Aware of his recklessness even in the heat of his own panic, he had the stray thought that some kindly angel must be watching over him, shepherding him safely home.

The apartment was quiet, the windows dark. Carrie's car was still parked out front. He didn't know how long she'd been home. Wishing for a gun for the first time in his life, Will sprinted across the street and crept quietly to his own front door. He pressed his ear against it, trying to siphon out the sound of the occasional passing car, the sound of the leaves rustling in a light wind. He was pretty sure it was quiet inside. He tested the knob to see if the door was locked. It was.

So much for sneaking up on the intruder.

Twisting his key in the lock, he gritted his teeth at the hard thunk of the bolt sliding back. He pushed the door open while remaining outside.

The lights were out. Nobody came to answer his presence.

"Carrie?"

Still nothing.

"Is anybody in here? Come on out."

By this time anger had occluded the fear. Someone had come into his house. With Carrie here. Jason's words tolled in his mind like a funeral bell.

He stepped in quickly, flipping on the lights. Two roaches scurried across the floor to hide in a deep crevice between the wall and the floorboards. "Carrie! Are you in here?"

Passing through the kitchen, he yanked open the cutlery drawer so forcefully that it hung from its runners like something disemboweled, spilling half of its contents onto the floor in a bright clatter. He retrieved a chef's knife from the pile, clutched it hard, and kept walking.

The familiar computer screen bleed of light seeped from Carrie's study. He strode to the entrance and there she was, as he'd found her last night, staring into the screen. She seemed unhurt: no blood, no signs of distress of any kind. She was dressed for bed. Something in the room stank.

"Carrie. Jesus Christ. Why didn't you answer?"

She did not seem to register his presence.

"Carrie?"

On the screen was the same image: the camera, still moving through the dark, wet hole. This time she'd turned the sound on: a distant, hollow wind, like putting your ear to a seashell. The fear settled back over him with a fluttering silence, like birds onto a tree. He put his hand on her forehead: She was clammy and sweaty. He realized with a twist of despair that the stink was coming from her: She had pissed herself and even now sat in a puddle of it.

"Oh fuck."

Facing her, turned away from the rest of the apartment, he felt as though he were standing with his back to the mouth of a bear cave.

Turning around, he said, "Who's here, baby? Is anybody else here?"

He left her sitting there, crept into the kitchen, and turned right into the living room. Enough ambient light leaked in through the windows that, after standing there for a moment, he could be reasonably sure that it was empty. But the door to the bedroom loomed beyond it, and no light intruded there.

Will clicked on a lamp in the living room. Shadows leaped and scattered, settling immediately into a picture of order and familiarity. The couch, the TV, the framed film stills Carrie prized so much. Light wedged into the bedroom.

"If anybody's in there, you need to come out right now. I swear to God, man. This is no joke."

When no one stepped forth, Will crossed the bedroom's threshold, peering in. The bed was unmade and the sheets were rumpled, which was typical. Neither of them had ever gotten into the habit of making it. A small pile of dirty laundry coiled in one corner of the room, spilling from a full basket. A comic book lay on the floor near his side of the bed, stacked notebooks and textbooks on hers. Nothing appeared out of the ordinary.

He flicked on the light switch, then knelt down and looked under the bed.

The apartment was empty.

Will sat on the bed, the tension unspooling from him in a long, shaky exhalation. He thought of Carrie sitting there still, in a puddle of her own urine, staring at that stupid loop on her computer. He thought of her sending him these pictures. Maybe she was losing her mind. He thought he recalled her mentioning that one of her grandmothers had suffered from some kind of mental breakdown once, living out a lonely end in a mental institution. Maybe that kind of thing ran in the family. He didn't know.

A terrible, gaping sadness opened in him, and he put his thumb and forefinger to his eyes to stifle the sudden tears.

The title of the book she'd been looking for floated across

his thoughts, unbidden and unwelcome: *The Second Transla-tion of Wounds.*

His phone chimed in his pocket, startling him so badly that he jumped.

Garrett's name was on the screen.

"Hello?"

That voice seeped out again: a shard of bone pushed through a throat. A welling of blood. Was it Garrett himself? The thing that had ripped out his teeth? Or something that had crawled out of him? Will listened with tears spilling from his eyes.

Carrie could not be coaxed from her chair until he shut her computer down, eliciting from her a small sound of loss. Her eyes, bloodshot and dry, finally closed. She sagged into him, utterly exhausted, and he held her head to his shoulder, wrestling to maintain his own outward calm. Inside, it felt as though pieces of himself were sliding away, like an iceberg calving into the sea. He was hunched behind a panic wall; just beyond it, he knew, must be a correct response. Something simple and easy. But there was also a howling chaos there, a black tumble of fear, and he couldn't face that just yet. He knew, in a distant way, that he was in shock, but he didn't know how to find his way out of it.

The first order of business was to restore sanity to his own home.

He lifted Carrie from her chair, heedless of the urine, and carried her calmly to the bedroom. She did not protest; he thought she had fallen asleep, until he glanced down and saw that her eyes were open and unfocused. He laid her on the bed, next to where he'd left his cell phone. He knocked it to the floor with an angry flick of the wrist, as though it were a cockroach that had crawled into their sheets. He ran hot water into the bath, and in moments he had her undressed and submerged to her shoulders. He talked to her while he bathed her, saying nothing in particular—just maintaining what he hoped was a steady, calming flow of speech.

Once the water began to cool, he drained it and guided her out of the bathroom. She seemed to have recovered something of herself. She unhooked her robe from the door and shrugged into it, binding it tightly around her waist. Then she sat on the bed and sighed deeply, still staring at the floor. But she was present this time; she had come back.

Will sat beside her and for a time neither of them said anything. He tried to imagine what might be going through her head, but couldn't do it. His phone, its screen now cracked, blinked at him from the floor. Three missed calls. All from the bar. He didn't even want to imagine what was going on over there; he'd left the place entirely at the mercy of the customers. He took it for granted that the job was lost.

"Shouldn't you be at work?" she said, finally.

"Yeah."

"Why did you come home?"

He looked at her. She was still staring at the floor, or at nothing in particular, and he couldn't gauge the weather in her voice. She was no less mysterious for having decided to speak to him. "Do you remember anything that just happened, Carrie?"

Her brow furrowed as she tried to think. "I was looking for something online. Doing some research. Then you called me."

"I didn't call you, Carrie."

"You did. I remember because you were at work and I wondered what it could be about."

"It wasn't me."

"Well, your number came up. After that . . . I don't know. It's hard to think."

The image of the figure sitting on their bed, its head weirdly distorted, floated to the surface of his mind. "Was anybody here tonight?"

She paused before answering. "I think so." Something in her voice slipped. "I told you before. I feel like something else is here."

"Who?"

Carrie shook her head. "I don't know. I was doing research. Your call came in. I remember talking to you."

"Goddamn it, Carrie, it wasn't me!"

She rubbed her finger against her temple—lightly at first, and then with increasing ferocity. He pulled her hand away. "Am I going crazy?" she said. "Do I have a brain tumor?"

"No, it's . . . no." He thought for a moment, wondering if he should push her. He decided he had to. "What's *The Second Translation of Wounds*, Carrie? And that file sharing site? What were you researching?"

Her face blanched; she leaned over, her head between her knees, and for a moment he thought she was going to puke. But she pulled herself together and sat up again. "It's a book. I was trying to figure out what those pictures were. It was on the table in the video."

The red volume. Of course. "What kind of book is it?"

She shook her head. "I couldn't figure it all out. Something bad. It's something bad. But it's about calling angels, I think. How can that be bad?"

"What about the tunnel?"

"What tunnel?"

"When I came home . . . two nights now. You were looking at a tunnel."

"I don't know." Her voice shook. She put her hands on his face and pulled at him, turning his face into a grotesque frown. "What did we see, Will? *What did we see?*"

He didn't say anything. The panic wall stood resolute. No option made sense.

After another moment Carrie drew in a deep, shuddering breath and quickly expelled it. "Okay. Well. You have to go back to work. We can't afford you to lose that job."

"Are you serious? I can't go back there tonight."

"At least call and make sure no one looted the place."

"Yeah. Okay." He retrieved his cracked phone from the floor; when he saw that there were no new texts or images waiting for him, he felt a giddy relief and almost laughed. He dialed the bar. Doug answered; apparently, somebody'd had the good sense to get him in early.

"Will, what the fuck? Where are you?"

"I'm home. It was an emergency. I'm sorry. I had no choice. How's the bar?"

"Everything's mostly fine. Are you okay, man?"

"Yeah. I'm good. I'll be back tomorrow night, if I still have a job."

"Relax. I got you covered."

He felt such a tide of gratitude that he had to fight back tears. "Thanks, man."

"Just do what you need to do."

Will was about to hang up when Doug started talking again. "Say that again?"

"I said Eric called, asking for you. Told him you went home early. I didn't know you guys were buddies."

"We're not. What did he want?"

"He wouldn't tell me. I gave him your number though. It's probably a booty call. I don't judge, brother."

Will barked a laugh. It sounded bad. "Yeah," he said. "Okay."

Sometime in the dark morning, while Carrie slept, Will crept into her workroom and activated her computer. The image of the tunnel flickered onto the screen, frozen. After a moment the computer reconnected to the Internet, and the image started moving again—drifting through the black tunnel. He glanced up at the URL line; it was blank.

The sound of wind still drifted gently from the speakers. Will was struck with the notion that the screen did not show a descent into the depths, but the perspective of something rising from them. Something dragging itself upward.

Will leaned back in the chair. An unpleasant energy coursed through him, filling him with an urge to action, but what that action might be he didn't know. He went to the freezer and retrieved a bottle of vodka, taking a few good slugs to calm himself.

It worked, at least partly. He was able to sit down again.

He took the yellow phone from his pocket and placed it on the desk. Then he took out his own phone and dialed Alicia's number.

After a long moment she answered. "Hello?"

"Hey," he said. "It's me."

"Hey, Will. You shouldn't call."

He leaned closer to the screen, trying to pull an image from the shadows.

"I know. I'm sorry to bother you. I'm just wondering if you're okay."

"I am. Thanks. How are you?"

"Good, I think. So . . . you told him, I guess."

"Yes. I didn't mean to. Or maybe I did. I don't know."

He thought that he could detect something—some scuttling presence—but it could have been just the pixels playing tricks on him.

"It's okay. Is he there with you?"

"Yes. In the other room."

"Is that a good idea?"

"There's nothing to worry about. Everything is fine. Look . . . I can't talk to you right now. I have to go, okay?"

"Will I see you tomorrow night?"

"I don't know. I have to go. Good night, Will. Don't call back."

He thought he heard another sound riding underneath the hollow wind coming from the speakers. He felt something ripple across his nerves, like a cool breath.

"Yeah. Okay. Good night."

She had already hung up. He put his ear next to the speaker. He strained to hear.

Later that morning Will broke things off with Carrie. He waited until she was fully awake and they were sharing their usual coffee at the kitchen table. He was abrupt and passionless.

"I think we should break up," he said. "This isn't working."

She did not immediately respond. His instinct was to keep talking, to fill the long silence with all the usual platitudes and excuses, but he stayed quiet.

He told himself that he was doing this to protect her. Whatever foulness had crept into his life was threatening her, and he wanted her well clear of it. He even allowed himself the small fantasy that after it was resolved—however that might be—he would tell her about why he did it, and although they would not be able to repair the hurt he was causing her now, she would at least come to understand his reasons and to hold him in a higher regard because of them. She would view this as a noble sacrifice.

He told himself, too, that he was just beating her to the punch. That she was going to dump him soon anyway, for Steve the English professor or for somebody else more accomplished than Will was, and for once he'd like to be on the delivery side of that particular bullet.

But all of that was bullshit, and even he knew it. Though what was happening to them might have catalyzed the action, the real reason was Alicia. He wanted her. He believed, at heart, that she wanted him too.

He waited for the tears and the anger. Carrie sat across from him, her gaze unfixed, almost contemplative. She took another sip from her mug, and he suffered a bad moment in which he thought he hadn't actually said anything at all, that he was still gathering the courage to do it. He felt slippage between himself and the world, like a soundtrack desynchronized from its film.

"Okay," she said.

He nodded dumbly. That wasn't enough. That didn't tell him anything. It didn't tell him what he needed to do next. He gave her a moment to elaborate, but she chose not to take it. So finally he said, "That's it?"

"Yup. That's it."

"Fuck." He leaned back, dismayed and hurt. "Well, fine then. 'Okay.' What a nice capstone."

She looked confused. "Why are you acting offended? You're the one who's breaking up with me."

"Yeah, but do you even care?"

"Not right now I don't. That'll come later. But you don't get to see that."

"I just can't believe how calmly you're taking this." He heard his own voice tremble, start to rise.

"It's been coming for a while. I know you want Alicia. It's too bad she doesn't want you."

"That's not it." He immediately regretted the lie, knowing it would be revealed as such within a matter of days.

"Then what is it? Are you threatened by Steve? Still think he wants to fuck me?"

"No. Come on. Will you stop with that shit?"

"Your words."

"I was being stupid."

"You're still being stupid, Will."

"Well, fuck you." He stared into his coffee, unable to meet her gaze. He felt the heat in his face, knew he was flushed. He tried to settle his breathing. "I'm sorry," he said. "I'm sorry. Will you just let me talk?"

She sat unmoved, watching him with an unearthly calm. "I didn't know I was stopping you. Please. Go ahead."

"It's not Alicia, okay? I wish you would stop with that, because it's bullshit, and it's always been bullshit. It's . . . it's this stuff with the pictures. The phone. It's dangerous. I don't want you around it."

Finally he got a reaction. Her face pinched in anger. "Really? You think you're protecting me? You're an action hero now?"

"What? No! Come on, Carrie."

"Can you hear yourself? I'm already 'around it.' I've been researching it, studying it. You've just been wandering around clutching that stupid phone like it belongs to you. This is all happening to *me*. You're just a goddamn spectator!"

"That's not fair."

"You're scared. You're a scared little boy. I'm scared too,

Will. But I would never have abandoned you to it."

He wanted to cry. This was going as wrongly as it could go. "No, that's not what I mean. Carrie . . ."

"No, fuck you. I wasn't angry until just now. I was disappointed. I was hurt. But I almost respected you for a minute there, Will. I almost thought you were doing the right thing. But now I'm pissed. So if that's what you wanted, congratulations. You got it."

"It's not what I wanted."

"You don't have any idea what you want. You know what I think you want? Nothing. I think there's nothing there to satisfy. I think you're a mock person, you're some kind of walking shell." She took a breath and brought her wrist to the corner of her eye to stanch a tear. "I guess you can find a place to crash until you get a new apartment, right?"

For some reason this hurt worse than anything else she'd said. "Really? Today?"

"What did you expect? That we'd cuddle? Besides, I might be *in danger*, right?"

"Fine." He got up. A terrible weight suspended between his lungs, threatening to upend him. He felt the heat of shame and grief gather in his face. It wasn't supposed to go like this. He made his way to the bedroom and excavated a crumpled duffel bag from the recesses of the closet. He began to shove clothes into it, heedless of what he might actually need. Just random things. When he walked to the bathroom to get his toothbrush and his razor, he heard a stifled sob in the kitchen.

This was the world he'd built. This was his kingdom.

It didn't appear as though anyone had been to Eric's door in the two days since Will had last stopped by. A fly-dappled recycling bin, topped off with beer bottles, had been shoved outside but not carried to the curb, suggesting that at least some effort had been expended in cleaning up inside. Will knocked on the door and waited. When no answer came, he tested the door, and it opened readily for him.

The place stank of sweat and rotting food. Flies buzzed angrily somewhere inside, and a few cockroaches ambled away, incurious and unafraid. Sunlight hacked into the dark interior, and heat spilled out in a thick collapse. The AC that had frozen him the last time he was here had apparently died.

So much for anybody cleaning up. "Christ," he whispered. Then: "Eric? Are you in here?"

He walked down the hallway into the kitchen, which bore evidence of continued neglect. Dishes were strewn around the counter space and piled in the sink, where an odor exuded from a stack of plates like an evil intelligence. Crumbs and stray bits of cereal crunched underfoot. Another handful of roaches perched like lookouts from their pot handles and their glass rims, their antennae waving in bored appraisal of this new element.

Eric's voice traveled from somewhere deeper in his apartment. It sounded like he was speaking around a mouthful of food.

The living room looked much as it had before, just a little more so: Clothes were draped across the back of the stained couch, socks gathered in little colonies in the corners and on the chair. A PlayStation sat in the middle of the floor, long cords extending in black umbilicals to the television and to the controller resting beside the couch.

There was a different kind of smell in here, something sweeter and fouler. It emanated from the darkened corner toward the back, which led to the bedroom. Will didn't want to go any farther; he knew what it was.

But the voice came again, floating out of the bedroom on a current of decay. "Will."

Will stepped into the bedroom. Eric had the blinds drawn, but sunlight leaked in through the slats, giving the room an odd, underwater feeling. Like the rest of the apartment, it was a mess. Eric was lying on the bed in his boxer shorts, the sheets kicked to the floor. He was sheened in sweat. He turned his head to watch Will enter, revealing the hideous wound distorting the left side of his face. It had gotten worse. Crusted with black blood, it had swollen and dried, reopened, dried again. Flies droned around his face, strutted boldly across his skin like little conquistadors. The stink of infection stopped Will at the door.

Eric tried to speak; the wound made it difficult for his mouth to move the way it was meant to. "What do you want?"

"I need a place to crash."

Eric apparently had nothing to say to this. Will couldn't really blame him.

"I need to stay on your couch," he said. "Just for a day or two. Just until Alicia's ready."

"No."

"I'm in a bad spot, Eric."

"No!" This effort caused him some pain, and he turned his face into the pillow.

Will shook his head. "It's going to be good. I'll even help you clean up a little bit. You'll see." He went back into the living room, ignoring the sounds Eric made. He made a space for himself on the same chair he'd sat in before, while shepherding Eric through his nightmares. He dialed Alicia's number on his phone.

It rang four times before she answered it. "I told you not to call back."

"That was last night! Are you okay? What are you doing?"

"Will—I am trying to fix my life, okay? I need you to stop calling me. It's not helping."

"I left Carrie. I broke up with her this morning."

There was a long pause on the other side. Alicia said, "I'm sorry. I'm sorry to hear that, Will."

"But—that's a good thing. Right?"

"I don't know. That's up to you, I guess."

"But—what? Alicia . . ."

"Will, I'm with Jeffrey. I love Jeffrey. Do you understand that?"

He shook his head, unable to accept what he was hearing. Unable to accept the magnitude of his mistake. "No, I don't understand it."

"I don't know when we're coming back to the bar. Maybe not for a while, okay? Don't call back. If you really care about me, don't call back."

With that, she hung up.

Will sat back on the couch, waiting for the right feelings to happen. The heartbreak, the anger, the tears. But he didn't feel any of them. What he felt instead was a terrible yearning. He didn't even know what for. But he felt it like a physical ache, like something on fire. He looked at the dark hole of Eric's bedroom, trying to will him into the doorway. They could address their pain with alcohol. Together—as friends. He just needed somebody.

And then, as though he had conjured him with a magic spell, Eric appeared there, leaning against the doorjamb, his flesh gray and loose. "You can't be here," he said. A fresh rivulet of blood had made a path along his jawline, and even now pushed lethargically down his neck.

A thought suddenly occurred to Will. "Eric, did you call the bar last night, looking for me?"

Eric's face clouded over. "No," he said, and turned to go back into his bedroom.

Will leaped from the couch and pinned him to the door frame, putting his face close. The stench of infection shoved its way into his nose, but he ignored it. "It came from here. Who called the bar?"

He was astonished by how weak Eric had become. Just a few days ago he would never have been able to hold him; Eric would have broken his teeth for even trying. But now it was like holding a listless child. "They did. Those freaks."

"What freaks?"

Eric turned his face, exposing the wound. It was spectacular. Will leaned in closer, a grisly curiosity overwhelming his aversion to the smell. It seemed outrageous, something too Hollywood to be real. The edges were swollen and damp with lymph, and they seemed rubbery, like the borders of a mask that could be yanked off. He peered more closely, wondering if he'd be able to see the teeth, the long ridge of the jawbone. As Eric tried to speak, Will could detect the movement of the tongue somewhere in the depths of the injury, like a grub rooting through offal.

"What freaks, Eric? Were they the kids from the bar that night?" Knowing already.

"They said they wanted to give you a present. Now get the fuck off me. I'll kill you. I will kill you." The sustained speech was agony, and Eric's knees buckled. Will caught him underneath his arms and half dragged him back to his bed, where he collapsed limply, curling up into the fetal position. He lay there, sobbing like a child, while Will stood over him.

It took him a few minutes before he understood what the present they'd left him was. When he understood, he had to lean his hand against the wall while a tide of vertigo swept through him. The wounds. The fingers extruding from the skull.

*It's about calling angels,* Carrie had said. *How can that be bad?*

They just needed a place to be born. That's all it ever was.

He knelt beside the bed, placing his hand gingerly on Eric's shoulder. "Can you feel it inside you?" he asked. "Moving around?"

A change came over Eric's face: It went still and pale, as though something essential to the function of life had been wrested from him, or had simply run down. He blinked, said nothing.

"You can, can't you." Will brushed the hair back from Eric's forehead. An intimate gesture. A kindness. Eric tried to pull away, but there was nowhere to go. "Is it going to come out through your face? Or do I have to make a hole for it?"

"Go away."

"People think you're such a nice guy," Will said, petting Eric's hair softly. "They don't see you the way I do. They don't see the way your eyes go flat when you're drunk. You're ugly in your heart. *I* can see it." He stared at him there, wasting away in his own bed, crawling with flies and marinating in his own stink. He'd always been ugly inside, and now, finally, anybody could see it. He wanted to drag him through the street, or down to the bar, and hang him from a hook on the wall. He wanted to make it plain to everybody. "It's okay. I'm ugly too."

*Is Heaven a dark place?*

"Do you have to be dead first? Or will it break you open while you're still alive?"

*Will I belong?*

Eric sobbed. Tears spilled from the corners of his eyes and

ran into his hair, his ears. He reached out and clutched Will's hand. He brought it close to his face, almost kissing it. "Please kill me," he said. "Please. I don't want it to come. I don't want to be alive when it happens. I'm scared."

"I wonder what would happen if I called it."

Eric's whimpering stalled. He fixed Will with a look of naked terror.

Will went into the kitchen and did a little search for a bottle of something, anything to smooth the edges of the experience. He found a third of a bottle of some basement-brand rum in one of the cabinets and walked calmly back into the bedroom, where he sat on the bed by Eric's side and dialed up Garrett's number on the yellow phone.

When the grotesque language began to spill into his ear, he put the phone on speaker and set it on the mattress. Eric mewled like an animal, curling into himself. Will felt the old, empty ache bestir itself again, and he welcomed it as one would welcome an old friend. They listened, and he drank, for some time. The heat crowded the air out of the room. At some point, when the light sliding through the blinds had taken on a golden color, he ran out of what was in the bottle. It fell to the floor, where it rolled under the bed. Shortly afterward Eric began to give birth.

Will set the phone to record.

Eric's body went rigid. A keening sound slipped through his teeth. Will leaned in close, watching the rupture in his face. It was a blood-rimmed crater into dark precincts. Eric's thin wail interlaced with the cracked slurry of words leaking from the phone, combining to produce a beautiful threnody, a glittering lament that landed in him like hooks.

Thick bone cracked, and blood spat from Eric's face, splashing in a sudden heavy river over his cheek.

Something struggled into the light.

Will felt the presence of it before he could see it. He felt an answer to the long ache. He leaned over Eric's shuddering body, brought his face close. He opened his mouth over the wound, touched his lips to its ragged edges. *Fix me,* he thought. *Please. Make me whole.* He closed his eyes, felt the billowing heat of it. Something moved against his tongue and he sobbed with a terrified gratitude as it probed the roof of his mouth, his teeth, and his cheeks. Filling his mouth. He opened wider and gulped it all in, blood leaking from the seal of his lips. Eric began to shriek, repeatedly and in escalating volume, and a host of startled cockroaches scrambled from their lairs, climbing up the walls and rising into the air with their dark, humming wings, a swarm of Christ-bound spirits.

# The Butcher's Table

## 1. Devils by Firelight

The Englishman stood on the beach, just beyond the reach of the surf, and stared out over the flat, dark plain of the Caribbean. A briny stink filled his nostrils. Palm trees heaved in the night wind. Overhead, a heavy layer of stars, like a crust of salt on Heaven's hull. At his back, the small port town of Cordova gabbled excitedly to itself: fiddles and croaking voices raised in raucous song, like a chorus of crows; the calling and the crying of women and men; laughter and screams and the rumble of traded stories. It sounded like life, he supposed. No wonder it made him sick.

Martin Dunwood was very far from home.

Approaching from behind came a heavy expenditure of breath, feet shuffling in sand; he turned to see a shape lurching from town: a small man, fat and stumbling, a rag-wrapped something clutched in his left hand. The smell of rum blew from him like a wind.

"Mr. Dunwood," said Fat Gully. "What're you doing. . . ." His words trailed off as he caught his breath.

"I'm taking some air," said Martin. "Please go away."

"No you don't," Gully said, his words sliding together and colliding. "No you fucking don't."

Martin controlled his voice. "No I don't *what.*"

Fat Gully meant to muscle up to him with his broad chest, but he miscalculated his footing and toppled back onto his posterior, air exploding from his lungs like a cannonball. His dignity, however, remained undamaged. He gestured with whatever item he held in his left hand, which Martin noticed was caked in dark blood. "No you don't take on no highborn airs with me, you fancy bastard. I'll peel you standing, fat purse or fucking not."

Martin wore his rapier, but he had seen Gully and his wicked little knife in action as recently as this afternoon, when they had been surrounded by four shipless sailors, attracted by Martin's moneyed appearance and anxious to settle the question of his worth. Fat Gully had acted suddenly, with a grace utterly at odds to his toadlike aspect; before a breath could be drawn, two of the men were attempting to keep their innards from sliding through their fingers and onto the filthy street. Martin was not eager to test him, even in his drunken state. Instead he turned his gaze to the gory rag in Gully's hand, leaking a thin black drizzle onto the sand. "What in God's name do you have there?"

Gully smiled and climbed slowly to his feet. The lights of the town cast him in shadow as he extended his arm and opened his hand. He looked like an emissary from an infernal province, bearing a gift.

Martin inclined his head forward to see, raising an eyebrow. It took him a moment to make sense of it: a tongue, freshly pulled from its root, saliva still glistening in the moonlight.

"The Society told me what you're here for," Gully said, a dull smile moving across his face. "I brought a snack for your new friends."

"I don't know what you mean by showing that to me, but I assure you I have no use for it. Nor do the people I'm going to meet. Get rid of it."

"You'll learn not to bark orders at me, Mr. Dunwood," Gully said, tossing his dreadful trophy onto the sand. A dull anger set in his face. If Martin hadn't known better, he might have thought his feelings were hurt. "Oh yes you will. You'll change your tune when we get there, I'll wager."

He'd met Rufus Gully at the London docks. Gully, no stranger to the cutthroat world of the Spanish Main, had been hired by the Candlelight Society to function as a bodyguard, seeing him across the Atlantic to Tortuga, where they now stood. From here they were to secure passage aboard a pirate vessel to the middle of the Gulf of Mexico, where they would rendezvous with a second ship, and the purpose of his journey. They had crossed the Atlantic in nearly complete isolation from each other; Martin had been provided a room near the captain's quarters—not the fine appointment to which he was accustomed, but the needs of the moment demanded certain concessions—and Gully among the rats and the scum before the mast. It seemed he had emerged with fresh ideas.

"We have to get there first," Martin said. "This Captain Toussaint is a day late, and I'm beginning to doubt that he'll show up at all. He's either been sunk, or he's a coward."

Gully smiled, his teeth a row of crooked headstones. "Never you fear, Mr. Dunwood. I've come with good tidings."

For the first time in many days, Martin felt something inside himself lighten. "*Butcher's Table* has arrived then, Mr. Gully?"

"It has indeed." Gully turned about and made his tentative way back into brawling Cordova, with Martin in tow. A pistol cracked in some ill-lit alley and a cry of pain rose above the cacophony of voices like a flushed bird. Gully lurched into the heated maw of that place, his purpose steady. "Come and meet our benefactors, Mr. Dunwood. We ship with the tide."

Gully slid into the city like an eel into a reef, steering his round body through the nooks and crannies of the crowd with a nimbleness that Martin both hated and admired. It was just another reminder that he could not allow himself to underestimate this squat little man. He was ungainly but quick, unintelligent but cunning. A sharp, murderous little villain.

Cordova was a ghastly place, alive with pitched debauchery. It was a constant maelstrom of noise and stench: roaring and howling, gunpowder and piss. Taverns spilled garish light. Women were passed around like drinking mugs from one lecherous grotesque to another, some cackling with abandon, some with the affectless expressions of dolls or corpses. He found himself surrounded by more black faces than he'd ever seen in one place, a fact that made him decidedly nervous. He understood that most were free men, though he found that hard to credit. A free black man was as alien to Martin's experience as a crocodile or a camel, and he stared like an idiot as Gully hustled him along.

A dim glow marked the docks: fires and lanterns alight on the shore, ship windows radiant as business of one sort or another was conducted within. The masts were like pikes struck into the earth; arrayed alongside this lurching little town, they gave an odd appearance of order. Gully crossed a muddy street, shouldering aside a man nearly double his size, and made his way to a two-story wooden structure across from the docks. It was an inn, and a busy one at that. A sign hanging above the door identified it as THE RED MAST.

"Mind your manners now," Gully said. He pushed his way into the building, and Martin followed.

The interior was close and hot. Several small round tables collaborated to make up a dining area. An arched doorway led into a kitchen, where dim forms toiled. A fire grumbled to itself in a vast, grimy hearth. The flue was insufficient to its task, and greasy smoke trickled up the wall and gathered on the ceiling like a dark omen.

Gully approached a table of three men, their backs against the far wall. His demeanor was much reduced, and when he spoke, it was with none of his usual bluster.

"I brung him, Captain Toussaint, like what I said."

Martin knew the men immediately for what they were: pirates. They were not likely to be anything else, here in Tortuga, but the shabbiness of their bearing would have made it plain besides. The man on the right was older, his gray beard hacked short and his face a jigsaw puzzle of scars. One eye sat dully in its socket like a boiled quail's egg, pale and yellow. The man to the left—a Chinaman, Martin thought—was slender and quite young, his gaze unfixed, his attention flitting through the crowd. Sitting between them was the man who could only be Captain Toussaint: a black man, broad-shouldered and broad-featured, his skin as dark as any Martin had ever seen. His beard was a shaggy bramble, and his hair grew in a dark shock around his head; Martin imagined the fear this imposing figure would strike into the hearts of his fellow Englishmen as he came leaping onto their decks, clutching a knife in his teeth and raging with all his barbaric energy.

They wore shabby, loose-fitting clothing, and they were

armed with steel. The Chinaman held a blunderbuss between his knees, and he tapped his fingers against it, as though eager to bring it to bear.

"Oh my, look at the pretty thing," the captain said, and the older man produced a chuckle, a sound that seemed unpracticed and awkward from him.

Martin stood straight, determined to suffer whatever insults to his person they might deliver. He knew he'd be traveling with base men, and he was prepared to acclimate himself to their lifestyle. "Captain Toussaint of the *Butcher's Table*, I presume."

"The very one. And you must be Mr. Dudley Benson of the Candlelight Society."

"I'm afraid Mr. Benson took ill and was unable to make the trip. He sent me in his place. My name is Martin Dunwood, also of the Society."

Captain Toussaint's eyes flicked between Martin and Mr. Gully. "Ill? How unfortunate. I hope the old fellow will recover. He seemed a lovely chap in our correspondence. You have a signed letter from him, vouching for your identity, no doubt?"

"I do not. I did not think it would be necessary."

"You were in error. It seems our business is concluded. How disappointing."

Martin's stomach dropped. All his plans, undone by such a stupid oversight! He struggled to maintain his composure. "Captain, don't make a mistake. You cannot proceed without my participation. Only a member of the Society can contact the Order of the Black Iron, and only a monk from that order can provide the map you need."

Toussaint seemed to consider this. After a moment he said, "There's the small matter of payment to be addressed.

You'll be eating from our stores, after all. Only fair that you should contribute. Surely, Mr. Benson will have told you, despite his unfortunate illness."

"Of course," Martin said. He had no doubt this wretch was exercising a crude revenge for being caught off guard. However, he was in no position to object. "I'm quite willing to contribute coin to the endeavor."

"Then produce it, Mr. Dunwood. Produce it, please."

Martin withdrew his purse and placed it onto the table, taking care to keep his hand steady, fearing one of these bastards might cleave the fingers from his hand for the simple joy of it.

The older man with the bad eye spilled the coins onto the table, where they thudded dully in the dim light, and counted them. All the while the younger man kept his eyes roving about the room. The blunderbuss, of course, was not for show. Meanwhile the captain's gaze had not wavered from Martin. When the sum of money was announced, he waved a hand idly, as though such concerns were beneath him.

"It seems I am forced to take you at your word, Mr. Dunwood, at least for the moment. The Society has a fine reputation, for a pack of diabolists, and right now that is all you have to support you. Be thankful it is enough. See that you do your job well, and we shall part as friends. Otherwise I will bury you at sea. Are we in agreement?"

Martin swallowed his pride. To be spoken to like that by this man—a thug who should be lapping water from a puddle in Newgate Prison—caused him a pain that was nearly physical in its intensity. But Alice awaited him further along this journey, and he could not afford the comforts of his own station. Not now. He would remember this wretch, however, and he would see him suffer for this display. That much he vowed.

"Yes, Captain. We are in agreement."

Captain Toussaint clasped Martin's hand and gave it a vigorous throttling. "You make me glad. Now Mr. Johns will show you to your berth"—he indicated the one-eyed man—"where you and Mr. Gully can nibble crumpets and giggle like ladies while I conclude the ship's business in town. Will that be fine?"

Mr. Johns permitted himself a chuckle.

Martin pulled in a long breath and nodded his acquiescence. "That will be fine, Captain."

"Mr. Johns, make sure *Butcher's Table* is prepared to depart the moment we return. We won't want to linger." The captain rose and quietly departed, the young Chinaman in tow. Mr. Johns, however, made no move to rise from his chair. He reached a grubby finger into the coin purse and liberated a few shillings. "Sit your arses down," he said. "I mean to be well and truly drunk before I take you devil worshippers aboard."

Martin and Gully had no choice but to comply.

Captain Beverly Toussaint and his first mate, Hu Chaoxiang, pressed their way through Cordova's crowded lanes as a cool wind blew in from the bay, carrying the sharp tang of lightning, the promise of rain and thunder. They made their way to a ramshackle warehouse, which stood a little too far from the docks to be considered of much use to anyone.

The warehouse was owned by a man called Thomas Thickett—known locally as Thomas the Bloody, due to his penchant for sudden, furious nosebleeds. A refugee from the Buried Church in the Massachusetts Colony, he'd won the building in a card game when he arrived in Tortuga several years ago. The man he'd won it from laughed as he signed over the deed, wishing him good fortune in housing cobwebs and rats. But Thickett, born in a cage and destined his whole life for the dinner plates of wealthy men, was accustomed to turning shit into gold. And there was no better place for that than a city of pirates. He capitalized on his particular knowledge of the Buried Church and its cannibal cult, making himself valuable to the men who did commerce with them. He stored their unmarked cargo for extended periods, and he provided specialized sails and timber to the quartermasters who came to him when they had to refit their vessels for unique purposes. As long as he did these things well, he was assured a livelihood in Cordova.

Captain Toussaint in particular had found him useful. He disliked dealing with the Buried Church; like the Candlelight Society, it was a pack of Satanists. But while Society members tended to be toothless storytellers in gentlemen's clubs, congregants of the Church commanded genuine institutional power—to say nothing of their cannibalistic appetites, kept sated through their hidden farms of human cattle. As a fugitive from one of these farms, Thickett proved an invaluable source of information. So Toussaint paid him handsomely and fostered a camaraderie with the man over shared drinks and wild dreams of the future.

Tonight it was going to pay off.

The warehouse was dark. The windows were shuttered, the door closed. The door was unlocked, and they pushed their way inside. The place was densely packed with mildewed crates, rolled canvas, bags of grain. A single lantern, balanced on a wooden barrel full of God knew what, cast a shallow nimbus of orange light, throwing strange, wide-shouldered shadows against the wall. Beside it was Mr. Thickett's closed office door.

In the quiet, Captain Toussaint could already hear the

hoarse whispers, a dozen or more voices attempting speech in the strange tongue of a different world. The voices crawled over the walls like cockroaches. He felt a thrill of excitement.

A small door opened to their right, and Thomas Thickett emerged from his office, where he had been waiting in absolute darkness. He looked frail and sickly, older than his thirty-seven years—that's what hiding from the Cannibal Priest would do to you, Toussaint assumed—but tonight there was a flush of vigor in his cheeks.

"Thomas the Bloody," said the captain. "Bless my bones."

Thomas nodded deferentially. "Captain. It's fine to see you again. Yes. I have the cargo right here, sir."

Captain Toussaint and Mr. Hu exchanged a glance. "Right to business then, is it? All right, Thomas, all right. Show it to me."

Taking the lantern in hand, Thomas Thickett guided the two men through the maze of crates to the other side of the warehouse. There was a large door here that would swing open to admit carriages drawn by mules or oxen, but it was secured fast, shutting out the din of the town. The whispering voices were louder here; Captain Toussaint felt steeped in ghosts. An old memory crowded his thoughts, and he forced it back.

The voices emitted from a crate about waist-high, sitting in the middle of the aisle. It was segregated from the rest, like a diminished little temple.

"I've secured a carriage. It'll be waiting outside," Thickett said. "At my own expense, of course."

"Of course, Thomas. Always reliable." Captain Toussaint nodded at the crate. "Open it."

". . . Captain?"

"I want to be sure."

Thomas glanced at Mr. Hu, as if seeking a better opinion.

Finding none, he fetched a crowbar from a shelf and set to, his body sheened in an icy sweat. Nails squealed against wood. After considerable effort, the top of the crate popped off. Thomas peered inside, and the pirates came up on either side of him. Together they leaned over, studying the contents like learned judges of the damned.

Inside was what looked like a huge anemone, its wide base crumpled and folded against the confines of the crate, resting in a thin gruel of blood and gristle. Its body tapered into a stalk, which culminated in a flowering nest of glistening tongues moving like a clutch of worms. Little channels of teeth and ridges of gum wended through the cluster, as though a single mouth had been turned inside out like the rind of a mango, yielding this writhing bounty. From this mass came a chorus of whispers in a language unknown to them.

Captain Toussaint clapped Thickett on the shoulder. "Seal it, Thomas." His demeanor was much reduced.

Thomas complied, nailing the lid back into place with trembling hands. The voices were muffled beneath the wood, though not sufficiently to suit any man present.

A lotushead. Captain Toussaint had experienced one once before, five years ago, when he was first mate to Captain Tegel aboard the ship he now commanded. They'd put it to good use: It enabled Toussaint to buy the ship, and it made Tegel a king. Or something very much like a king.

"I'll help you haul it out to the carriage," Thomas said, his voice elevated over the sound of his hammering. "I trust the next time I see you both, you'll be rich men!" He laughed nervously. "And perhaps you'll make me a rich man too."

Captain Toussaint put away thoughts of Tegel with relief. "The next time? My dear Thomas, you won't have to wait so long. You're coming with us."

Thomas paused, one long nail poised between his fingers. A dark coin of blood dropped from Thomas's nose onto the crate's lid.

He knew what that meant. Captain Toussaint wrestled down a sudden surge of self-loathing.

"Captain," Thomas said. He blinked tears from his eyes. He remained facing forward. "I arranged this whole thing. I procured the lotushead. I told you about the hidden cove. This whole venture is thanks to *me*. I'm sorry to be blunt about it, but it's true. Now, let's just load this into the carriage and you men be on your way. We had a deal. Let's just keep to it, shall we."

"Working with the Cannibal Priest comes with certain costs. You know that better than anyone, Thomas. This time, that cost was you."

More blood spattered onto the crate, and Thomas pressed a handkerchief to his face. The horror of the underground pens came rushing back to him: the thick stench of blood and fear, the close press of flesh, the chanting of monks. The sound of cleavers in meat.

"Who told them? How did they find me?"

"I did," said the captain. "I needed someone from the Candlelight Society. They were the ones who put me in contact. As long as I promised to deliver you to them."

Thickett turned to run. Perhaps he thought he could catch them off guard and make the exit before they had time to react. Perhaps he hoped they would kill him outright, and he would be spared his fate.

But Mr. Hu had anticipated this, and he swung the stock of his blunderbuss into Thomas's temple, dropping him to the floor. Thomas moaned and made a feeble attempt to crawl away. Mr. Hu trussed him while Captain Toussaint looked on.

"I'm genuinely sorry, old friend. If it's any comfort, I'm told they have grand plans for you."

Once Thickett was immobilized, Captain Toussaint slapped the crate. "Let's get it all on board, and smartly. I want to be gone before the jackals arrive."

Outside it had finally started to rain.

Alone in the second mate's quarters, which had been surrendered to him without a twitch of protest by the one-eyed Mr. Johns at his captain's order, Martin Dunwood lay in the cot suspended crossways across the tiny room and tried to acclimate himself to the deep pitch and tumble of *Butcher's Table* as it pushed its way across the cresting waves, bound for the open sea. Somewhere above him rain drummed over the ship. The lantern light stuttered as the ship plummeted down a steep trough. Martin snuffed it out before it could spill and light the room on fire. The sudden darkness was oppressive, as though someone had thrown a weight over him. The sounds of the water smashing into the hull mingled with the raw voices outside shouting to be heard over the storm, as the crew worked the lines and the sails with the precision—or lack of it—one might expect from a congress of pirates. Below, the carpenters worked on constructing a new set of rooms for Martin and their future guests. It seemed as though the whole ship's complement had suddenly crowded into his cabin and began knocking things about. Martin did not care to speculate on their abilities; he felt sick enough already. Instead he entrusted his fate to Satan's judgment and focused his attentions on better things.

*Alice.*

The promise of Alice pulled him across the sea, from the polluted stink of London to Tortuga and now to this criminal's vessel; he would have let it pull him across the whole of the world, if necessary, but he was struck again by the continually surprising thought that he would see her again in a matter of days, at which point a year's careful planning might at last come to fruition.

He remembered the first time he ever laid eyes on her: She had been standing on a corner outside a grocer's shop. Her fine clothes and her red hair were disheveled and there was a placid beauty in her expression, her face as pale as a daylight moon. Blood matted the expensive materials of her dress, caked heavily near the lower hem and arrayed in a pattern of sprays and constellations farther up her body, as though she had just waded through some dreadful carnage.

Martin, a newly minted agent of the Candlelight Society and a virgin to London itself, stood transfixed. He didn't know what catastrophe had befallen her, but it seemed she needed immediate help. He waited for a carriage to pass before he stepped out into the muddy thoroughfare, but immediately came up short—an older gentleman stepped out of the grocer and joined her at the corner. He too was well dressed, though his clothes were free of blood. He threw an overcoat around her shoulders and hailed a carriage. Within moments he bundled her into it, and with a flick of the driver's wrist she was whisked away, leaving behind an ordinary corner on an ordinary street. The drabness of the image seemed to reject the possibility that she had ever been there at all.

It was not until years later that he saw her again. By that time he had solidified his position in the Candlelight Society through a series of successful missions and had graduated to a more elevated social stratum. His success precipitated his invitation to a party thrown by a fellow Satanist, one who occupied a seat in the House of Lords. As Martin lurked unhappily in a corner of the glittering room—he was acutely conscious of his humble origins, sure that they were as plain as a facial disfigurement—he saw her again.

She was standing amidst a crowd of men, young and eager for her attention. She smiled at one of them as he gestured to illustrate some point, and Martin knew at once that none of the fools had a chance with her, that she was only wearing them like jewelry. He pressed his way through the crowd until he joined her little retinue.

If she noticed him as he approached she did not show it. He stationed himself in her outer orbit and just watched her. Although she was properly demure and maintained the comportment of a young lady of her station, something set her apart from everyone around her. She seemed carved from stone.

Martin could immediately tell that these men were normal, God-fearing Londoners, unaware of their host's secret affiliations. He was afforded a new confidence. At the first break in the conversation, he said, "Didn't I see you once outside a small grocer's in the East End? It would have been a long time ago."

Her pale blue eyes settled on him. "The East End? I rather doubt it."

"You would remember this," he said. "You were covered in blood at the time."

She betrayed no reaction, but even in that she revealed herself. No shock, no disgust, no laughing dismay. Just a cool appraisal, and silence.

One of the young men turned on him, his blond hair pulled back harshly from his forehead and tied into a bow. "I say, are you mad?"

"Not remotely," said Martin.

"It's all right, Francis," she said. "He's right. I do remember that day. It was quite dreadful. A horse had come up lame and had to be shot. It was done right in front of me and I think it's the worst thing I ever saw."

"Odd. I don't remember a dead horse," Martin said.

"Perhaps you weren't paying attention," she said. "So much occurs right under our noses."

Within minutes she had dismissed her pretty men and Martin found himself sitting some distance from the party, talking to this remarkable woman who seemed to fit amongst these people the same way a shark fits amongst a school of mackerel.

"Why did you say that to me?" she said. "What did you think would happen?"

"I had no idea. I wanted to find out."

"Hardly the environment for social experiments, wouldn't you say?"

"On the contrary. I would say it's the ideal environment."

She offered a half smile. "What's your name?"

"I'm Martin Dunwood. My father owns the—"

"Are you an anarchist, Martin Dunwood?"

He smiled at her, his first genuine smile of the night. "In a manner of speaking."

In minutes they were in the banker's bedroom, fucking with a furious, urgent silence. Thereafter they met often, and always clandestinely. She was even more contemptuous of the world than he, prone to stormy rages, and he found those rages intoxicating. They were wild and different and echoed his own sense of alienation from the world. Their illicit sex was as much an act of defiance as it was a hunger for each other. After a month of this she introduced him to the Buried Church, and he saw what she did there.

It was when he watched the blood drip from the ends of her long red hair that he knew he was in love with her, and that he would break the world to keep her.

Hours after *Butcher's Table* had left, the carrion angels arrived in Cordova. There were four of them. They emerged from a lantern-smoked alleyway, building themselves out of shadows and burnt rags. Seven feet tall, their thin bodies wrapped in fluttering black cloth, they listed back and forth as they walked, their bones creaking like the rigging of ships. Their faces jutted forward in hooked, tooth-spangled beaks, their eyes burned like red cinders, trailing smoke through the rain.

They stalked the avenues of the town with deliberation, keeping to the shadows, sending those who witnessed them shrieking and scattering like frightened gulls; some stopped and fired a few wild shots before running. The carrion angels were oblivious, their bodies accepting the violence the way a corpse accepts the worm. They swung their great heads at each juncture of road and alley, lifting their snouts and huffing deep breaths as they tracked the scent of their quarry.

They followed it to a darkened warehouse. The scent of the lotushead was strong here, but a quick inspection revealed that it had gone. Thwarted, they creaked slowly out of the warehouse, emerging from the interior like dim lamps.

The trail wended down toward the docks. The town had erupted in panic. Word of the carrion angels' presence spread fast. Narrow lanes were choked with men fleeing for their ships. Pirates and sailors careened drunkenly, lurching, stumbling, and trampling the fallen. Throughout the town, panicked men shot and stabbed at shadows, and the road to the sea was marked by the bodies of the dead and the dying. The angels came upon a fallen man lying across their path, the back of his head a smoking hole and his brains festooned across the packed earth. The stink of it made them drunk and they permitted themselves a brief respite, hunched around this glorious fountain of scent, this unexpected confection. They ate with a grateful reverence, the sound of wet meat and cracking bone rising in syncopation with the driving rain.

Most of the townsfolk stayed inside, shuttering the windows and locking the doors. Some followed the pirates to the docks, forgetting in their fear the true nature of these men, and remembering only when they were beaten back or shot as they tried to climb the gangplanks to safety.

The ships were alight with lanterns, riggings acrawl with sailors making ready for the sea. Boats were dropped from the side, towing the vessels away from port. Gun smoke hazed the air. The bloom of violence was a grace upon the town. The carrion angels walked in their slow, swaying gait through it all, like four tall priests proceeding safely through Hell, confident in their faith.

The scent ended at the docks. The lotushead had been taken to sea.

It was a small thing to sneak passage aboard a ship. The carrion angels dissolved into rags and dust, blowing like so much garbage in the wind, carrying over the water and into the rat-thronged hold of one of the several pirate ships, called *Retribution*. They settled amidst the refuse there, lying as still as the dead.

The captain of this ship was a hard old man named Bonny Mungo. He'd seen creatures like this once, several years ago, in a half-sunken stone church he'd stumbled across in a Florida swamp. There had only been two; they'd killed most of the men he'd been with and wore another like clothing, too small to properly fit. Catching a glimpse of them now, he was moved by an extravagant fear. Once *Retribution* achieved some distance from land, he ordered it to turn about, offering its broadside to the town. At his command the ship fired its full complement of guns in a devastating volley, sending cannonballs smashing through weak wooden walls and bringing whole buildings to the ground. Another ship took inspiration from this and fired as well.

Within minutes Cordova and its luckless residents were reduced to broken wood, and smoke, and blood. The pirates, satisfied by their own efficiency, rounded out to sea, disappearing into a curtain of rain.

The carrion angels slept in *Retribution*'s hold. The scent's trail was a road, even over the sea. They were sure of their way.

# 2. The Last Meeting of the Candlelight Society

Martin had only just achieved a precarious sleep when he was awakened by the harsh voice of a bent, pinch-faced man in his nightclothes. He stood in the narrow door and held a lantern at his side, casting his own face into garish shadow. "The captain wants you," he said. "Sharplike."

He pulled himself unhappily out of bed and fetched his trousers from the floor, noting the slow, easy roll of the ship over the waves. He must have fallen asleep during the storm. Perhaps he would make a seaman of himself yet. Still, an unbroken sleep would have done him good.

"Who are you?" he asked brusquely, reaching for his jacket.

"I'm Grimsley, and I cook your meals for you, mister, so mind your tone. I also see to the captain's whims. Which is you now, so be smart about it. Look at you fussing over your clothes like a proper lady. Leave off and do as you're bid, before his mood turns."

As it happened, Captain Toussaint's mood was generous. His quarters were at the aft of the ship, and the windows were open, affording him a salty breeze and a king's view. The clouds had dispersed, and although there was no moon to light the waves, the stars burned in great, glittering folds. Toussaint sat with his back to it, a shadow against the sky. He looked like an illustrated figure from the Old Testament. The table had been set up between them, with a kettle of hot water and two mugs.

"Did I interrupt your sleep, diabolist?" said the captain.

Martin took the seat opposite. He heard the steward shut the door behind him. "I know this is your ship, and you're lord of the high seas and all that, but I will thank you to call me by my proper name."

"I see your sensibilities are as delicate as your tender little hands." He leaned forward and pushed the mug closer. "Perhaps some tea will soothe your English heart."

"Thank you, Captain." Martin poured the tea into the mug and held it under his nose, breathing it in. He sipped, and found it surprisingly good.

Captain Toussaint smiled. "Privileges of the wicked life," he said.

"I suspect the privileges are many. Including summoning gentlemen from sleep to sit at your table upon a whim. What need do you have of me, Captain?"

"I have need of your context, Mr. Dunwood. I would like to know your business here."

"It is the same as yours, of course. We shall goad the lotushead into speech, and we shall cross into the Dark Water. Then I shall contact the Order of the Black Iron, and we will sail to Lotus Cove, where the Cannibal Priest will have his precious Feast. You'll fill your hold with lotusheads and I'll get my atlas. Everyone is happy. Is this a game, Captain? Why do you ask me what you already know?"

"It is not a game, Mr. Dunwood, but you continue to treat it like one. You are hiding something from me. Tell me what it is."

All the warmth generated by the hot tea dissipated. Martin put the mug back on the table and concentrated on maintaining his composure. The captain, damn him, watched him as carefully as he would an opponent in a duel; if that's what this was, Martin was already being pressed into a disadvantage. "Mr. Gully has been indiscreet," he managed to say.

"Mr. Gully has the eager tongue of a dockside whore, but I don't need him to tell me what's already plain. Something about you smells rotten, Mr. Dunwood. You're a pup, and I expected a grown man. The Candlelight Society does not send children to do men's work. I did not have time to question you before the carrion angels arrived, but now we're at sea, and time is something I have in abundance. So allow me to ask you again. And if you avoid my question one more time I shall summon Mr. Hu into the room, and he will do the asking on my behalf. Do you understand me?"

Martin's sense of control had evaporated. He was now simply afraid. It was a new and unwelcome emotion. "Yes, Captain, I think I do," he said quietly. He took a breath to steady himself. "There is a woman."

Captain Toussaint sighed, easing back in his chair. The ship crested a wave and through the great window behind the captain's head Martin watched the sea fall away; for a moment he was staring into the starry gulf of the sky. The cups on the table between them slid a few inches. "A woman. You mean *the* woman, of course. Alice Cobb."

"Yes. I do."

"So it's a love story then."

"If you like."

"All men of the sea enjoy a proper love story, Mr. Dunwood. Maybe it's because our own always end so badly. Tell me."

"I met her in London, some time ago. I was new to the Society. I'd had no dealings with the Buried Church; I'd only heard stories of it. I wasn't sure I even believed. When I met her, I . . . well. We fell in love, Captain. It's as simple as that."

"I doubt anything about it is simple. I'm shocked the priest tolerates this. She is his daughter, after all."

"He doesn't know. Alice and I would very much like to keep it that way. At the Feast, he will come to understand."

"I see. But Mr. Benson not only approves, but is so moved by your plight that he sends you upon the excursion of a lifetime in his place?"

"'Approves' would be putting it strongly. But we in the Society are storytellers, Captain, and it's in our nature to encourage the passions of the heart. We are romantic creatures, after all."

Captain Toussaint regarded him carefully. "So they send me an untested boy with a hidden ambition, so that he can run about my ship like some plague-addled wharf rat, with love corroding his blood like a disease. What's more, he has a secret which, if discovered by the priest, will not only scuttle the purpose of our voyage but very likely result in blood being spilled aboard my ship. Do I understand it correctly?"

Martin said nothing. Despite the cool air blowing in, the room felt close and hot. The pitching of the ship made a tumult in his gut; that, along with the new and very real possibility that this brute might interfere with his and Alice's plan, made it a struggle not to spew his last meal across the table between them.

"I love her, Captain. We are going to wed, there on Hell's shore. We will do this with or without her father's approval."

"A wedding at the lip of Hell. You amaze me, Mr. Dunwood."

"Love drives one to extravagant behaviors. Have you never loved anyone?"

Captain Toussaint fixed him with a searching look. "In fact I have. It too would have provoked disapproval, had it been widely known."

Martin pressed his advantage. "And if what I've heard of pirates is true, you would not have let something so small deter you."

"Not even death would deter me, Mr. Dunwood." The captain sipped from his tea. He seemed to consider for a moment. The stars heaved in the sky behind him. Finally he said, "All right. Your story does not set me at ease, but it does rouse my sympathies. We'll go on as planned. You may return to your bunk."

Martin nodded. "Thank you," he said, and rose to leave. His hand was on the door when Captain Toussaint stopped him.

"A word of caution: It's not *my* discretion you should worry about. That little villain you've hired to do your dirty work will sell you for a tuppence. You know that, surely?"

"Fat Gully," said Martin. "He's a creature of brute impulse, nothing more. He'll behave as long as he's paid."

Captain Toussaint smiled. "It's my experience that we all have a secret heart. Even brutes." He leaned back in his chair, drawing in a deep breath. "But perhaps you're right. Let's see what tomorrow brings us, shall we? Good night, Mr. Dunwood."

Martin retreated to his cramped quarters. He slept fitfully, and he was plagued by dreams of the Buried Church. He watched a cleaver rise and fall, over and over again, lifting bright red arcs into the air. He saw a stunned human face pressed against the bars of a metal cage. He heard a shriek so piercing that it launched him from sleep, upright in his swinging cot at some unknowable black hour of the night, panting and listening. He heard only the sound of the waves against the hull, the groan of wood straining against the deep. He closed his eyes again, and if he dreamed further, it was only of the abyss.

Six hours earlier, aboard *Retribution*, Bonny Mungo stared at the creature looming over his bunk and understood that he had only moments remaining before it extinguished him from the earth. He had fallen asleep perusing charts outlining the Hispaniola coastline, and so the lantern suspended over his head still shed a dim light. The carrion angel fluttered silently in its glow, its hooked beak opening, its red eyes spilling thin smoke.

If anyone had thought to ask him about the condition of his heart, Bonny Mungo would have said that it was bountiful with love. He had answered the call of his passions, leaving behind the diminished lifestyle of his parents on their Scottish farm and turning instead to the pursuit of his desires. He lived in a hot climate now, he waged glorious war in the ocean, and he indulged in women and drink on shore. What did not come to him willingly he took by force. The world was a heavy fruit. Life was the long satisfaction of impulse, and he would be a sorry man to complain about any of it.

He tried to set himself on fire. He would prefer to burn alive than let the carrion angel take him. His lunge for the lantern was too late, and his reach too short. The angel seeped through his skin and oriented itself in his body, fitting its eyes to Bonny Mungo's, cracking his joints and splitting his skull to accommodate itself more comfortably. Most of what made the pirate the man he was dissolved in the holy heat of the angel's presence, but enough rags of himself remained that he appreciated the smallness of his life's purpose until this point.

A new hunger grew in Bonny Mungo's heart. It was like gravity, bending every thought toward it. The passions of his former life were like a child's whims. Now he wanted only to eat.

The carrion angel guided Bonny Mungo like a clumsy puppet. He lurched from his cot on his new, broken legs, the knees snapping and bending haphazardly with each step. He maneuvered out of his cabin, the breach in his skull smoking, black rags fluttering from it like hair, his eyes sizzling like fat in a pan of oil. The angel opened its mouth to speak in its new tongue, and syllables spilled out like teeth. To hear them was to bleed. It would take some getting used to.

Down the hall, there were screams. The other angels were claiming their hosts. Following that, they'd have to spill some blood, but hopefully not much. The crew would obey. They wanted to live, after all.

The lotushead was somewhere ahead of them. The smell of it hurt Bonny Mungo in his bones. It turned his belly into a yawning hole.

Martin awoke early the following morning, roused by the commotion of work. The day was already warm. A crisp wind filled the sails, driving them west. He found Captain Toussaint standing aft, holding a spyglass to his eye. Martin squinted, but could see nothing through the glare of the early sun.

"There's a ship back there," said the captain, still watching. "The lookout spied it an hour ago. They're steering from the sun, hoping to buy some time before we spot them. A standard tactic."

"An enemy, then? How can you tell?"

"I can't for sure. But I'll wager it's the carrion angels, sniffing out our cargo. Once they get a scent they're bloody relentless."

"But they're beasts! Can they pilot a ship?"

The captain glanced at him. "Never seen one, have you."

"No."

"You will." Captain Toussaint left him, striding back to the deck and barking orders. Some of the men scampered up the rigging and started untying sails. Canvas dropped and billowed. The man at the helm adjusted the great wheel a quarter turn to the right, and the ship surged forward, sending white foam crashing over the bowsprit.

Martin lingered at the railing, eyes locked onto the horizon. Though he still couldn't see anything, the sense of threat soured his stomach. He'd heard of the carrion angels in Society meetings: holy cockroaches, gorging themselves on anything from Heaven or Hell that might have become lost in the mortal world. The lotushead would be a fine morsel, no doubt.

Not for the first time, Martin doubted the wisdom of this venture. The captain was right: He was too young and too inexperienced. Here he stood, sturdy as a fencepost, and still he felt a consuming fear. He wished to be home in London, with its dark libraries and lantern-lit alleys, with his pipe and his brandy, surrounded by the Society's flickering candles and devil-haunted shadows. There he would feel safe. Out here, in this briny, sun-wracked environment, he felt exposed and bewildered. A moth lost in a delirium of light.

After nearly an hour of waiting and watching, he could still see nothing on the horizon. If this was a chase, it was the dullest one he'd ever heard of. He made his way belowdecks and found the galley, where the man who had woken him from sleep a few hours ago—Grimsley—toiled over his fire. Beside him was a small table covered in chopped vegetables, strewn with cured meat. The kitchen would be freshly stocked from the visit to Cordova, and the food was as fresh as it would be all voyage. Martin heard the clucking of chickens coming from some way off, and a barnyard stink—two pigs and a goat—mingled with the welcome smell of cooking meat and coffee.

The steward cast him a glance over his shoulder. "His Highness arises."

"I'm hungry. Give me something to eat, Cook."

"You've missed vittles, so you can make do with a biscuit and a slice of pork." Grimsley threw the items onto a plate and pushed it toward him. "Sorry—not the type of meat you're craving, I gather. I know some pygmy tribes in the Pacific could help you."

"I am no cannibal."

"Of course not, Your Highness. You just share a table with them, is all. Why should one draw conclusions?"

Martin tamped down a flash of anger. "Coffee," he said.

Grimsley directed him to the pot with a lift of his chin, and then turned his back on him once again, resuming his chore.

"Wretch." Martin took his meager breakfast to the mess hall next door, which was empty save for his own Mr. Gully, lounging like a lord with his back against the bulkhead, digging a nugget of food from his teeth with a fingernail. Gully winked and presented an unsightly grin.

"We're going to have a party soon, so I hear," he said. "Another ship stalking us like a hungry shark. Best stick close to me, if it comes to a fight, lad. I've got to earn my keep, you know."

"There will be no battle. The captain is quite competent." In fact Martin had no idea if this was true, but it made him feel better to say it.

"Did he pry your secret from you last night?"

"How did you know I spoke to him at all?"

"Why, I'm your protection, ain't I? It's my business to know what you're up to, Mr. Dunwood."

Martin passed a hand across his face. "I told him what I needed to. He gains nothing from betraying my confidence."

"Maybe, maybe not." Mr. Gully took another bite of his biscuit, chewing as he spoke. "He has secrets of his own, our captain does."

"What do you mean?"

"He's got a man locked up in the hold. Weeps throughout the night."

Martin smiled, enjoying the opportunity to display his superiority over his awful companion. "You're like a child sometimes, Mr. Gully. It's almost charming. That man is no secret. That man is the Feast."

Something like thought seemed to pass across Mr. Gully's face. "Him? But he's nothing. He's a nobody."

"For once, I agree with you. Congregants of the Buried Church are an odd lot, though. They care about the nothings, or at least they claim to. For them, the Feast is the ultimate expression of love, and Satan is egalitarian in His appetites. Even a beggar may suffice."

Mr. Gully considered this in silence.

Martin, pleased, enjoyed his coffee in peace.

The final meeting of the Candlelight Society's London branch remained one of the signal moments of Martin's life. Six gentlemen convened, as per usual, in the Brindle Mare

Club. They retired to a private room prepared according to their specifications: the table polished to a high shine, reflecting the light of fifty candles arranged in clusters throughout the room. The curtains were tied open, and through the window one might watch the streets of London at night. Coats and wigs were hung by an employee of the club, who retreated from the room immediately, and who would not return until summoned. A decanter of brandy waited on a serving table in the corner, and Mr. Dunwood—at twenty-four years of age, the youngest member present—assumed the duty of filling each man's snifter before addressing his own. Pipes were lit, and conversation eased into life.

The Candlelight Society met bimonthly, and at these meetings it was a selected man's duty to relate a story to the other members, recounting what he had done to further Satan's cause in society. Often these stories involved considerable risk to the teller of the tale; if there were occasional embellishments, well, surely they were only symptoms of enthusiasm for the cause. The atmosphere at these meetings was unfailingly collegiate and warm, and the men had forged a familial unity over the years.

Conversation was permitted to wander for a time before Mr. Benson summoned everyone's attention with a gentle clearing of his throat.

Martin's heartbeat increased, and as he held his snifter, he studied the level of the brandy inside to see whether he could detect a tremor in his hand. He found none.

"Gentlemen," said Mr. Benson, "I'm afraid we shall have to forgo the stories this evening. I know it's a disappointment."

In fact, it wasn't. Mr. Withers had been scheduled to speak tonight, and his stories were always a chore to sit through. The events were all well enough, but he spoke without pause or inflection, as though he were reading market reports on Turkish figs. Anything that might delay that experience was to be welcomed.

"At our last meeting Mr. Dunwood surprised us all by telling us a wonderful tale of his visit to the Buried Church. The friendship he struck with Miss Alice Cobb facilitated an exchange of letters between myself and her father, Abel Cobb. London's own Cannibal Priest. Because of that—indeed, because of your initiative, Mr. Dunwood—the Candlelight Society is presented with its grandest opportunity since its acquisition of the Damocles Scroll, some two hundred years ago."

"Hear, hear," they said, and glasses were raised all around. "Greater even than that," offered one of them, and there were murmurs of agreement.

Martin smiled humbly, raising his own glass. "Thank you, gentlemen. All I seek is to bring honor to the Burning Prince."

"I shall speak your name to Him," assured Mr. Benson. "This I promise you."

Martin smiled. Mr. Greaves, a portly, middle-aged man sitting directly to his right, clapped him on the shoulder. "I know you wanted to be the one to go, Dunwood. Very good of you to understand."

"I defer to Mr. Benson's authority, of course, and to his many long years of service. If any man here has earned the privilege of being the first member of the Candlelight Society to tread Hell's shore, it is he." He waited for all the tedious affirmations to settle before he continued. "I only fear that the journey may be dangerous."

Mr. Benson made a dismissive gesture. "Never fear. I don't trust the Buried Church any more than I trust those southern pirates. I've hired a bodyguard to accompany me. I am told he's quite capable."

"What's the name of this fellow?"

Mr. Benson paused, and chuckled. "Do you think you would recognize it, Mr. Dunwood? I daresay you travel in different company."

Martin produced a laugh. It sounded sincere, even to him. How easily the lies came, these days. "Not at all. But should anything happen to you, I would like to know whom to hold responsible."

"Risk is a natural component of our endeavors here. We all know that. Should I fall in my duties, I trust the Society will continue its business unflagged. Nevertheless, if it will please you to know it, the man is called Rufus Gully, and I am told he can be found lurking about Whitechapel or at the docks. You may deliver whatever retribution seems appropriate. Now, if that's settled, I would like to move on to the question of Miss Alice Cobb."

Martin compressed his lips, unable to hide his discomfort. He felt keenly the scrutiny of the others. "What do you mean?"

"I know this is uncomfortable, Martin, and I'm sorry for that."

The sudden informality caught him off guard, and he felt a curious wash of goodwill toward Mr. Benson and all the gentlemen here. They were the best family he had ever known, and the few years he'd spent doing the Devil's work at their side had been the proudest of his life.

"I know you feel strongly for the girl," Benson continued, "and the Society has always honored great passion. The Burning Prince is not called such after a simple fire, after all."

Someone said, "Hear, hear."

Martin nodded, acknowledging this.

"I only wish to remind you of what's at stake. Miss Cobb,

enchanting as she may be, is the daughter of a Cannibal Priest, and therefore in pursuit of a different cause. We may all bend the knee to the same Lord, but we honor him in different ways. I go in place of you not only because of my position in the Society, and not only because of your youth, but because I know I will not be distracted by my heart. Do you understand?"

Martin nodded, the goodwill of a moment ago entirely evaporated. "I do."

Mr. Benson gestured to his depleted glass. "I wish to make a toast. If you would, please."

"Of course." Martin rose and turned to the decanter. Behind him, Mr. Benson addressed the group.

"Multiple purposes are converging here, and if every man is honorable there will be no difficulties. The pirate wants to fill his hold with lotusheads, so he can cross into the Dark Water at will and do trade with the cities on Hell's border. The Cannibal Priest wishes to hold a Feast there, and hopes to entice Satan Himself to the table. I admit I hope very much that he succeeds. I can imagine no greater honor than to sit at that table. And I, of course, have my own purpose." He waited until Martin had finished replenishing the brandy snifters. Once this was accomplished, he raised his glass. All followed suit. "I shall bring to the Society an atlas of Hell," he said. "I shall bring to us the means to study the true face of our Lord."

"To your success, sir," said Mr. Greaves. "And to the Candlelight Society."

"Hear, hear," they said, and all but Martin drank.

Mr. Benson beamed. "Hail—" His throat closed around the phrase. He brought his hand to his neck with an expression of bewilderment. The others sputtered and coughed briefly, and then a gravid silence spread over the group. Their faces turned a turbulent red. Blood flowed from their noses, their eyes. Their faces, Martin thought, looked like holy masks.

He overturned his raised glass. The brandy spattered onto the table and ran off the edge. He met Mr. Benson's bulging eyes and held them for as long as it took for the light within them to expire.

"Hail Satan," Martin said.

# 3. The Cannibal Priest

They sailed a week without incident. Martin browned in the tropical sun. He dined at the captain's table in the evenings but kept as much to himself as was possible during the long, bright days. His only true moments of apprehension came when he observed a crewman training a spyglass behind them, reminding him of their pursuer. But Captain Toussaint surmised that that ship had laden itself with stores for a long raiding campaign, while *Butcher's Table*—with only the lotus-head and the unfortunate Mr. Thickett in its hold—carved a quicker path through the sea. They kept an easy distance.

So it was that the first ship Martin beheld with any clarity was not their pursuer, but a colonial schooner called the *Puritan*, its Union Jack fluttering crisply in the southern breeze.

Martin leaned over the railing, straining his eyes to see if he could make out anyone on the deck. He felt the proximity of Alice in his blood, and if he'd believed he could get to her more quickly by swimming, he would have jumped overboard on the instant. The thought was already half formed in his mind when a hand clasped his shoulder, startling him so much that for a moment he thought he had actually done it.

"It'll be a few hours yet," said Captain Toussaint. "She'll wait for you."

"Hours?" They appeared so close; it seemed outrageous.

"Indeed. The eye travels faster than the wind will carry us. We'll meet with them before the sun goes down, be assured. I'm only grateful for the reinforcements." He cast a glance behind them, where the other ship lurked on the horizon like a mote in the eye.

Martin followed his gaze. "Surely they won't attack all of us together? They'd be mad."

Toussaint cast him a sidelong glance. "It's past time you became accustomed to madness, Mr. Dunwood. But don't fear. They are far enough behind that I believe we'll make the crossing before they catch us."

"But the *Puritan* won't be crossing with us. What of them?"

"They shall have to fend for themselves. If their captain is intelligent, they'll be rigged for speed."

Unsettled, Martin retreated to his cabin, hoping to pass the hours going over the particulars of his task. As much as he looked forward to seeing Alice, and as much as he anticipated the thrill of the passage into the Dark Water, he was already feeling nostalgic for the past week's quiet journey. He'd grown used to the rolling waves and the slapping of the water against the hull as he settled in for sleep each night. He fancied himself becoming a proper man of the sea.

He opened his valise and removed a package wrapped in oilcloth, which he set beside him. He felt a nervous flutter in his breath and took a moment to compose himself. He unwrapped the cloth, exposing three tall, inelegant candles, dull yellow—more like some waxy excrescence than things designed by human hands—with long black wicks like eyelashes. He should not have them out; they were as crucial to the success of the mission as the lotushead, drowsing somewhere below him. He had taken all three from the Society's stores, as a safeguard against accident, but even that seemed a brazenly small number.

The door opened and Martin jumped in alarm, though every man aboard knew what he carried.

Fat Gully stood framed in the door, staring with naked interest. "That's them, isn't it? The hellward candles."

Martin wrapped them carefully again. It seemed somehow grotesque that Gully had seen them—as though they'd been sullied. "Yes."

"Ugly little things."

Martin slid the oilcloth back into his valise, which he tucked beneath the cot. "They are not meant to please the eye, Mr. Gully. What do you mean by barging in on me?"

"We've nearly arrived. We're in shouting distance."

Martin felt a pulse of excitement. Still, that did not justify the intrusion. "Thank you. I'll be up presently. You may go."

Mr. Gully moved fully into the room then, shutting the door behind him. The quarters were close at the best of times; with his wide and malodorous presence, they became oppressively small. "It's time we spoke clearly, Mr. Dunwood. I was going to wait until later, but what with that other vessel coming on behind us, it seems there might not be time."

Martin shifted uncomfortably. "Why don't we go above and—"

"We'll stay down here, Mr. Dunwood, where it's nice and private, yes?" Gully leaned over him. Martin couldn't leave without physically pushing past the man, which he did not wish to attempt.

"Very good, Mr. Gully. What's on your mind, then?"

"It's about your lady, sir. It's about Miss Cobb. I want you to arrange a meeting between us."

Martin flushed, both angry and frightened. "You have no business with Miss Cobb."

"Oh, I do."

"*What* business? Is it the Society? Did they give you some instruction?"

Martin was unable to hide his frustration, and Mr. Gully made no secret that he enjoyed it. "No, it ain't the Society, Mr. Dunwood. And even if it were, you took care of them, didn't you? Nothing they told me matters anymore. No, it's just me. Just dear old Gully. I got something I want to ask of your precious lady, and you're going to make sure I get the chance."

"You're mad. Of course I won't do it."

"You will, sir."

Martin attempted to stand, but Mr. Gully shoved him roughly back onto his cot, where he swung wildly, nearly spilling backward. As he struggled to right himself, Mr. Gully gripped his throat and dug his fingers in. Terror overwhelmed Martin; he gripped Mr. Gully's thick forearms, but he was too weak to do anything but clasp them tightly, as if he were grasping the arms of a welcome friend.

"Now look here, dog. I've got you to rights, I do. I know all there is to know about you. You do what I say or I tell the Cannibal Priest about your designs on the girl. Her father's the top man, ain't he? Won't he be fascinated to learn what became of the Society, and that the whelp who done it is here to fuck his daughter right under his nose. You'll be keel-hauled, Mr. Dunwood, or worse. You do what I say or I make sure you're dead before the sun sets."

". . . bastard . . . you bastard . . ." Martin struggled to breathe. His face was going red.

Mr. Gully smiled. "Are you questioning my parentage, Mr.

Dunwood? Why, I've never been so insulted. What *shall* I do." He relaxed his grip just slightly, allowing Martin to haul in a ragged breath.

"You've crossed a line, Gully. You were paid to protect me. You have no idea what—"

Mr. Gully cut him off again with a squeeze of his hand, like a man turning a valve. "You're nothing to me. You've always been nothing. The Society was just a bunch of wanking old men telling dull stories to each other because no one else would bother to listen. You're all as threatening as a litter of kittens." Martin felt a sharp pain near his groin; Gully had slipped the blade of his knife through his trousers and pressed its edge against the pulsing artery. "You'll say nothing to anyone. You'll do what the fuck I say and you'll be quick and quiet about it. Tell me you understand."

He loosened his grip. "Are you going to hurt—"

"Tell me you understand."

"I understand."

Gully released him completely this time, leaning back, and Martin slid to the floor, curling into himself and coughing. The pitch of the ocean, a soothing rhythm only moments ago, tried to wrestle the breakfast from his belly.

Before the rage had time to bubble up, Mr. Gully addressed him from the door. "I've no doubt you'll be performing your little ritual after dinner tonight, so there won't be much time. Arrange my meeting before all that happens."

"Perhaps I'll just have you killed before we get there," Martin said. He regretted it immediately, but the threat gave him satisfaction.

"Aye, you might. Who would question a gentleman condemning a scoundrel like me? But let me tell you something, Mr. Dunwood. If your friends in the Candlelight Society thought there was safety aboard this ship, my contract would have expired once you were taken into Captain Toussaint's care. But it didn't, did it? Has it occurred to you the captain doesn't need you at all, once you've performed your duties tonight?"

Martin shook his head. "We have an arrangement. I've even paid for passage."

"You put a great deal of stock in your 'arrangements,' don't you? As much as Mr. Benson did, do you think?"

Martin said nothing.

"Once you've crossed into the Dark Water, there's nothing to stop them from dumping your carcass overboard. Nothing but me, that is. The Society knew it. That's why Benson paid me for the whole journey. So you can turn me over if you like, Mr. Dunwood, but if you do you'll be joining me down a shark's gullet soon enough. Do what I tell you, though, and everything will continue as it was, pretty as you please."

He departed, leaving Martin shivering on the floor.

Late afternoon found *Butcher's Table* joined with the *Puritan* in the calm Gulf waters, sails furled and launch boats plying the short distance between them. Stores and personnel were ferried from the colonial vessel to the pirate ship in preparation for the crossing. Captain Toussaint stood on the aft deck, in the company of Mr. Hu, Martin, and Fat Gully, where they received Abel Cobb—the Cannibal Priest himself—accompanied by his bodyguard, a Virginian soldier called Randall Major. Abel Cobb was an older gentleman with a heavy white moustache, his round belly an indication of his wealth, his white clothing crisp and smartly tailored. One might imagine he'd just stepped out of a club, and not spent a week at sea.

Cobb grasped Captain Toussaint's hand and shook it coolly. These were two men who, under any other circumstance, would be happy to watch the other hang. Then he turned his attention to Martin, whom he greeted with genuine warmth.

"Mr. Dunwood, it's a pleasure to have a member of the Candlelight Society join us at the Feast. I believe it's been more than fifty years since the last time such a thing has happened."

"I believe it's been that long since an invitation has been extended," Martin countered, and the two men permitted themselves a chuckle. In truth, though they ultimately served the same master, certain doctrinal differences forced a rivalry between their organizations, to which bloodshed was not unknown.

Captain Toussaint interjected. "You do not seem surprised to see Dunwood, whereas I had been expecting old Benson. I do not like feeling shut out, Mr. Cobb."

Abel smiled indulgently at the captain. "You have not been shut out, I can assure you. Mr. Benson sent word along to us that he had fallen ill. You, well . . . your particular business makes you rather more difficult to reach."

"And yet here we are," Toussaint said, but he let the matter rest. "Enough pleasantries, I think. Let's attend to business."

"Why the haste? We have an abundance of time."

"Mr. Cobb, we are pursued."

Abel Cobb peered into the horizon beyond Toussaint's shoulder. The sea appeared empty and quiet.

"They are perhaps a day out, but they are not under a natural command. It would be a mistake to linger. Come below, and I'll show you what we've rigged for you."

The captain led Mr. Cobb away, followed by Hu and the Virginian. Martin and Gully lingered on the aft deck. The afternoon was hot, and the sun cast bright shards over the waves. They watched as Mr. Johns supervised the intake of materials, much of which seemed to be rare foodstuffs, spices, and animals, in preparation for the Feast on Hell's shore. Finally, though, he saw what he had been waiting for. She seemed a jewel in the sunlight, the launch that carried her lifting and dipping over the gentle waves, six men laboring hard at the oars.

Interminably long minutes later, Alice Cobb was assisted aboard *Butcher's Table*. Her hair was done up in a bun, and she wore a somber black dress. She navigated the crowded deck gracefully, and she seemed to Martin as out of place on this ship as a nightingale flitting through an abattoir. Not a single head turned; every man aboard this ship kept to his duty, and he wondered at the fear she instilled, that she could quiet their grosser instincts. She mounted the stairs to the aft deck and approached him, her smile radiant, her skin ruddy with the sun. Martin felt as though every inconvenience, every crime, every humiliating slight had been nothing more than prelude to this heart-filling justification.

"Alice," he said. Every impulse in his body urged him toward her, but he resisted. Though no one would stare at this woman outright, he knew that the corner of every eye was attuned to them.

"Mr. Dunwood," she said. With her back to the crew, she was free to give expression to her joy. "It is fine to see you again." She looked at Mr. Gully. "And who is this?"

"This is Rufus Gully. He is my companion on the journey."

She arched an eyebrow at the little man. "Surely not the whole journey?"

Mr. Gully stepped forward and executed a clumsy bow. "Absolutely the whole journey, Miss Cobb. Martin and I are the dearest of friends. Isn't that so, Martin?"

Martin stiffened. "Mr. Gully was hired by the Society to serve as my protection."

"Protection? Not from us, I'm sure!"

Martin shook his head. "Of course n—"

"From everyone," Gully said, presenting his full, gap-toothed grin. "We don't know what awaits in the Dark Water, after all, and you lot might get hungry."

Alice smiled down at him. All pretense of warmth had gone. "I do like a plain speaker. If we do get hungry, I daresay there's more meat on your bones than his, rancid though it may be."

To Martin's horror, Gully giggled shamelessly at this, as though she'd just performed the most outrageous flirtation.

Alice was indifferent to him. To Martin, she said, "I regret we do not have more time, but there is still much to be done before tonight. I shall see you again at dinner." She nodded politely, letting her gaze linger with Martin's for a delicious moment, and then turned away.

She'd gone a few steps when Mr. Gully turned to Martin and fixed him with a cold stare. "Don't you dare test me, sir."

Martin, face flushed, called out to her. "Miss Cobb. If you please."

She turned and paused.

"Mr. Gully has a point of business he must discuss with you."

"Does he now." Her face was unreadable. "Spit it out then, little morsel."

Gully grinned again, but this time he maintained his composure. "In private, if you please."

"If you think I'm going to be shut into a room with you, you're mad."

"Right here will suffice. Give us a moment, Mr. Dunwood."

Presented as an order. Martin felt lightheaded. He considered that if he acted quickly he might surprise the man and wrestle him overboard. If it became a struggle, perhaps others would come to his aid. But he knew there was no realistic hope of this, and that such an action would only result in his own guts spilling onto the deck, there to cook in the hot sun. Worse, the same fate might come to Alice. So he swallowed his anger and said, "Be quick."

He walked to the railing and turned his back to them. From this vantage point, he could see the *Puritan* poised nearby, its own decks alive with activity. The traffic between the two ships had slowed. He peered into the southeast, but there was still no sign of the pursuing vessel. Perhaps they'd given up.

He would not have time to spend with Alice before the crossing, but he consoled himself with the promise of her company afterward. In a few days' time, they would be married. With a little good fortune, perhaps they could even secure her father's blessing, though they would certainly proceed without it. He did not think Abel Cobb would find cause to refuse him, even considering their natural animosities. He felt confident that the ritual following dinner tonight would put any possible objections to rest. It was all very well to call the Candlelight Society a toothless gathering of storytellers, but let him see Martin work with a hellward candle, and he would adjust his thinking.

"Come on then, Mr. Dunwood."

Mr. Gully stood at his side. Martin turned in time to see Alice wending her way through the crowded deck and disappearing down the ladder into the interior of *Butcher's Table*. She did not spare him a glance. Martin grabbed him by the shoulder and shook him once. "If you've threatened her in any way, I will kill you for it!"

"Take your hand away. I did no such thing. All I did was ask for a place at the table."

Martin needed a moment to understand what he'd just heard. "A place—you mean at the dinner tonight? Preposterous."

"Not tonight's dinner," Gully said. "Another one."

Martin's mind reeled. He meant the Feast. Even under normal circumstances, it was remorselessly exclusive; few outside the diabolist circles even knew of its existence. The notion that some miscreant from the gutter might be welcomed tableside simply by exhibiting a bit of bluster offended him on a foundational level. "You don't even have the right clothing for it," was all he could think of to say.

"I don't think it'll be a problem." He patted his employer on the arm. "Now, let's get below and get you ready, Mr. Dunwood. You done what I asked, and now God help anyone who crosses you while I'm about." He considered a moment, then gave him a wink. "Well . . . God, or whoever."

Fifty leagues to the southeast, what remained of Captain Bonny Mungo stalked the decks of the *Retribution*, calculating the time it would take to catch *Butcher's Table*. The captain existed as a fluttering scrap of thought in a body that had once been his but was now broken and expanded to house the carrion angel that lived there. The bones in his face had unlocked and pushed outward to accommodate the angel's presence. The flesh was swollen and bruised black; occasionally some pocket of trapped blood would find its way out and trickle down his face in an oily stream. When the captain issued orders to his crew, his Scottish burr pushed through altered vocal cords to create a sound that terrified them and left them wholly subservient.

The other three carrion angels had surrendered their hosts

as soon as the crew had been tamed, and now roosted in the masts, black silhouettes fluttering against the hot sky, occasionally drifting down to feed on one of the bodies spread like a red feast on the decks. The crew had been trimmed to its barest essentials. Everyone else was provender.

Bonny Mungo retained enough of himself to remember Scotland, to remember standing atop a seaside cliff and watching the ships leave that cold rock for adventures under a foreign sun. He remembered a childhood spent thieving from the shops, waylaying passing carriages and unfettering the fops inside from the bags of coin weighing them down. The years spent in and out of gaols, escaping the hangman's noose long enough to finally find passage aboard a ship full of bloody-minded young men like himself, brothers all. He hacked and beat and bought his way to a position of prominence among them, to a captaincy, to respect and fear and a rolling home thousands of miles from the fog-clapped cliffs of Scotland, in a part of the world where the sun hammered its devil's eye onto hot sand and clamoring Spanish ports. Bonny Mungo retained enough of himself to remember all of that, and to provide the angelic cockroach splitting his body like a too-small jacket with the requisite knowledge to keep enough men alive to sail his ship, and to point it in the direction of its prey. After that, he and all that remained of his crew would just be gruel in the trough.

The scent of the lotushead drew them across the waves. It was getting closer, but the rag that was Bonny Mungo knew that it was not quickly enough. Because he knew it, the angel knew it too.

It spoke a word that fractured the jaw of its host, registering the pain as a curiosity. Upon hearing the word, one of the roosting angels took flight, rearing against the sun in a flare of black feathers, and plummeted into the sea, where it sank from sight like a corpse weighted with stones. The angel descended quickly, a dark-feathered ball, until it passed beyond the reach of sunlight and the water grew cold and black. It fell more deeply yet, oblivious to the atmospheres pressing against its body, its eyes pulling from the lightless fathoms darting shapes, shifting mountains of flesh.

It found a host, made a bloody gash and wriggled into it, and filled the beast with its holy spirit. Skin split in fissures along the length of its form, and it jetted forward with fresh purpose, its tentacles trailing in a tight formation behind it, its red saucer-shaped eyes incandescent with hunger.

"Tell me," said Abel Cobb, as Captain Toussaint led him through the cramped corridors below.

Toussaint bulled his way toward the ladder that descended into the hold. He spoke over his shoulder as he walked. "I believe we're pursued by a carrion angel. Perhaps a host of them."

If this rattled Cobb's resolve, he disguised it well. "I suppose it was to be expected. Tracking the lotushead, no doubt."

"No doubt."

The hold, lit generously with lanterns, bustled with activity as crewmen filled the larder with the meats, spices, and vegetables that would supply the Feast and afterward sustain them on the short journey back to the colonies, where all parties would go their separate ways. Beyond this, toward the aft, were the rooms the carpenters had added to house Abel and his retinue. The scent of recently cut wood filled their nostrils. Abel peered into his own room and sniffed with disdain.

"These are barely adequate."

"Your other option is the open deck. I'll leave that decision to you."

Cobb turned away. "Show me the runner."

Toussaint gestured farther down the passageway. No lantern hung there, and it ended in a swell of shadow.

Cobb hesitated.

"Don't be nervous, now," said Captain Toussaint. He smiled.

Cobb proceeded without a word. About twenty feet ahead the corridor ended in a closed and locked door. Sound was muted here; the loading activities behind them seemed to come from a more distant place, and the chill of the water, so near to them, shivered their blood. The captain gestured to the door. "In there, Mr. Cobb. Would you like to see him?"

Cobb only nodded, and the captain shouldered by him with a key. He couldn't shake the unpleasant notion that he was taking orders aboard his own ship. Abel Cobb was one of those men who inhabit power the way other men do a suit of clothes.

The door pushed open and they discerned a shape on the floor, which slowly materialized into the crumpled form of Thomas Thickett, lifting his face into the meager light. He blinked and held out a hand to block it out. "Yes? Yes?"

Cobb swelled as he drew in a deep breath. "There you are at last," he said.

Thickett froze as he recognized the voice. He scrambled back into his cell's darkest corner. "No."

Abel Cobb knelt at the room's entrance. When he spoke, his voice was gentle, almost kind. "You are the most fortunate of men," he said. "Do not flinch from this honor."

"*NO!*"

Cobb backed out of the room and shut the door. Captain Toussaint locked it again, muffling the sound of Thickett's sobs. They were an assault on his heart, and it took him a moment to harden himself against them again. He passed the key to Cobb, formally transferring custody.

"You feel sorry for him," Cobb said.

Captain Toussaint straightened himself and walked back down the corridor, not sparing the man a glance. "He's made his own fate. I have nothing more to do with it."

"I've heard rumors that you're a sentimental man," said Cobb, following behind. "I just wasn't sure I should credit them."

"Sentiment is a dangerous quality on the sea, Mr. Cobb. So is a credulous nature. Be wary of rumors."

"Ah, then the stories about Captain Tegel and yourself are lies, invented to destroy your character. What a relief, sir, I must tell you. So there will be no sentiment, then, to spoil the Feast."

They arrived at the door to Cobb's new quarters. Captain Toussaint stopped there. "I will not be dining with you at the Feast," he said.

Cobb smiled beneath his moustache. There was no warmth in it. "I thought your kind were less discriminating. Do you tremble at the thought of tasting the human animal? He was bred for this, after all." He flicked his eyes over Captain Toussaint's solid form, as though sizing up a slab of beef. "I assure you, you are as different from one another as a dog is from a pig."

Captain Toussaint felt a familiar heat rise in his chest. It had been growling like a low fire since the priest had boarded the ship. He'd expected to dislike the man and was not disappointed on that front. But he did not know how long he'd be able to keep the fire banked if Cobb insisted on making provocations. "I want nothing to do with your barbaric Feast. I am not one of your cultists."

"'Cultists,' is it? We are an old order, sir. Older than the Candlelight Society, older than whatever groveling thing you Haitian beasts fashion your altars to. We are bound by traditions. A man like yourself may have no regard for such things, but I assure you they are the very bedrock of civilization."

"'Captain.'"

"I'm sorry?"

"You will address me as 'Captain,' sir. You're aboard my ship. You will address me properly. You will not attempt to recruit me or any of my crew into your brutish practices. And what's more, you will not speak the name of Josiah Tegel again. You're not fit to. The rumors you've heard are true. I loved him. I still do. You may titter behind your handkerchief in private, but do it where I can see you and you'll learn what punishment looks like to a pirate crew."

Abel Cobb nodded absently, seeming to consider. His eyes shone in the lantern light. "Thank you for your candor. Allow me to return it. A man like you can only give orders to white men aboard a ship that has already surrendered itself to chaos. No vessel in the Royal Navy would tolerate it. Not even the colonists would endure such a thing, and they are known to fornicate with savages. I need your ship, *Captain* Toussaint; I don't need you. You would be wise not to forget it."

Captain Beverly Toussaint smiled. "And now we understand each other. Good day, Priest." He turned his back to the man and made his way to his own quarters, where a mugful of rum would help calm his anger. That, and the knowledge that he would see sweet old Tegel again very soon. Even now he awaited Toussaint in the Dark Water, ready to enact a plan they'd agreed upon years ago.

Toussaint cast an eye over the empty space in the hold.

There probably wasn't enough; but he could always throw some Satanists overboard, and make more.

Meetings of the Candlelight Society were convivial affairs, defined as much by the sharing of good whiskey and brotherhood as the sharing of Satanic devotions. There was not a member of the Society who could not claim to be a gentleman, so Martin Dunwood felt distinctly out of his element as he sat at the captain's table, surrounded by criminals and cannibals.

Walls had been taken down by the carpenters to make the room more spacious. The curtains were pulled back from the bay window, admitting a cooling, salty breeze. Twilight was falling over the waters; the sky was a smear of pastels. Two candelabras sat at either side of the table, filling the room with a warm light. Grimsley busied himself with taking away the plates from the meal, and replacing them with a sheaf of paper, a quill, and an inkpot.

Dinner had been intimate and quiet. Himself, Captain Toussaint, and the Cobbs. Their companions—Mr. Gully, Mr. Hu, and Mr. Major—dined in the mess with the rest of the crew. Conversation at the table had been muted; Martin detected a tension between Captain Toussaint and Mr. Cobb, though he was too preoccupied by Alice's presence to give it much thought. Alice was formal and polite with him, nothing more. He found it difficult to restrain himself from offering the occasional illicit smile, or to touch her foot with his own underneath the table. He did none of these things.

Once Grimsley had finished and retreated from the room, all eyes fell to Martin. He pulled in a steadying breath and removed the cloth-wrapped candles from an interior pocket. He placed one into a silver candleholder as the others watched.

"It's ghastly," Alice said.

Now that his moment had come, Martin was nervous. But a breeze carried the scent of Alice's perfume to him, warming him with the memory of their secret nights in London. This, along with the slow rocking of the ship and the heave of the waves through the open window, conspired to produce a feeling of pleasant intoxication, steadying his hand and calming his nerves.

"Gentlemen—Miss Cobb—I'm prepared to light the hellward candle. It is customary for a member of the Candlelight Society to tell a story before applying the match, but—"

"For pity's sake," Abel muttered.

"—considering that we are pressed for time, I will forgo it." With a flourish, Martin lit the match. The smell of burning phosphorous tickled his nose. Flickering orange light lit their faces; the skin appeared to crawl over the bones of their skulls. He glanced at Alice; he could not read her expression. "While this candle diminishes, its sister in the Black Iron Monastery, on the border of Hell, will rise in counterpoint. During that time I will be in communication with one of the monks in residence there. We will arrange a meeting place. It's crucial that I not be interrupted. Everyone must remain silent."

The match hissed in his hand. He paused, feeling his inexperience keenly. He'd been present at the lightings of hellward candles before but had never performed the ritual himself. It occurred to him that if he botched it, the entire expedition would be undone. He would lose Alice as a certainty, and he would probably also lose his life.

Captain Toussaint leaned forward in his chair, sliding his hand across the table toward him. He did not touch Martin, but he breached the distance between them: It was a calming gesture. "We won't interrupt you. Light the candle, lad."

Martin touched the flame to the wick, and the candle flared to life. Martin sat. He aligned the parchment comfortably before him, and dabbed the quill into the inkpot, careful to let the excess drop back inside before positioning his hand over the paper. The hellward candle began to smoke, its acrid plume drifting out through the open window. Abel Cobb retreated a step, covering his nose with his sleeve. A trickle of melted wax began to drip down one side of the candle.

Martin closed his eyes—it was important to establish a sympathetic blindness with the monk—and spoke. "My name is Martin Dunwood, of the Candlelight Society. I request an exchange with the Order of the Black Iron, according to the protocols of the Coventry Accord."

The effect was immediate. A trapdoor opened in his mind and Martin seemed to drop out of his own head, plummeting down a dark tunnel with terrifying speed. Though he was bodiless, the terror of impact was quite real, and he found himself reaching with arms he no longer possessed to grab for purchase on a wall that did not exist.

Horror consumed him. He suddenly believed that his worship of Satan had been a terrible mistake; that every promise offered to the Society, to the Buried Church, to any of a thousand practitioners of obeisance, had been a lie. All had been fooled, all were destined to be swallowed into this endless black gullet. His little soul was nothing more than a crumb of the great human feast for the Burning Prince. Martin wanted to scream, but there was nothing left of him to do it.

The Black Iron Monks take a vow of darkness upon entering the order. Of all the people existing on Hell's borders, they alone cross into the final country. Upon taking the vow their heads are fitted with black iron boxes, which they wear until death. They experience no need for sustenance, no need for air. The boxes allow them to pass into Hell unaffected by its influence. Each passage into its territory is a pilgrimage; some monks go in solitude, though most go in a linked procession, guided by a native beast. The monks are the cartographers of Hell; all excursions are, in the end, illuminations.

Martin felt the closeness of the iron box around his head. He smelled the stink of flesh long unwashed, of a mouth filled with teeth left to rot. He existed as little more than a ghost in the monk's consciousness. Whatever epiphany he experienced moments ago was forgotten in the exultation of success. He was here, in the Black Iron Monastery. What he wouldn't give for the monk to remove his iron cage, so that Martin might see the interior: the maps and charts that he imagined must hang from the walls like illustrated curtains, the walls made of stone dug from Hell's earth, the quality of light that came not from the sun but from Satan's burning hide, unknown leagues away.

He felt a wordless pulse of thought: not so much a welcome as an acknowledgment of his presence. It was disorienting, and he was briefly overcome with nausea. The monk's mind recoiled, followed by another pulse, this one a mixture of surprise and curiosity.

Of course. He had been expecting Mr. Benson. Martin could not keep the memory of what he had done out of his mind, and it spilled across the Black Iron Monk's thoughts like flaming oil: the deception at the table, the poisoned brandy, the members of the Society expiring in puddles of their own blood.

Betrayed by his inexperience, Martin quailed. He had not meant to share that information. He feared that the monk would cast him out, dooming their expedition. But the

ancient agreement between the Candlelight Society and the
Black Iron Monastery superseded whatever crime he'd committed. He'd performed the ritual properly, and so the monk
had no choice but to honor it.

Degrees of latitude and longitude seared into Martin's
mind like hot iron pressed into flesh. It was the place they
would retrieve the monk from the Dark Water. Martin's hand
scrawled the coordinates onto the parchment, untethered
from conscious thought.

And then another pulse: a demand. The price that would
balance their equation. This time Martin received it as words, a
sentence built by a being far removed from the use of language.

**Tell me about sunlight.**

The yearning in the monk's voice filled Martin with a kind
of sadness he could understand: the wanting for warmth, the
ache of skin waiting for the touch of a kind hand. The need
to fill a hole that only grew deeper. Martin filled the monk's
mind with a vision of sunrise over a field of barley, the air
bright with drifting motes. It was summertime. Birds kept a
quiet chatter. A girl was there, who smiled when she saw him.
It hurt in the most beautiful way.

The hellward candle guttered out, plunging the room into
darkness. Martin slumped onto the table, his fingers grasping weakly against the wood, tears gathered in his eyes. Abel
Cobb took him by the shoulders and pushed him upright.
"You're all right then, Mr. Dunwood, you're all right."

Martin stared at the coordinates he'd written on the parchment, and then lifted his gaze to Alice. "I did it," he said. "I
did it."

Captain Toussaint opened the door and called down the
hall. "Mr. Johns! It is time."

~ ~ ~

The sea grew increasingly restive. *Butcher's Table* and the *Puritan* bobbed over the waves. Heavy clouds blotted out the moon and the stars, and the ships looked like floating chandeliers in all that darkness.

The crate had been brought onto the main deck. Mr. Johns and a contingent of deckhands positioned themselves around it, hooks and spikes held in defensive postures like medieval instruments, while Hu Chaoxiang and Randall Major watched from a modest distance. Mr. Hu and Mr. Johns had sailed with Captain Toussaint for years; they had served with him under Captain Tegel's command and had previous experience with a lotushead. To the rest, it was a new experience. Fear buzzed around them like a cloud of flies.

A tattooed, shirtless man pried off the lid and leapt back, swiping the air in front of him with a hook, as though an African jungle cat had launched for his throat. In fact nothing emerged from the crate, and the others laughed cautiously at his performance. Chastened, he approached again, wedging iron into a corner and leveraging it free. Twice more and two sides fell away. The lotushead slumped like a huge dead plant on the deck. Its trunk looked like an old man's flesh, gathered and bunched at its base. Its tapered neck sagged into itself, the glistening bundle of tongues that crowned it limp and gray. A light rain began to mist, dappling its flesh with beads that reflected gold in the lantern light.

"It's dead," the sailor said, looking back at Mr. Hu with something like hope.

"It ain't," said Mr. Johns. "Stop your ears, boys." He removed the wax plugs from his pocket and stuffed them into his ears, while around him the others did the same. The dull roar of the ocean became a distant hiss. The light patter of rain on the deck faded away, becoming only a cold sensation on his skin. Once this was done, he addressed the man who'd opened the crate. "You've got to coax it, lad. Give it a poke." He could not be heard, but he illustrated his meaning with a gesture toward the creature.

With a few shouts of encouragement, the sailor approached the lotushead again. He extended the hook slowly toward its bunched flesh; in the last moment, with a flash of courage, he lunged forward and pricked the beast's skin with the point of the hook. He leapt back into the fold of the other men, and this time no one laughed.

Muscle rippled along the length of the creature, and with a shiver of life it inflated to its full height, nearly six feet. Its body looked like an amalgamation of plant and animal, as though the stalk of some jungle growth was comprised of thick joints and rolled meat, with no thought to structure or function. Its cluster of tongues, only moments before hanging in a sagging wreath around its apex, began to writhe. The sailors stepped well back from it, apprehension plain on their faces.

Only Mr. Johns stayed his ground. He cast a glance at Mr. Hu, who nodded his assent. "Make it sing, Mr. Johns!" he cried, and the old man moved to obey. He extended his hand, and someone placed a meat cleaver into it. He stepped closer with a nervous twinge in his blood.

The squealing sound of wood being torn and splintered filled his senses; a moment afterward came the screams, and then the bucking of the deck beneath him as the ocean surged in a mighty wave. Mr. Johns fell to the deck, his senses disoriented. The cleaver slid away from him, toward silent lotushead.

"What the devil—"

He turned to see the *Puritan*—barely discernible in the

rainy night though not a hundred yards distant—keeling to port, its masts forty-five degrees to the ocean's pitching surface. Something seemed caught in its rigging, as though it had flown there, and it took Mr. Johns a long moment to make sense of it in the light of swinging lanterns.

It was a squid, a deep-sea monstrosity with tentacles nearly as long as the ship itself, and it was inverted in the sky. Its arms pulled the sails from their masts, yanked yardarms free of their moorings. People slid from the deck and into the churning water. The squid hovered in the air, its skin split lengthwise, revealing the white flesh of its interior, as though something within itself did not fit. Ragged black feathers jutted from the wounds. Its tentacles splayed in the air around it, a corona of horrors. Its glaring eyes smoked in the beating rain.

"Holy mother of God," said Mr. Johns. It was a carrion angel. Mr. Johns pissed down his own leg.

"Mr. Johns! Now! Do it now!" It was Mr. Hu, holding on to the railing. His voice carried through the screaming din, through the wax plugs in his ears, and recalled the old sailor to his duty. He found the cleaver on the deck and crawled toward it. The carrion angel was here for the lotushead; it would tear through the *Puritan* like a flimsy box and then move on to *Butcher's Table*, where it would devour the lotushead while every soul aboard sank to the cold bottom.

Mr. Johns grabbed the cleaver and staggered toward the creature. The deck lurched beneath him and he fought to keep his footing. A hand gripped his shoulder from behind, and Randall Major shouted into his ear. "No! Not yet! We have to save them!"

Mr. Major had come from the *Puritan*, and he knew its people. Sentimentality drove him to madness.

"They're dead already!" Mr. Johns shouted. He jerked his

shoulder free and swung the cleaver with his full might into the lotushead's flesh. The creature bucked, knocking Mr. Johns backward. A sound emitted from somewhere beneath the mass of tongues, staining the air like blood seeping into cloth. The creature's tongues stirred, wriggled, flailed. In tandem they articulated the seventeen dialects of Hell, they intoned the Bleeding Harmonic, they recited the cant of the Angelic Brutalities.

Randall Major raged in protest. He threw Mr. Johns to the deck, knocking the wax plug from his right ear. Mr. Johns's fingers scrambled to find it. His hand shook, tears filled his one good eye. He'd turned his back to a man caught in the grip of madness; he cursed himself for his beginner's mistake. The voices filled the sky, occluding every other sound. Mr. Johns turned his face away from the milling tongues, but the language poured into his ear like boiling oil. Mr. Johns died in a paroxysm of joy, his eyes pouring out of his head in pale, heavy streams.

Around him, a quiet descended over the crew. The lotus-head's speech stuttered into silence. The sea beneath them was black and calm, the sky cloudless and spangled with red stars. Whatever grave the *Puritan* had sunk to existed in a place unreachable to them now. *Butcher's Table* had crossed into the Dark Water.

# 4. The Darling of the Abattoir

Alice remembered the first time she'd taken Martin to the Buried Church beneath London. There were seven in the world, each a small series of chambers hacked from the raw earth, connected by tunnels and lit only with torches, if they were lit at all. Here they raised their human cattle—some stolen from cradles, some purchased in the smoky rooms of state power, some bred in the dark for their fates. These latter were the most desirable, with eyes and flesh unstained by sunlight. She had guided Martin through the pens, and he had been struck mute by the sight of them shivering in their cages. A few stared into the light with a terrible, manic look; but most turned away, as though from something holy.

The experience cowed him, as she'd known it would. Members of the Church had always been disdainful of the Candlelight Society, figuring them for little more than dandies playing at worship by swapping tales in front of polite fires in polite hearths. Alice always assumed they were something more than that—she was not susceptible to her father's prejudices—but no matter how serious they were in their devotions, the brute reality of the Church practice made everyone quail.

"How can you do it?" Martin asked, kneeling beside one of the cages and staring at the boy inside, no more than fifteen years old. The boy was one of those who stared back, though he did it from the far side of his cage. His mouth moved, as though he wanted to speak but couldn't remember how.

"Because we love them, and we love our Prince."

Martin shook his head. "They're people, Alice. They're people like you and me."

Alice knelt beside him. "Precisely so. We're slabs of meat for Satan's plate, waiting to be laid open by the stroke of His knife. We bleed onto His plate, ride gratefully upon the fork into His mouth. We are split between His teeth."

Martin stared at her, the torchlight turning his eyes incandescent.

"There is no greater expression of love for our Lord than to devour the human animal. To be the one devoured is to be the vessel of that most beautiful expression."

She could see him struggle with this. He wanted to align himself with her way of thinking. His love for her compelled him to.

"Let me tell you a secret," she said. She retrieved a key from a chain around her neck and slid it into the cage's lock. The boy inside watched this with rapt attention.

"What are you doing? He'll escape!"

"Not with you here to keep him subdued, surely."

The look of fear that passed over Martin's face almost made her break her composure. She touched his hand. "It was a joke. Forgive me." She opened the lock and swung the cage door wide. The boy hesitated, then approached, keeping low to the floor. Almost crawling. "The secret," Alice said, "is that my father can barely stomach the taste. He prefers to have his portion cooked."

Martin could not understand, of course, but that hardly mattered. What it meant was that her father's faith was weak. He had become drunk on his position in the church, and his ambitions were about power, not service. Sometimes she dreamed of informing the congregation that the Cannibal Priest himself was a fraud, a weakling who applied fire to the meat lest his delicate palate be overwhelmed by its potency. His blasphemy both shamed and disgusted her.

The boy reached them and sat back on his haunches. He turned his eyes up to the cave's black ceiling, and the firelight played over the angles of tendon and muscle in his neck. An artery pulsed there, bearing the heart's red tide.

A cleaver hung from a hook beside the cage, and Alice took it down. "It's always best when they're willing," she said, and then she went to work.

She'd fed Martin that day with her own hands, and though they'd eaten lightly, it was enough to confirm what she'd hoped: she could love him. He could bear the weight of it.

~ ~ ~

Martin slept. Since not all of Abel Cobb's retinue had survived the sinking of the *Puritan*, the old man had allowed him to move into one of the new rooms in the hold—an improvement from his previous berth. Mr. Gully stationed himself outside. At some point early in his fitful rest, Abel Cobb pounded on the door of his quarters, enjoining him to go topside. "How can you linger down here?" shouted Cobb through the door. "We've arrived in the Dark Water! Come up with me, Mr. Dunwood. Let us see this new place."

But Martin was exhausted by his ordeal. Furthermore, he was beset by a doldrum of the spirit; here, on the brink of his greatest achievement, he wished only to hide from his fellows, to bury his head beneath his pillow and slip into a dreamless abyss. Perhaps this was a common side effect of using a hellward candle. He instructed Mr. Gully to keep the Cannibal Priest away.

And so he passed some hours that way, bobbing along the surface of sleep like a cork at sea, until the door creaked open and Fat Gully's head intruded from the hallway. "Are you awake, Mr. Dunwood?" he whispered.

"I am ill. Send him away."

"Not this time," Gully said, and he opened the door for his visitor. Alice stood in the darkened door frame. She looked like a ghost, her white gown limned in lantern light from down the hall, her face obscured by shadow.

"Alice!" Martin sat up, collecting his bedclothes about him. "Come in! Hurry! What if you're seen?"

Alice stepped inside, and Gully closed the door behind her, remaining outside the room himself.

"Do you think I'm a fool?" she asked. With the door closed he could barely tease out her shape in the darkness. He felt her sit beside him on his mattress. He leaned over and lit a candle beside the bed, providing them with a little island of light.

"Of course not."

"It's been hours," she said. "They've drunken themselves to collapse. They imagine they've done a great thing, and they're celebrating."

"Haven't they done a great thing? Haven't we all?" Martin was still tired, but he felt a twinge of apprehension at Alice's choice of words.

"We've only crossed the border. Others have done so before. Greatness, if we're going to find it, will be found in Lotus Cove."

That might be true, but it made him impatient to hear it. He was the first member of the Candlelight Society in generations to cross into the Dark Water. Surely some acknowledgment had been earned.

Perhaps he would just take it for himself. He took her by her shoulder and pulled her near, for a kiss. She allowed herself to be drawn closer, but resisted the final inch by buttressing her arm against the mattress. A few loose strands of her hair tickled his cheek. The smell of perfume filled his nostrils, and with it came the memory of the last time he had seen her—her body glazed with someone else's blood. He leaned toward her, but she stopped him with a finger to his chin.

"Not yet," she said.

"But why? Alice, it's been a year. Do not hurt me like this."

"You know why. If we're discovered, you'll be executed. Your part in this is done. It's only the strength of the contract that keeps you alive now."

"You forget. I have Mr. Gully to protect me."

She smiled at that. "Mr. Gully has his own purpose here, Martin. And it isn't protecting you."

Martin sat up, forgetting his desire. "What do you mean?" He recalled their secret conversation on the deck with apprehension. "What did you two talk about?"

"That is my business, and his."

"What? How can you say that to me? We're about to be married!"

"What does that have to do with it?"

"Well . . . you should obey your husband." He tried to present it as a joke, but he didn't really mean it as one, and they both knew it.

She sat upright on the bed. "You're making some dangerous assumptions, Martin."

He tried to sound conciliatory. "I'm not, really. Only I don't understand why you're being secretive. I have a right to know."

"It has nothing to do with you," Alice said. "I know you find that shocking." She leaned over him and graced him with a kiss. Just a small one; she withdrew before he could open his lips.

"Very well. I trust you, Alice."

"Do you now. We sail ever closer to Hell. It is not a place for generous inclinations."

Emboldened by this—as though she had issued a challenge—Martin fell back on the bed again, gripping her arm and yanking her down with him. His other hand snaked into her hair, pulling it loose from its stays so that it spilled in a bright tide from her shoulders. "Stay. I want you right now. I want them to think it is Satan Himself rutting in the hold, splitting the goats apart with His lust."

Alice pushed his head back, baring his throat. She took his chin between her teeth and bit gently. "I know what you want." She extracted herself from his grasp and stood up. She took a moment to fix her hair as it had been. She turned to leave, paused, and gave him a small smile. "When we're finished, there will be no more rules." She leaned down and blew out the candle.

Martin wiped the sweat from his face, breathed deeply to slow the blood in his veins. She stood so close. A black pillar etched in the faint red light creeping in around the closed door, where Mr. Gully stood guard outside. They were surrounded by threat, by coiled violence, and by the possibility of extravagant fortune. He felt as though he rode on the crest of a towering wave. He felt like a usurper, like a new and terrible king.

"I think this is how the Burning Prince Himself must have felt," he said. "Before His grand rebellion."

Though he could not see her face in the darkness, he saw the shape of it change; he thought it must be a smile. Then she opened the door and disappeared down the corridor.

Mr. Gully watched her go, then leered in at him. "Everything all right then, Mr. Dunwood?"

"Shut the door," said Martin.

Mr. Gully did so with a chuckle. Martin consoled himself with images of the little man bleeding to death at his feet.

Rufus Gully waited until he could hear the snores issuing from Martin Dunwood's room before he crept down the hallway. He felt a twinge of apprehension; he did not like leaving Mr. Dunwood unguarded. Now that his part had been completed, the rich fool was vulnerable to the murderous whims of the others. Civility may hold them in check—even the pirate seemed beholden to it—but Gully knew thieves. They did not like to share.

And yet. Miss Cobb had instructed him, and he was no

stranger to his own heart. If Mr. Dunwood must be left unguarded in the wolves' den so that he could meet with her, then so be it.

Mr. Gully glanced into the main body of the hold. The light of a hanging lantern illuminated the stacked crates, the stores swinging in their netting, the mounds of burlap sacks. Goats and chickens were penned on the far side, and though he could not see them, their stink was overwhelming. He turned in the opposite direction and made his way down the corridor, between the new rooms built for the Cobbs. The ship pitched on a rough sea, and he lurched into a wall, barking his elbow. He cursed life on a ship, remembering fondly the London docks. If anything, life there was even more precarious, but at least the ground didn't leap under your feet.

"Mr. Gully." Miss Cobb's quiet voice, somewhere ahead. "You lumber like a gorilla. Come, you're almost here."

He pressed on into the dark and found her, waiting patiently by the locked door at the very back of the ship. He waited until his eyes acclimated enough that he could read her face, and then he whispered a quiet greeting.

Miss Cobb unlocked the door, ushering him in ahead of her. Not until she secured the door shut did she light a match, touching it to the wick of a small candle. The light flared and there in the corner cowered Thomas Thickett, naked now, shaved hairless as a salamander. He recoiled from the light, curling into a fetal position. He wrapped his arms around his head. Goose bumps peppered his skin.

"This is the Feast," said Miss Cobb.

Mr. Gully knelt beside the shivering man. He wanted to touch him but was afraid. He glanced up at the lady, the candlelight highlighting her pale skin and her red hair, and he felt the shudder of a complicated emotion. He became suddenly aware of his own ugliness: his squat, toadlike frame, the unappealing arrangement of his face. Alice Cobb was beautiful, as though she had just stepped out of a sonnet. Even Thickett was an expression of beauty: a vessel of Satanic love. The stink of his fear was gravy to the meat.

"Our presence here is a transgression," she said. "He is not meant to be seen again until he is brought to the table."

Gully did not understand. He felt he was in the presence of something holy, and his very proximity was spoiling it. "I've made a mistake. I'm sorry. I don't belong here."

Miss Cobb said, "You belong, Rufus."

Mr. Gully started at the sound of his Christian name. He had not heard it spoken aloud, especially by a woman, in a long time. It was always Fat Gully at the docks, Mr. Gully to his employers, or coarser names than those. He became freshly conscious of his position here, crouched in folded shadows with a beautiful woman and a beautiful man, the spare golden light of a candle giving them form, and he the lone wretch. The flaw in the art. "Why, Miss Cobb?" His voice cracked. "I'm ugly. I'm stupid. Why did you bring me here? Why did you listen to me?"

"Because all your miserable life, no one has ever loved you. Because yes, you *are* ugly, and you're mean, and you're lonely. I knew you for who you were the moment I saw you. Are you a Satanist, Rufus?"

"I've never given religion much thought, miss."

"You should be. Love is Hell's breath. You crave it. Your whole soul shakes with it. *You* are suitable for the Prince, Rufus. Not this coward." She looked at Thickett, shivering naked on the floor. "He runs from the honor. He's perfectly suited to my father's weak palate. There's nothing left of him but fear." She prodded him with her toe. "I'm almost sorry for you, Mr. Thickett. You won't even get that, now. Your whole life was wasted."

"Please." It was Thickett, wrapping a hand around Mr. Gully's ankle. Blood ran from his nose and dribbled down his chin.

Gully extracted his foot and knelt beside him. "What is it you want then, aye?"

Thickett's hands continued to grasp for him, one on his knee, the other reaching for his hand. "Get me out."

"I'll just let you go then, shall I? And what of Miss Cobb?"

"Kill her. Kill her right now. Please."

"That's not very charitable."

"You don't know what she is."

"No? What is she?"

Thickett swallowed. His eyes fixed on Gully in a mad, hopeful stare. Did he sense some distant possibility here? He clutched Gully's sleeve. "She's a monster. They're all monsters."

"All of them!"

"Yes!" Thickett waited for some action. When it didn't come, he began to understand that Gully was toying with him. Watching his small hope crumble was a remarkable experience. "Don't kill her then. Don't kill anyone if you don't want to. Just open the door and I'll run. I'll swim for shore. I'll swim for it. I don't care if I drown. I just don't want this."

Gully slapped his hand away. He grabbed Thickett's lower jaw and squeezed, turning his head to the side. "Don't *want* it? You thankless shit. You don't *deserve* it."

He slipped his knife from its sheath and pressed it against the artery in Thickett's neck. Miss Cobb stopped him with a light hand on his shoulder.

"Not yet, Rufus."

Gully withdrew the knife with some difficulty. The

contempt he felt for this cowardly little man almost over-whelmed his better instincts. Thickett didn't even put up a fight. He just slumped back to the floor, curling into himself again. He shivered with cold or with fear.

Miss Cobb leaned closer to Gully from behind, her lips close enough to his ear that when she spoke it tickled his hair and stopped his breath. "Love must be earned, Rufus. With restraint, and with silence. Wait until the Feast. Do it when they have no choice but to turn to you instead. And then it will be your turn, Rufus. Your turn in the light, at last."

Gully wiped a tear from his cheek.

*You're out there somewhere*, Toussaint thought. He scanned the horizon, obscured by darkness and a pitching sea. The sky and its pinwheeling stars provided no light.

Captain Toussaint, Mr. Hu, and Mr. Johns had been to the Dark Water once before. Six years ago, when he was simply Beverly Toussaint, first mate to Captain Tegel, who commanded *Butcher's Table* with vicious and bloody effi-ciency. They had found a lotushead on an English merchant vessel they'd captured off the Carolina coast. A member of the Church of England had custody, and he was quick to sur-render his secrets when Captain Tegel displayed for him all his various instruments of persuasion, glinting in the hot sun. Upon learning what he wanted, Tegel had the man flayed anyway, as a rebuke against the God he represented. "Let us see how much of your blood I have to spill before He decides to make Himself known to me."

In fact he spilled all of it, and God remained absent.

Captain Tegel commanded Mr. Johns to hack into the lotushead's flesh, provoking the strange cries that opened the way from the Atlantic Ocean to the Dark Water. From there they sailed to Hell's coastline, and it was there that Beverly Toussaint first laid eyes on the galleons of the Black Law, enforcers of the infernal order. It was there that he learned of the secret commerce that transpired between Hell and his own world, right under the Black Law's nose.

Captain Tegel had found a place where he could unleash his cruelest aspect and be celebrated for it. He decided to stay behind, breaking Mr. Toussaint's heart. Toussaint feared he would never hear of him again, but over the years word began to trickle back to him: of the captain who commanded the brigantine *Angel's Teeth*, carving a cruel path through the dark sea; of the captain who left ships burning in his wake, whether pirates or vessels of the Black Law; of the captain who garlanded the rigging of his own vessel with the bones of his enemies, so that others told stories of hearing their clatter carried on the night wind, signaling his passage. Toussaint knew that his old lover was flourishing.

And unlike these men muttering stories under lamps of whale oil, he knew Tegel's true purpose, one they had agreed to share all those years ago: smuggling the Damned out of Hell and back into the world. Toussaint because he would spit in the eye of any god or devil that tolerated the enslavement of human beings; Tegel because he wished only to usurp the order of things. Any order at all.

And now Beverly Toussaint was a captain himself, and he stood at the prow of his ship to honor the contract he'd made with the man he loved.

He heard a familiar tread approaching from behind.

"I'm sorry, Mr. Hu," he said, without turning around. "I know you and Mr. Johns were close."

Mr. Hu leaned onto the railing beside him. He did not speak for a long moment, watching the dark horizon instead, where lightning bellied the clouds. "Well," he said. "It was the Virginian."

Captain Toussaint looked at him. "What do you mean?"

"The one called Major. He got in Johns's way, tripped him up. Wouldn't have happened otherwise."

Captain Toussaint took a moment to absorb the information. "What did you do about it?"

"Nothing. You know me better than that. We have a job to do."

He nodded. "I'm grateful for your restraint. You'll have your chance later."

"With respect, Captain, I don't need your permission for that."

"No. I understand." Mr. Hu and Mr. Johns had a long and complicated history, and the captain did not presume his own authority could outweigh it. Mr. Hu would handle the Virginian as he saw fit, and that was the end of it. "What about the lotushead?"

"Secured again, for the trip home." The return trip would likely kill the creature; they were notoriously fragile.

"And our friend Mr. Dunwood?"

"He's below, in the new accommodations. He and the priest are sleeping on soft beds tonight. Soft beds for soft men. I look forward to seeing the end of them."

"Soon, Mr. Hu. Very soon."

Mr. Hu shifted, and there was a hitch in his breath. Captain Toussaint observed him from the corner of his eye. "Say it," he said.

Mr. Hu deliberated for a moment. "Has it occurred to you that he will be different?"

He was talking about Tegel. Toussaint turned to face him. "Different," he said.

"Yes. He's been here *six years*. The whole atmosphere on this ship has turned sour just by the presence of that gang of Satanists we're carrying. What happens to a man who's chosen to live here?"

"You pick an interesting time to voice your concern, Mr. Hu."

Hu Chaoxiang put his hands on the railing and looked at them when he spoke. "I wouldn't have. But Johns was apprehensive too. He didn't want to do this. Now he's dead, so I have to say it."

His first mate was practical and efficient; in that way he reminded Captain Toussaint of Tegel. And he was a killer, too, but unlike their old captain he was always cool in the act. He possessed an admirable self-control, an ability to separate himself from the red moment with a thoroughness that had preserved his life many times. And so his nervousness now was almost charming.

Almost.

"Yes, Mr. Hu. It has occurred to me that he will be different."

Mr. Hu was still. After a moment, he nodded.

"Do you still have the stomach for this?"

"Yes, Captain. Yes, I do."

"Good." He slapped his old friend on the shoulder. "Put some fresh eyes in the crow's nest. We have to be sharp, now."

Mr. Hu turned and went about his task. Captain Toussaint returned his gaze to the strange sea, still looking for a glimpse of his heart's object, ringing with bone chimes and flying a black flag.

At the coordinates provided by the Black Iron Monk, the rounded head of a giant protruded from the pitching sea, its skin as black as an inkpot, its pale white eyes irisless and blind. The lower half of its face remained beneath the waves. Martin stood beside Captain Toussaint at the prow of the ship, the questing tendrils of an oncoming storm whipping them with wind and rain. He stared at the vast creature through the captain's spyglass. The surge of waves made fixing the beast with the glass a difficult prospect, but it was large enough that at no time did it leave his vision. Martin's heart thrilled at the reality of the experience. Communicating with the monk through the hellward candle was one thing, but here was a creature of Hell in the flesh, in service to the Order of the Black Iron, which was in turn—for the moment—in service to him.

*. . . I think this is how the Burning Prince Himself must have felt. . . .*

Captain Toussaint said, "By God, is that him?"

Martin smiled. "No indeed. It is the vessel by which he arrives."

That seemed to be good enough for the captain. His voice boomed: "Drop the launch! Smartly now!"

The launch boat struggled through the waves toward the giant, six men heaving at the oars to the very limits of their strength, Mr. Hu perched at its prow, a coil of rope wound about his right arm. If any of them were afraid of the great beast, Martin could not tell.

The launch boat pulled up a dozen yards short of the giant. Mr. Hu stared at the monster, rocking with each pitch of the boat with all the ease of a man standing on solid English earth. After a moment, the head lifted out of the sea, runnels of water streaming like a heavy rain. The water churned around it in a vast radius, encompassing both the launch boat and even *Butcher's Table* itself, its decks thronged with spectators.

Jet-black tentacles rippled along the surface of the waters, propelling the head closer to the launch. It opened its mouth to reveal a red tongue, which it extruded toward the boat, and upon which stood the Black Iron Monk, standing as still as a pillar, his black robes fluttering about him. A black iron box encased his head: the physical manifestation of the order's Vow of Darkness, and the device that protected them during their sojourns through Hell.

Mr. Hu had no need of his rope. The beast's tongue touched the tip of the launch with delicacy, and the monk stepped into Mr. Hu's grasp like a gentleman alighting from a carriage. The launch returned to the ship as the beast slipped beneath the waves again.

Once on deck, the Black Iron Monk was left to Martin's care. He reeked of Hell: char and smoke and, underneath it, something delicately sweet. Martin guided the figure belowdecks to the first mate's quarters, which he'd recently vacated. Since Mr. Johns had met his end, the room had been deemed unlucky, and no one had moved in to take his place.

It seemed a ridiculous setup. The monk was a figure of awe, even terror: someone who had actually passed across the border into Hell's radiant fields and recorded what he witnessed there, in whatever way the monks could witness a place. He was practically a figure of mythology to Satanists the world over, and now Martin had brought him to a small, cramped room, where he must sit on a box or swing on a hammock like any normal fool.

"Forgive me," Martin said, not even sure the monk could hear him from inside his iron box. "The accommodations are rough. We are ill prepared for someone of your standing."

The monk gave no reaction. He simply stood in the center of the room, unconcerned with the furnishings. Martin had the unnerving thought that he was like a broom that had been tucked back into its closet, there to remain immobile until fetched to perform his function.

A step sounded behind him, and Martin turned to see Fat Gully standing there, his expression subdued for once, a hint of wonder in his eye.

"This is him, then, aye? The man from Hell."

"Not *from* Hell. The Order of the Black Iron resides along its border. They are cartographers."

"Does he talk?"

Martin felt a flush of shame at Gully's performance of ignorance. "The monks communicate differently. Please stand outside, Mr. Gully. But do not go far. I must speak with you."

"I'm never far, Mr. Dunwood." He gave the monk another lingering glance, and retreated from the room.

Martin retrieved parchment, quill, and inkpot from a drawer. He placed them atop a box and said, "If you'll be so kind as to produce the map. As specific as you can, please. Also, the routes of the Black Law's patrol. We must not be discovered. I know you understand."

When the monk neither moved nor spoke, Martin decided that he must leave him to it and simply trust that it would be done. He left the cramped room, securing the door behind him, and found Mr. Gully waiting for him there as promised.

Gully opened his mouth to speak, but Martin silenced him by grasping his bicep and ushering him farther down the tight corridor. "When we arrive at the cove, upon my order, you will sever the monk's head from his neck. Regardless of whether the priest endorses our wedding, Miss Cobb and I will not be returning with you. The head will serve as our atlas, and we will take it together into Hell. And you will be released from your contract."

"What, you and the lady are just going to wander off into Hell together? You've lost your senses."

"Well, it is love, after all. And what would you know of that?"

When Martin revisited the monk's quarters a short while later, the parchment he'd left behind was covered with instructions and a detailed map. Martin thanked him and carried the information to Captain Toussaint, who studied it carefully. Within the hour, he had plotted their course, wending carefully through the patrol lanes of the Black Law. He was convinced he could guide them through unnoticed.

*Butcher's Table* filled its sails with wind, pushing through the rough waves and the whipping rain. Black clouds boiled overhead. Martin could no longer distinguish night from day. Alice stood by his side. She seemed happier than she was the previous night, even unconcerned that her father might notice their attachment to each other. He was curious, but he had learned long ago not to press her. She would tell him what she wanted to, when she wanted to. He was content with that.

Fat Gully hovered nearby, never out of eyesight. That his engagement with him was fast approaching its end gave Martin the will to bite back a curt dismissal. He was so tired of the little man's grotesque appearance, his sneers and his effronteries. Leaving him behind to fend for himself would be one of the greatest joys he'd ever known.

Behind them all the crew labored in eerie silence. The white sails had been taken down and black ones raised in their place. Captain Toussaint had issued an order that no man should speak aloud, all communication to be done through hand signals. Although the constant storm made it unlikely that the sound of their passage would reach the Black Law, he took nothing for granted.

Martin peered into the white foam below, conscious of the vast creature that had delivered the monk to them only hours before. He imagined whole civilizations beneath them, cities of such monsters with heads bent in contemplation of alien philosophies, engaging in wars, creating strange art. The thought both thrilled and appalled him.

Alice touched his arm, breaking his reverie, and pointed ahead. He squinted into the spitting rain, seeing nothing but the rolling waves, the spray of water, the shifting clouds. After a moment's patience, though, he saw it: land. A jagged coastline, like teeth from a jawbone, barely discernible in the turbulent air. Excited, he turned to alert the crew, only to discover that they all saw it. Men hung from the rigging, or paused on deck, and stared. Captain Toussaint, standing on the aft deck, held his spyglass to his eye. Mr. Hu stood at his side. Martin turned to look again, his heart leaping. Here was Hell's coast.

He felt a kind of fear he could only describe as ecstatic.

Alice whispered into his ear: "Soon, my love."

He took her by the waist and kissed her recklessly, heedless of the consequences for either of them. Inviting them, even. He felt that old surge of power, that kingly entitlement. This time, she did not resist him. Perhaps she was no longer afraid of her father. Perhaps she was unable to resist the magnetism he felt exuding from his bones like an elemental energy.

Let Abel Cobb come for him. Let Fat Gully, let Captain Toussaint, let them all descend upon them with knives drawn. He would christen Hell's ocean with their blood.

They sailed several leagues down the coastline. At no time did Martin see a place they might make landing; the land was jagged stone and tall cliff, the waves breaking themselves against great, toothy rocks well before the shoreline. If he did not place so much faith in the infallibility of the Order of the Black Iron, he would have begun to despair already. He could already see the doubt kindling in the eyes of the crewmen who passed him as they performed their duties. He doubted them before he doubted the map; how long would Captain Toussaint's influence keep them on task?

Mr. Gully seemed to share his apprehension. Always close, he now seemed fastened to his side like a barnacle, the hilt of his knife prominently displayed where it protruded from his belt. Alice, for her part, seemed completely untroubled. Whether in the company of himself or of her father, she expressed nothing but delight at their imminent success.

What they were seeing was not the landscape of Hell itself. That existed farther in, beyond a range of mountains that could not be crossed without protections and guidance. What they were seeing here was just borderland. Scrub. Martin understood there to be small settlements through-out, and somewhere in there, close to the mountains, was the Black Iron Monastery.

And yet, they caught glimpses of things on the shore that could have had no other provenance. A pinwheel of arms and hands, connecting in a knot of tissue bearing one staring blue eye, kept pace with them for hours, leaping in what appeared to be play, sometimes disappearing behind rocks for a mile or more, only to be spotted again as the landscape evened out; a small shack at the base of the cliff, with three charred black figures, paused in their construc-tion of a wooden pyre to fix them with a red glare as they sailed past, while something small and frightened bucked beneath the pile; a great centipede, twice the length of their ship, descended from the crags and slipped into the crashing sea, where it disappeared to join whatever horrors lived in that briny abyss.

After a time even these sights became mundane. Martin turned away from the wonders unfurling alongside him, his thoughts turning inward. He found himself thinking ahead to the crossing of the border into Hell, hand in hand with Alice, with the atlas to guide them. They would take no protections from the environment, as the monks did; they would let the atmosphere work its effects on their flesh and on their minds, transfiguring them into whatever shape or condition pleased the Burning Prince. Alice assured him that the purity of the Feast would grant them favor.

A cry came down from the crow's nest: "The cove! Lotus Cove, Captain!"

Alice rushed to the port railing, Martin following. Mr. Gully approached as well, his flat little eyes alight with wonder. Behind them, the entire crew went silent.

The rocky shore stretched on, seemingly interminable, but for a break in the line, which showed where an inlet lay hidden; Lotus Cove must be around that bend. But how, wondered Martin, could the lookout be sure? What did he see?

Alice saw his bewilderment and put her fingers on his chin, turning his head incrementally to the left. His gaze shifted, and the blood drained from his face.

Dangling over the edge of the near cliff, so large he mistook them for earthen formations, were the enormous upturned fingers of a left hand. Now that he saw them he could not fathom how he had missed them before: alabaster and smooth as stone, they might have been mistaken for a statue were it not for the damage they had taken: a pink wound, like an incision, along the meat of the thumb, from which some dark-rooted trees seemed to have sprung; and the snapped digits of the first and second fingers, the latter broken so thoroughly that splintered bone—a dingy yellow in comparison with the pale flesh—jutted into the air like cracked wood. The hand seemed luminescent against the dark flow of clouds overhead. Martin found himself short of breath. He lowered his head, closed his eyes, and concentrated on the work of his lungs.

"What is it?" said Gully, cowed with awe.

Alice said, "I daresay it is an angel's corpse, Mr. Gully."

Martin turned to look at the captain. Toussaint had trained his spyglass not at the cove, but back toward the sea, as if waiting for something to materialize behind them. Most likely he was only concerned about being discovered by the Black Law. Still, it seemed odd that his attention would be distracted at this moment.

Rounding the bend into Lotus Cove took the better part of an hour. Once the turn was made, though, they might as well have passed out of the Dark Sea and into the Caribbean again, or someplace stranger and more beautiful. The cove was large enough that it might have given shelter to a small fleet of ships the size of *Butcher's Table*, and the water here was calm, clear, and bright blue. Schools of fish flitted beneath them, and large, eel-like shapes undulated just beyond the range of vision.

Dominating everything, though, was the angel's corpse. It lay on its back, a luminous wreckage. Its head—as large as one of London's great warehouses—lay shattered and half submerged in the water, a hole in its side gaping like a cavern, large enough to sail the ship into. The rest of its body stretched on a sharp incline of earth, spread out in a mangled heap on the barren plain above. Martin tried to make out some sense of order to its body, so that he might intuit what shape the creature would have had in full flight, but it was a hopeless task. It was a tangle of broken limbs, exposed meat, and a score of torn wings.

The water proved deep quite close to the shore, enabling Captain Toussaint to maneuver *Butcher's Table* to within a few hundred feet of the angel's broken skull. He ordered launch boats dropped, and within minutes the ship was disgorging its crew and materials to the shoreline, where Abel Cobb's retinue worked quickly to assemble the banquet table. The angel's corpse was so large that there was little room to either side of it, so the site of the Feast was to be the interior of the skull.

The skull's contents had long ago spilled into the cove, leaving dry planes of bone covered by curtains of seaweed. Clusters of rooted plants grew in bunches where remnants of the brain survived, bearing pink, bulbous growths, which sagged like the heavy heads of kings. Chairs were ferried over, as well as a white tablecloth, and numerous sets of silver cutlery and dinnerware. Abel Cobb's own chef, one of the first to arrive on shore, presided over the whole business, barking orders with as terrible a mien as any Caribbean tyrant.

In the meantime Captain Toussaint sent a contingent of sailors, led by Mr. Hu, on a steep climb up the side of the angel's ruined head. By means of ropes and grapples they would achieve the creature's upturned chin, from which point they would descend into its open mouth and down its throat. There they would dig out the lotusheads, which grew in profusion in the place where the angel formed its speech. The captain had no interest in joining the Feast; his business was the harvest. And, perhaps, something else; Martin noted that he still seemed more interested in what might be coming behind them than what lay before.

Beside him, Alice had no eyes for the preparations: She

looked instead up the long slope to the vast, dry field that separated them from Hell's true country. It would be an arduous crossing—but the monk's guidance would make it possible.

# 5. The Feast

At last, the table was set.

Alice took her place at her father's right hand. Above them, the angel's curved skull blocked the sky. The bone was completely covered in hanging vines, moss, strange growths that pulsed with light, and suspended sacs gravid with ochre liquid. Animate life crawled through the foliage, hidden to the eye but emitting a low, constant susurrus. From this vantage point she could see the bright blue water of the cove, so unexpected in this setting, and *Butcher's Table* anchored in the distance. Randall Major had taken a launch to fetch Thomas Thickett to the dinner plate and should be returning any moment.

The table was laden with food. Cobb's chef had toiled mightily in Grimsley's kitchen, preparing a modest but worthy repast—better, in any case, than anything they'd eaten since leaving the colonies nearly a week ago. Roast pheasant, carrots and onions, and blood pudding crowded the table, along with boats of gravy and carafes of red wine, situated in such a way that a large oval of space was left free in the middle.

Martin sat across from her, to her father's left. Beside him, though of course he would not be dining, sat the Black Iron Monk, inscrutable in his stillness. On her right were the only two other members of the Buried Church to survive the sinking of the *Puritan*—typical church functionaries, as uninteresting to her as roaches haunting an alleyway. Mr. Gully sat on a rock some distance away; her father would not welcome a man like him to this table.

One seat remained empty, positioned directly opposite Abel Cobb. It was reserved for Satan Himself.

Alice watched the sea for the return of the launch. Soon enough, she saw it. Mr. Major worked the oars, bringing Thomas Thickett to the table.

Captain Toussaint watched Mr. Hu and the others descend into the angel's open mouth, the small team provisioned with rope and leather, knives tied to their waists or clenched in their teeth. They would return with half a dozen lotus-heads, and no more. The rest of the hold was reserved for the Damned.

Once they were out of sight, he turned his spyglass back out over the cove, where it opened into the ocean. A chiming carried softly over the water—the hollow music of bones knocking into each other as *Angel's Teeth* heaved across the waves. Beverly Toussaint stared into the white mist beyond the cove's lip, waiting for the ship to materialize. He felt the working of his heart in his chest, could feel it too in the pulse in his fingers, each heartbeat a jostle against the spyglass, a shuddering of the world it contained. When the ship parted the fog, he exclaimed quietly to himself. It was as he had been told: Skeletons hung from the rigging, separated bones suspended from ropes and masts, clacking into one another in the ship's steady motion. An ornate chair, fit for an island governor, had been affixed to the bowsprit, and the skeletal remains of some fallen regent reposed there. Antlers grew from its sagging head, and seaweed draped its body like a vestment. Standing at the bow was the outline of a man. He could not discern its features with any clarity, but he knew the shape of Josiah Tegel as well as he knew his own.

He felt that old bruise in his heart.

When he barked his order, though, his voice carried all the usual power. "Prepare to receive them, boys!" he said. "Smartly! Smartly!"

Another voice came down from the crow's nest. "A ship, Captain!"

Toussaint stared up into the rigging, trying to catch sight of the idiot. "I can see it, you damn oaf! What's your name?"

"Not *Angel's Teeth*, Captain! To larboard! Look!"

A chill washed over him. Captain Toussaint did look, his spyglass pressed to his eye again.

Another ship pushed through the mists, about a mile out. Sails and hull so dark that the eye wanted to slide right off them, as though it were only the night coming. But it wasn't the night; it was the Black Law. They had been discovered.

Abel Cobb struck a fork against his wineglass, summoning the company's attention. Thomas Thickett lay on the table between them, breathing shallowly, his eyes unfocused and wandering. Blood trickled from his nose: an aesthetic blemish to the proceedings, which Martin fixated upon, to his lingering discomfort. It seemed a teasing glimpse of what would shortly fill their plates, like a bead of fat perched upon a boar's roasted carcass. Martin's stomach rolled over sluggishly, and he wrenched his gaze away from it, fixing it onto his folded hands instead.

"My friends," said Cobb, "whether you are members of the Buried Church or honored guests"—here he nodded once at Martin and once at the Black Iron Monk, standing a small distance away, like some terrible obelisk—"you have the privilege of sitting at the table of the most significant Feast in our history. Tonight, we dine at the lip of Hell. Tonight we honor the Burning Prince with living flesh, and invite Him to join us at the table."

He looked at the empty chair across from his own position: carved of black wood, a single staring eye painted red at the peak of the chair back. Before this chair a table setting, cutlery polished and ready for use. Thickett's head lay nearest this setting, in an inversion of the typical arrangement. The Cannibal Priest surrendered the honor of the skull's sweet morsel to the true head of the table, should He arrive. It was Cobb's hope that the Prince would be there to crack it open himself.

"At this table, we honor the rutting goat, the feasting worm, and the ache of unanswered yearning. We honor the bruise in the heart. To honor Satan is to honor love itself," said Cobb, and he gestured to Alice. "If you would, please, Daughter."

Martin watched the woman he loved rise from her chair and take a long, slender carving knife from the table. She placed its tip near Thomas Thickett's left shoulder. She pressed the blade down and drew an incision to the midpoint of his chest. Thickett shrieked, and blood spilled in a sheet. Martin fought the urge to put a hand over his eyes. Alice repeated the gesture from the right shoulder. Once the two incisions met, she carved a new line from their meeting point down to his groin. Blood ran in a heavy tide, flowing onto the table and running off the edges. Thickett's scream filled the hollow of the angel's skull.

A gunshot cut it short. Martin's ears rang with it. A warmth spread over his body and he looked down to see that Thickett's brains had splashed across the table and the guests, all his red fears sliding onto the soft earth.

Mr. Gully stood some distance away, a flintlock pistol smoking in his hand. He stared at the table with an expression of dismay or wonder, like a child might wear. He said something that made no sense to Martin—"I done it, miss! I done it!"—but all his attention was focused on Thickett, who was still alive despite his fatal wound, writhing in mute agony between the dinner plates.

A wind blew in from across the plain, hot and sand-ridden. It slipped into a fissure in the angel's corpse and through its cavities until it funneled through the angel's throat, shivering its old vocal cords. Hu Chaoxiang and his small company, suspended on rope ladders and hacking lotusheads from their bases, froze in place as the sound of it carried over them. It passed through them like a razor, and each man wiped a trickle of blood from an ear or a nostril. The sound shaved little memories away, slivers of themselves they would never recover nor even miss.

And then the sound of a single cannon shot reached them. Captain Toussaint's signal: The Black Law was coming.

Mr. Hu shouted orders, but they were unnecessary. The men were already hoisting themselves to the angel's lip, leaving several lotusheads hanging by fibrous threads. They would take what they had. It would have to be enough.

A wooden plank dropped between the two ships, and the Damned began to cross from *Angel's Teeth* to *Butcher's Table*. They did not look like men anymore. Rather they looked like gross imitations, clay roughly shaped. Their skin was gray and soft, and it hung from their faces like wet laundry. They shuffled slowly. Captain Toussaint resisted an impulse to hurry them; they were beyond any human directive. They were cattle now, and the captain just another human trafficker. The irony was not lost on him.

But he was no cannibal, and he was no slaver.

Once on board they were directed into the hold by the

crewmen. They offered no resistance, nor even acknowledgment. Toussaint hoped that they would remember their lives once they returned to the world; but perhaps they would never be more than living corpses, staring into the sun with pale, Hell-haunted eyes.

But he had more concerns than only the Damned.

Behind them stood Josiah Tegel. He still wore his old brown greatcoat, now frayed and scorched; his long beard had turned white as the moon. Whatever chaotic impulse had driven him near to madness in life served him well here. He seemed almost incandescent with power. He was a creature of the Dark Water now, and it made him magnificent.

Tegel spoke to him, and though they were separated by hundreds of feet and the clamor of the crews preparing for the Black Law's arrival, Toussaint heard him as clearly as if he had whispered in his ear. "Come with me, Beverly."

Perhaps he would. Perhaps, when this was finished, he would allow himself what he wanted.

Captain Toussaint turned his eye to the approaching ship. It seemed to move with an impossible speed. He swiveled his gaze to the angel, where his men were emerging from its mouth, securing what they were able to gather. They moved so slowly, and the Black Law was so fast.

"Ready the guns," he said.

The sound of Alice's laughter snapped Martin from his stupor. Thomas Thickett was staring at her. The bullet from Mr. Gully's shot had passed through the top of his skull and into his brain, and now he leaked jelly onto the table. He still lived. Martin rose from his seat, suddenly conscious of the red scramble on his shirt. He brushed at it, as though he might flick it away with a napkin.

"Alice, what's happening?" he said. She looked at him, and he saw pure delight. Whatever this was, she had orchestrated it. Why hadn't she told him?

Mr. Gully let the pistol fall from his hand. "I'm ready, Miss Cobb." He began to tug at the laces of his shirt.

Abel Cobb left his place at the table's head, dazed, and started toward Mr. Gully. His arms were extended, his hands prepared to accept Gully's throat into their possession. Alice interceded, the carving knife extending from her hand like a talon. She opened a seam beneath his great belly in a quick, confident motion. Cobb gasped, clutching her arms. "Alice," he said. The weight of his spilling guts pulled him to his knees.

Martin reeled. He grasped the edge of the table to steady himself. Behind him, Randall Major stood transfixed where he had been stationed, either as shocked as Martin himself, or—more likely, he realized—loyal to Alice, and already privy to her intentions.

"But the Feast," Cobb said weakly, gathering his innards into his arms as they slipped out of himself. He started to weep. "My Feast."

"There it is, in your hands," she said. "Eat it, or starve."

It dawned on Martin that the greatest obstacle to their plan had just been dispatched. He looked toward the shore. In the cove, *Butcher's Table* was receiving human cargo from a second ship. Smoke curled from one of its starboard guns, aimed harmlessly over the dead angel. A signal shot had been fired. As if on cue, Mr. Hu and several crewmen hustled toward it farther down the beach, hurriedly dragging a collection of bound lotusheads behind them. They made for the launch boats beached on the shore.

Randall Major, silent until this point, was goaded into

action at the sight of this. "They're leaving us! The traitors!"

Martin said, "You'd better stop them, I think."

The Virginian needed no further incentive. He pulled his pistol from his belt and ran after them, shouting invectives. At the boats, Mr. Hu turned from his work and observed his approach. He waited patiently for his arrival, as behind him the first of the launch boats pushed out into the cove.

"Alice," called Martin. "Now is the time. Let's go." He was giddy with anticipation. Everything was so close.

"The monk," she said, climbing to her feet.

Of course. The Black Iron Monk stood by the table in terrible silence, indifferent to what transpired before it. Martin turned to Gully, who stood mutely transfixed by the proceedings.

"Mr. Gully! The monk! See to the monk!"

Gully was staring in bewilderment from Alice to Martin. He had managed to strip off his shirt—what the devil had he been thinking of?—but now he stood stunned, as if struck by a hammer. "No, you're not leaving. She promised me." He sounded like a little boy whose greatest hope had just been dashed.

"She promised you what?"

"It's me. I'm to be the Feast. I'm the one. It's supposed to be me."

On the table, Thomas Thickett tried to crawl away, but he could get no purchase—his hands kept sliding in his own blood. By this time most of the contents had leaked from his head; there was little of him left aside from a mute recognition of agony.

"Do what I tell you!" said Martin.

Mr. Gully recovered himself. He withdrew his little knife and pointed it like a finger at Martin. "I told you you would come to regret that tongue," he said. "Now I'll carve it out of you."

Martin took a step backward. "Do what I tell you, Mr. Gully."

Gully strode toward him, the knife thrust ahead like a guiding element. Martin retreated and stumbled to the ground. For a moment all he saw was the curved arch of the angel's skull above him, grown over with vines and hanging plants. Then Gully filled the world. He had time to scream Alice's name before Gully stuffed his fingers into his mouth with one hand and pushed the knife in with the other. Pain spiked him in place, and his throat filled with blood.

"Rufus, no." She said it quietly, almost casually. He could not hear her, of course, bent over his bloody work, his back to her. She approached him calmly, her knife dripping in her hand. Dimly, she heard the sound of skirmishing carrying across the water behind her, and coming from the shore where Randall Major engaged Mr. Hu and his cohort. But she focused on Gully now, working his knife into Martin's mouth. Only Gully remained to be dealt with.

A quick glance toward the Black Iron Monk stopped her. It no longer stood by the table, where Thickett still sluggishly moved. Her stomach dropped. Without the monk's head they would be lost. It would all be for nothing.

There it was: heading in the opposite direction of the launch boats, wading now in shallow water, meaning to leave the angel's skull and presumably walk back to its monastery.

Very well. She was the butcher of the Buried Church. She would do this work herself. Martin's garbled screams echoed through the skull. He would have to fend for himself. Her father grazed her leg with one bloody hand as she passed, letting his armful of viscera slide heavily to the earth. "Alice," he said. "Is He coming?"

She caught up to the monk in the shallows. He was short but difficult work. He did not attempt to flee, had no idea what was coming for him. He was like a lamb in that way. Alice swung the knife into the soft flesh just beneath the iron box. A sheet of blood sprayed her face. The monk staggered backward, all sense of awe and mystery dissipating as it crashed into the water, hands pressed against its throat as it scrabbled for life. Alice set her foot on the box, holding it in place. She hacked at the neck, sending the monk's fingers rolling like little pegs. Blood greased her hands and forearms. The surf turned red.

A thin, reedy noise escaped the monk: air whistling through a torn throat. The sound of it was like a small razor sliding through her brain. Her eyes started to bleed. This was the language of Hell, the language of her Prince. Love's sweetest vocabulary. She worked furiously until the head was entirely separated. The hissing air stopped. A panel slid shut underneath the iron box, and whatever the monk said now was contained inside. She made her way back to shore, taking the box with her.

Several feet away, Gully rose from where Martin lay prone beneath him, his ghastly trophy oozing between his clenched fingers. He stepped over Martin and held it out to her, like a gift.

"Here's a liar's tongue," he said. "Now I'll take yours."

Martin spat blood from his mouth, but more came in torrents. He curled into himself, shuddering in pain. He was obscurely aware of the others around him, satellites to his own experience, but Alice occluded them all. It was Alice to whom he extended his bloody hand. He watched Fat Gully approach her: an avatar of death. He tried to push himself to his feet but collapsed each time. He could do nothing to save her. All of this, for nothing. All of it broken at the feet of some dockyard scum.

His tongue. His speech. His means of worship. No more stories told, ever again.

He rolled onto his back. Blood backed into his lungs and he watched arcs of it leap from his mouth as it choked the life from him. Beyond it was the curve of the angel's skull, and he found himself wondering at the brain that once resided here. What terrible dreams still haunted this place? Were they living one out now, like vessels possessed by ghosts? The thought gave him a strange comfort.

Martin closed his eyes and allowed himself to be consumed by this idea. He became separated from responsibility and consequence. He was only a figment of a dead dream, carried away by his own red current.

Gully closed on Miss Cobb, his volcanic anger already cooling. The monk's body rolled in the surf behind her, its limbs moving slowly. In her right hand she held loosely the carving knife with which she had performed all the work of her life. Gully moved toward her in a delirium of heartache. Thomas Thickett, Abel Cobb, and Martin Dunwood lay in a bloody tableau behind him. That Thickett and Cobb still lived was an undeniable miracle, whether due to their presence in the angel's hollow skull or their proximity to Hell's border he could not say and did not care. What it meant was that if she had kept her promise to him, he would have lived as they feasted on his body. He would have experienced the translation of his solid flesh into an expression of love; to come so close to acceptance and to lose it was more than his mind could bear.

"Why?" he said, when he arrived beside her. The knife was ineffectual in his hand. He could not kill her. No one here could die. The gravity of his failures pulled him to his knees. "You said I could be loved."

"I lied," she said. She walked around him and headed toward Dunwood, carrying the head of the Black Iron Monk.

Let them have it, then. Let them love each other. That was never for him, and he accepted it now. He pulled himself to his feet and headed for the boats.

There was no time left. Captain Toussaint ordered the plank between ships to be withdrawn. They had taken about three-score of the Damned. Fewer than he'd hoped. Captain Tegel held his gaze from his own ship. Toussaint had always known they'd be hurried, had always known there would be no time for anything more. And yet he had allowed himself to hope. The sting of it hurt beyond all reason. He wanted to shout across to him that he would come back, that next time Tegel should return with him—or that next time he would accept Tegel's offer and stay.

He turned his gaze one last time toward the beach, where the worst people he had ever known had gathered for their terrible feast. The people who came here to worship the very hook in Toussaint's heart. Slavers, conquerors, murderers, gluttons—they gorged themselves in celebration of everything that stank, everything that was rotten in the world. It would be a pleasure to leave them all beached on Hell's shores, but it was not enough to satisfy. He commanded the starboard guns to fire, and they did so, hurling enough iron at the feasting table and everyone around it to shatter a frigate's hull.

~ ~ ~

The cannon fire hit the beach without warning, and Gully found himself airborne. He landed hard, half submerged in water. Through garlands of smoke he saw severed limbs, splashes of blood, splayed viscera. The table had been smashed to flinders. Spread across and beside it were human remains, still quivering with life. One hand extended skyward from a bloody morass, fingers grasping for something or someone it would never find. Miss Cobb crawled across the beach. Her legs were gone just above her knees, yet she was undeterred. She wore a terrible grin. He heard Mr. Dunwood's wail somewhere beyond his sight; surely it was to him she crawled.

Gully surveyed his own body. Aside from superficial injuries, he seemed unharmed. A wave pushed in from the cove and submerged him, so he crawled farther up the shore. Pain flashed through his body with each movement; he felt as though his joints had been fitted with knives.

A few feet away from him lay the severed head of the Black Iron Monk, still contained in its box. Gully fought his way to his feet, gasping at the effort, and pulled the box from the sand. If Dunwood and Miss Cobb would go into Hell, they would do it without their precious atlas. It was the only revenge available to him.

He staggered toward the last of the launch boats, some distance away. Mr. Hu was attempting to push it out into the water. The Virginian floated faceup in the surf close by, a gunshot wound in his chest, his face battered and broken. His mouth opened and closed as he struggled to produce words. They were beyond him now. The tide pulled him farther out with each wave.

Gully heaved the iron box into the launch boat and put his shoulder to it; between them, he and Hu succeeded in getting it past the breakers and floating free. They climbed aboard, not a word exchanged, and put themselves to the oars. Farther out, *Butcher's Table* turned toward the cove's entrance as two other ships skirmished nearby. Gully had no idea what was going on; he only wanted back on board. He only wanted to be rid of these narcissists, these traitors, these grovelers. He wanted the familiar odor of the docks, its comprehensible confines, its knowable hierarchies. He wanted to go home.

The Black Law was almost upon them. Figures stood gathered at the rails, waiting to board. Their skin smoked, obscuring whatever features they had. They seemed composed of cinders. They wanted only to burn.

Captain Tegel maneuvered *Angel's Teeth* between them; he would buy him what time he could. The crewmen herded the Damned and all the lotusheads save one belowdecks. Captain Toussaint was prepared to give the order to slash the creature and provoke the crossing back into the Gulf of Mexico, when a cry from the crow's nest stayed his tongue.

"Captain! Mr. Hu is approaching!"

And indeed there he was, working the oars of a launch boat, Rufus Gully rowing beside him.

Behind him, *Angel's Teeth* was boarded by the Black Law: The air grew heavy with the sound of clashing blades and gunshots, with the smell of burning meat. The man he loved was risking everything to buy him time to escape.

"Captain, we have to go now."

"We'll wait for Mr. Hu," he said.

"But—"

"We'll wait."

In those short minutes, *Angel's Teeth* fell. Josiah Tegel went down beneath their weight; he would not die, but there were darker fates in store for those caught here. Toussaint turned away, tears stinging his eyes. Half a dozen of the Law threw grappling hooks toward *Butcher's Table*, their iron spikes hooking over the rails and digging into the wood. They were living cinders; their very proximity caused the wood and canvas to smoke.

Mr. Hu and the little wretch beside him came alongside *Butcher's Table*, and men were ready with a rope ladder. Mr. Hu climbed quickly; waiting hands grasped his shirt and hoisted him aboard. Fat Gully retrieved the iron box with one hand and made an awkward attempt to scale the ladder himself.

"Cut him loose," Toussaint said.

With a flash of knives the rope ladder was severed at the railing, and it fell in a loose tangle over Gully as he stumbled backward into the launch. "No! NO!" he screamed, but the captain had already turned his back.

"Do it now," he said.

A hatchet sank deep into a lotushead's trunk. Its tongues flailed to life. *Butcher's Table*, once more, made the crossing, pulling Gully's launch in its wake.

Martin opened his eyes. Alice was beside him. His chest had been cracked open like a walnut in the cannon fire. She dipped her hands into him, removed a glistening portion and fed it into her mouth. Her stare was unwavering. There was no intelligence behind it, no recognition. Nothing at all. Alice was gone. There was only brute impulse at work now. He tried to say her name and was rewarded with an overwhelming pulse of agony.

He did not want this. This was not love; it was an atrocity.

*Please,* he thought, *let me go mad. Let me go mad. Please let me go mad.*

~ ~ ~

The Black Law passed through the sinking ruin of *Angel's Teeth* and poured into the open chamber of the angel's skull, where the members of the Feast still twitched and struggled in the lowering light. Abel Cobb, Thomas Thickett, the drifting body of Randall Major, the surviving parishioners of the Buried Church, Martin and Alice: They shivered in the red mud, each sobbing plea or groan of pain a supplication to their Lord. Their bleeding bodies were His portrait, their wailing throats His opening eye.

The carrion angels waited for them in the gulf. *Butcher's Table* manifested at the precise point from which it had disappeared, Rufus Gully's launch pitching against its hull as the waves heaved beneath them. *Retribution*, arriving at last while they'd been gone, immediately flew canvas to bring their guns into position. Captain Toussaint was unprepared. Still reeling from Josiah Tegel's loss, still disoriented by the crossing, he lost fatal seconds staring at the enemy ship, and at the misshapen thing that had once been Bonny Mungo perched in its rigging like a hellish vulture. *Butcher's Table* received a full broadside from *Retribution*; masts snapped in two, sails were torn, and rigging fell like a net. A flying cannonball sheared the head from a sailor standing directly beside him.

Mr. Hu grabbed his captain and hauled him away from the side, but there was nowhere to turn. The carrion angels shed their human costumes in bloody sheets; the one still wearing the squid's body wrapped its great arms around the belly of the ship and tore it in half. The sea filled with the wreckage, with flailing crewmen, with harvested lotusheads, and with the rescued Damned, sinking into the blue fathoms like heavy stones. The carrion angels darted after them, the water boiling in their wake.

One of them detoured to Rufus Gully's launch, pitching and yawing in the frothing sea. It grasped the black iron box in a claw, tearing a rent in its side. A tumbling spar slammed into its body as it fell, driving it underwater. The box tumbled back into the boat. Panicked, Gully grabbed the oars and pulled away from the sinking vessel, his muscles screaming in protest.

Eventually he eased his rowing and watched as *Butcher's Table* sank beneath the waves. Scattered survivors clung to floating spars or planks of wood. Their calls floated across the water. He did not answer them.

*Retribution*, divested of its occupying forces, drifted at the whim of the sea. What crewmen remained found themselves with no desire to exert their will upon the ship. Their brush with the divine had ruined them. There was nothing left inside but a mute passivity. Eventually a lantern slid from its place on a table and smashed into the hold. Within an hour the whole ship was ablaze. Gully watched it burn for hours. When twilight fell, he had drifted leagues away, yet still he could see it shining like a torch against the early wash of stars.

Gully did not know how to read the constellations. There was no sail on the launch. He rowed weakly for a while, then surrendered himself to fate. He closed his eyes and listened to the lapping of the water against the hull, and it was not too difficult to pretend it was the sound of the Thames lapping the posts of the London dock. He dozed somewhere in the night, and dreamed of a whispering voice. The voice spoke in a language he couldn't understand, but it filled his brain with thoughts he recognized well enough. Red thoughts, murder thoughts. He dreamed of his mother, sitting quietly in the dark of their small flat, rocking incessantly in her chair. She told him a story of a witch who lived in the chimney, who crawled out at night, all covered in black, looking for a little boy to eat. His mother would not touch him or comfort him. He dreamed of his father, distant and harsh, driven by some nameless rage, dead of an exploded heart while still a young man.

Gully awoke to the glare of the sun. The voice whispered still. He peered into the bright air around him, his eyes gummy, the heat blistering the naked skin on his back. He called out for his parents. When he remembered himself, he went quiet. He kicked at the black iron box, rolling it over. He saw the gash the angel had rent in one side. The whisper leaked out of it. His skin had cracked and charred at the fingertips. He wiped at his eyes and saw that it was blood that made them sticky.

"What are you?" he said to the box.

Eventually he remembered what Martin had told him. The monk's severed head was an atlas of Hell. It recited its dreadful litany, listing all the landmarks of that burning country—the Breathing Mountains, the Love Mills, the Grieving Fields. It outlined the paths of the travelers there—the Crawling Eye and the Voyeurs, the pilgrims and the priests, and all the roaches of Heaven. He understood none of the words, but he saw these places clearly. Rufus Gully listened to the atlas speak for all the time it took for the sea to push him across hot open leagues of the Gulf, to the swampy shores of New France, in a district called La Louisiane.

By the time the launch became entangled in the trees there, the voice had transformed Gully into something far different from what he used to be. Tumors and growths blossomed across his body—from inside his mouth, from beneath his eyelids, from his ears, from under his arms and around his neck. His body was burnt, both inside and out. Smoke trailed from his nostrils in an unceasing plume. Only in his mind was there life, as he soared over the landscape of Hell, exulting in its bleeding vistas.

In time the boat would decay, and the iron box sink deeply into the mud, where its voice would be silenced for generations. Before then, though, Rufus Gully lay prostrate in its bottom, his body a glorious feast for the swamp's vermin. They ate him while he lived, and he sighed with gratitude beneath a carpet of flies.

"I love you," he said. "I love you, I love you, I love you."

# ACKNOWLEDGMENTS

First and foremost, thanks go out to my daughter, Mia, who listened to me work these stories out from their earliest beginnings; endured my anxieties, self-doubts, and dark days; and who gamely participated in ridiculous conversations ("So I'm thinking about a scene where an angel possesses a giant squid . . . is that too much?"). She's my compass, and I love her absolutely.

I want to thank my agent, Renée Zuckerbrot, and her assistant Anne Horowitz at Massie & McQuilken Literary Agents, who gave this manuscript a rigorous edit in record time, making me look much more polished than I actually am. Renée has already done more for me than what I had dreamed possible.

Thanks to Joe Monti, Bridget Madsen, Gary Sunshine, Beth Adelman, and Michael McCartney at Saga Press, for taking on this book and turning it around so quickly—and, most of all, for their faith in me. I'll do my best to honor that.

Thanks to my film agent, Sean Daily, who changed my life. By extension, thanks to Babak Anvari, a brilliant writer, director, and friend, whose long conversations with me about "The Visible Filth" helped me improve the novella even as he made the story his own for the movie. And thanks to

Lucan Toh, Christopher Kopp, Kit Fraser, Andrew Harvey, and the whole team at Annapurna Pictures for always making me feel welcome and involved.

Thanks to early readers who offered insight, critique, and general support during the writing of these stories: Dale Bailey, Matthew M. Bartlett, April White, Heather Wiscarson, Alicia Graves, Heather Clitheroe, Karen Tucker, Mary Laws, Luke Fore, as well as all the writers at Sycamore Hill and Arrowmont.

I want to offer a special thanks to Jeremy Duncan, who provided wonderful black and white illustrations for "The Butcher's Table" years ago, when it was just a personal project called "The Cannibal Priests of New England." Maybe one day we'll get to release an illustrated edition, Jeremy!

Thank you to the editors who bought or reprinted these stories and helped me make them what they are now: Ellen Datlow (who grew me from a bean), Kelly Link and Gavin J. Grant, Christopher Golden, John Joseph Adams, Joe Hill, Michael Kelly, Kathe Koja, Randy Chandler, Cheryl Mullenax, and Michael Wilson and Dan Howarth.

Particular appreciation is due to Kelly and Gavin, whose support and generosity enabled this book to take its own unusual journey, culminating in the volume you hold in your hands right now. I'll never forget that.

Thanks to my mom and my brother, whose support has been constant and unwavering.

A profound thanks to everyone who bought *North American Lake Monsters*, or talked about it, or pushed it on a friend. That was the little book that could, and it's all down to you. I'll do my best to honor that gift.

Finally, thanks to my dad, who passed away in late 2015. He was the rock of my whole life. I wish he could have seen the movie happen. I miss you, Dad.